CHERIE FEATHER

HEAT
New York

THE BERKLEY PUBLISHING GROUP
Published by the Penguin Group
Penguin Group (USA) Inc.
375 Hudson Street, New York, New York 10014, USA
Penguin Group (Canada), 90 Eglinton Avenue East, Suite 700, Toronto, Ontario M4P 2Y3, Canada
(a division of Pearson Penguin Canada Inc.)
Penguin Books Ltd., 80 Strand, London WC2R 0RL, England
Penguin Group Ireland, 25 St. Stephen's Green, Dublin 2, Ireland (a division of Penguin Books Ltd.)
Penguin Group (Australia), 250 Camberwell Road, Camberwell, Victoria 3124, Australia
(a division of Pearson Australia Group Pty. Ltd.)
Penguin Books India Pvt. Ltd., 11 Community Centre, Panchsheel Park, New Delhi—110 017, India
Penguin Group (NZ), 67 Apollo Drive, Rosedale, North Shore 0632, New Zealand
(a division of Pearson New Zealand Ltd.)
Penguin Books (South Africa) (Pty.) Ltd., 24 Sturdee Avenue, Rosebank, Johannesburg 2196,
South Africa

Penguin Books Ltd., Registered Offices: 80 Strand, London WC2R 0RL, England

This is an original publication of The Berkley Publishing Group.

Cover photo by Robert Whitman/Veer.
Cover design by Lesley Worrell.
Text design by Tiffany Estreicher.

First edition: June 2008

Library of Congress Cataloging-in-Publication Data

Feather, Cherie.
The art of desire / Cherie Feather.—1st ed.
p. cm.
ISBN 978-0-425-22160-0
1. Women museum directors—Fiction. 2. Women artists—Fiction. 3. Indians of North America—Fiction. 4. Man-woman relationships—Fiction. 5. Diaries—Fiction. I. Title.
PS3623.H5798A78 2008
813'.6—dc22

2008008109

PRINTED IN THE UNITED STATES OF AMERICA

10 9 8 7 6 5 4 3 2 1

To Karen Solem and Cindy Hwang,
for believing in this book. To my family,
for their love and open-minded support.
To Chris Marie Green and Judy Duarte,
for being there every day.

PROLOGUE

TEXAS
1895

The first time I saw him he was naked, morning-dappled water lapping at his skin, swirling around tendon-tight calves. His rifle, a gun he'd probably stolen from a rancher, was at the edge of the stream, well within his reach.

A hawk soared above his head, screeching like a red-tailed devil, creating a strangely spiritual arc. Mesmerized, the Indian followed its every move.

I knew he was unaware of me. Although I was no more than twenty to thirty steps away, I was crouched amongst a copse of cottonwoods. Earlier I'd been napping there, and upon awakening, I'd lifted my head and spotted him through a branch-scattered gap in the foliage, a stunned gasp locked in my throat.

Was this my punishment for dozing in the sun? Or my reward? I'd gone to that location to work, to sketch the scenery.

I longed to draw him instead. But I couldn't find the will to move, to do more than stare. Curiously handsome, his bluish black, cheekbone-length hair framed the hollowed angles and mysterious shadows that sculpted his face. Muscled ridges and flat planes defined his body, with wide shoulders and a powerful chest. His thighs, I decided, had been built for straddling the horse that grazed nearby. A stolen mount, no doubt. A prize that went with his rifle.

Taking a swift breath, I centered my gaze, filling my vision with his penis. I measured the length and fullness, but I imagined how it would look fully erect, with his testes drawn tight, his foreskin pushed back, and the sensitive head exposed.

Queen Victoria shame me.

In my own country, I was a rumored bohemian, London-born, Paris-schooled, an artist seceding from conventionality, an upper-class girl who'd cast her morals to the wind, who'd stroked many a cock with her hands, even with her ruby red mouth.

But the gossip wasn't true. Not completely. I fantasized about those carnal acts, but the only cocks I dared stroke were with a collection of Asiatic marten brushes.

The hawk flew away, abandoning its circling post. The Indian snapped out of his trance and continued his bath. My heart pounded like the drums of his people. I knew who he was. He was an Apache prisoner of war who'd escaped from a military fort in Oklahoma Territory. Last week U.S. Army soldiers had scoured this area in search of him. They'd ridden into town with a photograph, asking if anyone had seen him. They'd gone to ranches and farms, too. When they'd come to my house, I'd gazed curiously at his picture.

And now here he was.

I should have remained motionless until he went away. But somewhere in the peril of my soul, I found the strength to sit upright, to lift a piece of charcoal from my ready-made paint box. The paper clamped to my stretching board was cold-pressed, better suited for rough effects than a detailed portrait of a bared man. But I was willing to compromise. Desire burned like a hot-wick candle beneath the folds of my skirt.

I had moved to America to study its ethnic, geographic, and religious diversity, to paint its fading frontier. So why not study him? Make him my secret project?

"Atacar." I whispered his name. It was of Spanish origin, and in English it meant "to attack."

Suddenly he went still, his dark gaze shooting through the trees like an obsidian-tipped arrow. He couldn't have heard his barely audible name on my lips, yet he'd found me out.

The charcoal slipped from my fingers; my paper remained blank.

Our eyes met, and he reacted like a hound on the heels of a fox. Before I could blink, he grabbed the rifle, jammed it against his water-damp shoulder, and aimed it at me.

I did the unthinkable. I looked at his penis again, challenging the air between us. His face remained an indiscernible mask, devoid of emotion, of any kind of lust. But in his fire-ready stance, his stomach muscles jumped, giving him away, making his cock stir.

From there, neither of us moved.

Finally he motioned with his chin, ordering me out into the open. I didn't hesitate. I lifted my arms in surrender and walked toward him.

Praying he would take me.

CHAPTER ONE

Dirty sex with a dirty boy.

That was all Mandy Cooper, the proper, professional, highly organized director of the Santa Fe Women's Art Museum, could think about.

She was addicted to Jared Cabrillo, Atacar's great-great-nephew, a man who sizzled in the art scene, who was notorious for having public liaisons, who wielded his celebrity like the party-on-the-edge charmer he was.

Mandy could feel him watching her from across the museum. She and her staff were hosting a summer reception, and he'd crashed the event.

She tried to avoid him, but she couldn't. His gaze was too strong, too persistent. She gave up the fight and looked at him, too.

Their eyes met, and he lifted his wine and toasted her before he put the glass to his lips and drank the bloodred liquid.

She gripped the silver chain on her evening bag, locking it

around her wrist like a handcuff. He was drop-dead, imprison-a-woman gorgeous. There was no other way to describe him. He walked toward her, and her panties stuck to her skin, making her want to rub her thighs together.

"Nice party," he said, as they came face-to-face.

"It's going well." She'd been sleeping with him for almost a month, yet she couldn't stop herself from staring.

He sported a retro-style, black Western shirt, decorated with white piping and tucked into crisp jeans. His face, diamond-blade dazzling and stone-quarry tough, mirrored his heritage. Both ears showcased tiny silver hoops. He had an intimate body piercing and tribal tattoos, too.

He was everything she shouldn't want. At thirty-eight, she was supposed to know better. He was ten years younger than she was, but he wasn't her boy toy. He controlled their affair, enticing her into carnal situations.

He set his empty glass on a nearby table. "You look beautiful, Mandy."

"Thank you." Her black dress scooped modestly in front, and the delicate silver and turquoise cross around her neck offered a hint of adornment.

Aside from their naked urges, they didn't know each other very well. They didn't have meaningful conversations. But at least she knew he wasn't seeing anyone else. He didn't cheat on his lovers. Of course that didn't change who and what he was. He treated monogamy like a courtesy, not a commitment.

Needing a diversion, Mandy turned toward the famous portrait of Jared's ancestor. They were standing in front of Atacar's exhibit.

He was the museum's most prized possession, a Catherine Burke treasure, a portrait remarkable for its depth and passion, for its stunning realism. But Atacar was more than Catherine's greatest work. So much more. The nineteenth-century artist was rumored to have loved him, just as he was rumored to have loved her.

But no one knew for sure.

Catherine had abandoned her Texas home, never to be heard from again, and soon after she'd disappeared, Atacar had been shot and killed by a trio of soldiers.

As Mandy looked into his eyes, an air-conditioned chill blasted from the ceiling, sending goose bumps along her arms.

He was an imposing figure, his head cocked just so, his expression dark and serious. Positioned in a straight-back chair, he gripped the barrel of a Winchester rifle. She tried to imagine him sitting for Catherine while the daring girl painted his image. His clothes consisted of Anglo gear, reminiscent of ranchers and farmers, but he was Chiricahua Apache, an enlisted army scout who'd become a prisoner of war.

Mandy blinked, but Atacar's gaze remained constant. The museum had acquired his portrait nearly forty years earlier. Prior to that, it had been hidden inside the walls of the farmhouse where Catherine had lived.

Upon its discovery, their romantic legacy had begun. Rumors spawned that they'd been lovers. That she'd disappeared because of him. That their desperate hearts would remain forever entwined.

But once again, no one knew for sure.

The only ray of hope was that Catherine had kept a secret journal, writings that had never been found.

By now, most of the art world thought the journal was a

myth. But Mandy chose to believe otherwise. She had the museum historian searching for it.

Suddenly Jared moved closer, close enough to invade Mandy's space, to attack her senses. She could smell the spicy notes of his cologne. She turned to face him, his ancestor fading into the background.

"Why did you come here tonight?" she asked.

He smoothed the front of his hair. He wore it plaited into a single braid, leaving the hardened angles of his face unframed. "To fuck you."

Her addiction jabbed her hard and quick, like a needle to a starving vein. "I'm working, Jared."

"That's what makes it so fun." Fun or not, he didn't smile. He just looked at her with the same driven expression as when he'd toasted her with his merlot or cabernet or whatever he'd been drinking. "Like when we do it at my work."

She didn't respond. He was a highly successful breeder, trainer, and showman who managed his own horse farm. Banging each other's brains out in his barn wasn't the same as getting naked at the museum.

His gaze turned darker, more intense. "You could take me to your office. You could make me do things to you."

Hedonic chills vibrated her spine. By now, they were just inches apart. He kept moving closer, drawing her in to his seductive sphere, doing what he always did.

"What things?" she asked.

"You could take off your panties, order me to my knees, and lift your dress in front of my face. You could make me taste how sweet you are."

The room started to spin. She wanted his mouth between her legs. But envisioning herself standing in front of him, *making* him do it was almost more than she could bear.

"Does that excite you?" he asked.

"Yes."

"What else turns you on? What other games do you want to play?"

"I don't know." Her voice shook. "I honestly don't know." At the moment she just wanted to crawl all over him, to fall like a sugared gumdrop at his feet.

"I'll bet she did it," Jared said.

"What? Who?"

"Catherine." Jared moistened his lips. "I'll bet she lifted her skirts in front of Atacar's face. I'll bet she came all over him." His voice was soft and low, dangerously demanding. "Do it, Mandy. Be bad for me."

Heat flooded her lungs. If her guests weren't milling around, eating canapés and socializing, she would've removed her panties right then and there.

"Meet me at my office," she said. "But give me a head start. I need to unlock the door."

His demeanor didn't falter. "Hurry up."

"I will." She did her damnedest to regain her composure, to not give away what she was about to do.

She walked toward the stairs, moving quickly so no one stopped her, so she didn't get trapped into small talk. Finally she ascended to the second floor, her low-heeled pumps assaulting terrazzo-topped concrete, ringing like bullets in her ears.

Her office door came into view, and she fumbled with her

purse. What if she got caught? Her affair with Jared wasn't a secret, but doing it at work . . .

She removed her keys, and footsteps sounded. She nearly jumped out of her skin.

"Easy, baby, it's me."

Jared. He'd barely given her a head start. Mandy glanced his way, her heart thudding between her thighs.

He came up behind her, bumping his fly against her rear. "You're so conventional. So ladylike. But here you are, wanting this as badly as I do."

He had no idea. She crammed the key into the lock and pushed open the door. Her drug of choice was crashing in on her, rushing perilously through her veins.

They crossed the threshold and locked themselves inside. Her office housed an executive desk, a sofa, and matching side chairs. But she didn't move in that direction. She paused just beyond the entryway, beside a floor-to-ceiling bookcase, with a security light burning low.

Caught in a sexual whirlwind, she reached under her dress and removed her panties. She wasn't wearing hose. Her legs were bare.

"Get on your knees," she told him.

He dropped down with a grateful thud. Gorgeous Jared with his head tipped back, his jaw jutting forward. While he waited, a thick, naughty beat of silence swallowed the air.

One. Two. Three. Let him see.

She hiked up her dress, bunched the fabric around her hips, and exposed herself.

"Damn." His voice pulsed, the tendons in his throat strained.

He was staring at her. Ravenously. Mandy gripped her hem a little tighter. She knew he liked her Brazilian. He thought the process that left a small strip of pubic hair above a woman's vulva was hot and sexy. He'd talked her into getting waxed, convincing her that it would make her feel prettier, even when she was alone. He'd told her to touch herself and think about him when he wasn't around, to make it her guilty pleasure. She couldn't begin to count how many times she'd followed his advice, imagining that he was watching her.

She moved closer, teasing Jared with her guilty pleasure, widening her stance to give him a better look, to show him the cleft of her labia. But that wasn't enough. Anxious, she took her dress completely off, dragging it over her head. Her basic underwire bra came next. She wanted to be naked, all the way bare, except for her conservative black pumps.

He swallowed, eager to taste her. He looked half-starved.

"Do it," she commanded, spreading herself for him. "Do it."

He didn't waste a second, not one delicious moment. He went right for her clit, sucking hard and fast, then slowing to deliberate strokes. He knew how much pressure to apply, how much saliva to spread. Excitement gathered low in her belly.

She watched him lavishing every taut, tingling taste. The sight was roughly, fiercely erotic. His hungry mouth. Her damp, swollen sex. She pitched forward, and he made a primal sound. Mandy got even more aroused.

"Are you hard?" she asked, trailing her hands through his hair and snagging his thick, silky braid.

He paused to answer her question, moisture glistening on his lips. "I'm so turned on, I could come in my pants."

Her knees nearly buckled. "I'm going to do this to you. When you're done with me."

"What if I don't want to stop? What if I want to keep going?" He snaked his tongue so she could see him make contact with her clit. He banged her with his fingers, too.

All the way in. All the way out. He even rubbed his sticky digits down the front of his shirt and along his bulging fly, smearing himself with her juices.

Dizzy, she rotated her hips. Sooner or later he would have to stop; if he didn't, she would explode into a pool of pollinated liquid.

Reaching out, she grappled for something to brace the blinding pleasure and fisted the edge of a shelf. A moment later, she caught the binding of a hardback book and clutched it between her white-knuckled fingers.

He made a sudden move, cupping her rear and pulling her toward him. They both went crashing until she landed on top of him, sprawled across his handsome face.

This was even wilder, she thought. Sexier. She rode his mouth, her body flexed, her back bowed in a fluid arc. She'd never felt more graceful, more ladylike. The irony should have made her laugh. Instead, she came in convulsing waves.

All over her dirty boy.

Jared and Mandy sat on the floor and gazed at each other. He wiped his mouth with the back of his hand. He'd just devoured her orchid-soft, pussy-sweet flavor, enjoying every warm, wet, orgasmic taste.

"That was the hottest thing ever," he said, before she got shy and glanced away. "So don't even think about blushing."

She lifted her chin. "I'm not."

Sometimes she did. Regardless of how nasty they got, she still had an innocent quality. Her mink-colored hair skimmed her shoulders, and her eyes were framed with sweeping lashes.

She was the first proper girl he'd fucked, and he was hooked. He didn't know for how long, and he didn't want to know. For him, it was easier living from day to day, walking the sexual tightrope that drove him.

"Now it's your turn," she said. "Take off your clothes."

"Are you still going to blow me?" he asked, upping the ante on the offer she'd made. "Are you going to suck me as deep as you can? Deeper than you ever have?"

"Yes." She released a shuddering breath. There was a damp spot on the carpet beneath her, where some of her wetness had leaked onto the floor. "I am."

His nerve endings went electric. He got to his feet and offered her a hand. She stood up, and he grabbed her and swung her into his arms.

"What are you doing?"

"Carrying you to bed."

She looped her arms around his neck and kicked off her shoes. "It's a sofa. Not a bed."

"Close enough." He tossed her onto the sofa in question, planted his knees on either side of her face, and shoved down his boxers and jeans in one fell swoop.

His penis sprang free, and he felt good enough to grin. The head of his cock was pierced, and he knew it fascinated her.

"Up close and personal," she said.

"Just for you." He imagined her tongue sliding over the curved barbell. He got harder just thinking about it. Not that he wasn't already rock solid, not that he hadn't meant what he'd said about creaming his jeans earlier.

"I like touching it," she told him.

"Then what are you waiting for?" He wanted her to get aggressive.

But she didn't. She traced the barbell with the tip of her finger. Softly. Tentatively. He thought he might die.

"You never told me what it's called."

"It's a PA." His own breathing engulfed him. "A Prince Albert. They pierce it from the outside of the frenulum and into the urethra."

"Is this the frenulum?" She gestured to the band of tissue under the head of his cock, where a portion of the barbell was.

He nodded. "It's a common piercing for a guy."

"Not in my world." She touched him again. No, not him. The jewelry. "Every time I see it, I keep thinking that it hurt."

"When I first had it done? It didn't. No more than getting your ears pierced." His stomach muscles jumped. He wanted her to lean forward, to give him a silky blow job. Her gentleness was exciting him. "It takes about the same amount of time to heal, too. But I've had it forever." Since he was a rebellious teenager, seeking a rite of passage, a way to define who he was.

"If feels amazing when we have sex," she said. "I didn't expect it to. But it does."

"It's supposed to give both partners more pleasure. Not painful pleasure. Tingling sensations. It increases the sensitivity."

Mandy looked up at him, and their eyes met, making him more aware of his erection popping in her face, of the promise she'd made.

They moved toward each other at the same time, at the same exhilarating instant, and she parted her lips, taking the tip of his cock inside.

She toyed with the barbell, creating a rippling sensation, then pulling back to lick him, to run her tongue along the underside of his shaft and over the top, until she nursed the head again.

He fought the urge to relinquish control. But he didn't. He held on, letting Mandy play, letting her decide when she would take him deeper. While she experimented, he watched her, heightening the game.

It got better from there.

She shoved his jeans farther down his hips. "Lie on your back," she said. "I want to crawl between your legs."

Who was he to argue?

He did what she told him to do, even though they had to fight the sofa to make it happen. Once he was in position, she opened the snaps on his shirt and exposed his chest and stomach.

She took her time, kissing his abs, leaving wet marks on his skin. By now he wanted to push her down and make her suck him all the way to the back of her throat.

He didn't wait for long. He tried, but he couldn't. She put her mouth on him again, and he lost the battle. He did what he was craving to do. He pushed her down.

She made a girl-hungry sound. She liked his roughness, he thought. Jared spread his legs and lifted his hips, grinding one booted heel into the cushion and planting his other foot on the floor, supporting his weight. He set the rhythm, and she took over, sucking greedily.

She was sowing her blow-job oats, reaping him for all he was worth, the way he'd wanted her to. But even so, he didn't spill into her mouth. Not because he was being polite. He loved watching her swallow. But tonight he wanted to come inside her. So he lifted her up and told her to stop, whispering gruffly in her ear, telling her it was time to fuck.

Mandy watched him undress. Her eyes were bright, and her hair was tumbled. She was still feeling her oats.

Anxious, he ditched his boots and went to work on his jeans, then his pricey Western shirt, tugging the sleeves to get himself out of it. He hadn't brought protection. He and Mandy were clean and safe. They'd talked about it on the night they'd first gotten together.

"I love your tattoos." She pawed his triceps, where he had matching armbands. "Do you have any idea how exotic you are?"

"Do you have an idea how hard I'm going to give this to you?" He nudged her with his steel-tipped sword.

"I'm ready."

"You better be." He told her to straddle his lap in a reverse cowgirl position, so he could see her ass, so he could reach around and cup her tits, so he could pinch her nipples.

His lover accommodated him. She turned around and spread her thighs nice and wide, creating the slick leverage she needed.

He gripped her waist, and she went rodeo, giving him a thrill. Not only could he admire the curve of her ass, he got an erotic view of her sliding up and down, milking his cock.

She gulped her next breath. "It feels so good."

He knew she meant the barbell. The sensation rocked him, too. Her pussy caressed him, and he nearly growled, his heart machine-gunning his chest.

"Touch yourself." He struggled to steady his voice. She kept riding him, only now she was going slowly, forcing him to feel every luxurious glide. "Do it the way you do it when you're alone."

She moved her hand, and he could tell that she was rubbing her clit. He couldn't wait to bring her deeper into his realm, to seduce her even more.

"Turn around," he said. "I want to see."

They made the switch, with her sitting forward on his lap, stroking her sex.

He watched her come, thinking how incredible she was. She smiled when she was done. Her lashes fluttered, too. How pretty could she be? Warm and soft in the barely-there light.

"Is that what you wanted to see?" she asked.

He wasn't about to respond, not now, not in the wake of wanting her so badly. Desperate for more, he pushed her down and opened her legs until they were almost straight in the air. She gasped, and he thrust full hilt, pumping hard and fast.

She had another orgasm, poised like an acrobat. Her stomach quivered, and she reached out and clawed the back of the sofa.

When she wrapped her legs around him, the familiarity of being this close to her shattered his mind. Jared tunneled his hands in her hair, heat surging through his blood and burning his loins. He went off like a geyser, coming deep inside her.

In the minutes that followed, she clung to him, breathing

softly against his neck. He wanted to be gentle for her, to hold her close, but he didn't know how to pull it off, not without getting out of his comfort zone. So he settled on a quick kiss, got dressed, and went downstairs ahead of her.

Once he hit the party, he didn't have another drink or wait for Mandy to reappear. He left the museum, and on his way out, he frowned at Atacar, knowing the other man would've stayed.

CHAPTER TWO

"Turkey with avocado and coleslaw on the side. Pink lemonade, lots of ice."

Kiki Dion, the museum's colorful historian, placed Mandy's lunch on her desk. The other woman's wavy red hair peeked out from beneath a geometric-printed bandanna-style scarf, and freckles dusted her nose.

"Thanks. It's been one of those days."

"For me, too. We deserve a moment to rest our bones." The redhead sat across from her. She'd also gotten a sandwich, cramming in a quick lunch together.

"How's the research going?" Mandy asked.

"I don't have anything new to report, but not from the lack of trying. I'll keep working on it."

"I know you will." The journal quest was still in its early stages. Mandy had worked at the museum for a little over a year, and Kiki had only been there for eight months, so it had taken some time for them to settle into their jobs before they'd made the journal a priority. But now that they had, they weren't letting go.

The historian unwrapped her food. "So what's up with you? Any more hot romps with Jared?"

"Not since the party." Mandy wasn't surprised by Kiki's blatant question. She'd been confiding in the other woman about her affair.

They seemed like unlikely friends, but they weren't. Although Kiki was closer to Jared's age than to Mandy's, they'd both survived mundane marriages, with ex-husbands who'd left them wanting more, not just sexually but emotionally. Not that Jared came anywhere near to fitting the emotional bill for Mandy. But she kept telling herself that wicked sex wasn't supposed to be steeped in life-altering conversations and hand-holding walks.

Kiki glanced at the sofa and shot her a teasing grin. "I hope you had that cleaned."

She smiled, too. "I did. Right away." But the memory of him remained. She'd been focused on Jared all week, anxious for him to call, to tempt her into another be-bad-for-him encounter. "I spilled coffee on it the next day to cover my tracks."

"Good thinking." Kiki dived into a grilled roast beef and swiss, eating heartily, crumbs falling onto her napkin-draped lap. "Why don't you ever call him?"

"I don't know. Maybe I like waiting for him to get in touch with me." Mandy removed a pepperoncini from her sandwich and bit into it. The juice squirted into her mouth, the spicy hotness reminding her of her lover. "Maybe it's part of my addiction. Part of the thrill."

"He is exciting. Remember the first night you slept with him?"

"How could I ever forget?" Mandy had always been keenly

aware of Jared's reputation, but she rarely saw the art-celebrity bad boy out on the town. They didn't run in the same circles. Then last month, she'd been seated next to him at a hotel ballroom charity dinner, and sexual sparks flew. "I told him that I was half in love with Catherine and Atacar."

"And he used that to seduce you."

"Yes, he did. By the end of the night, he'd convinced me to check into a room with him."

"You were the talk of the town. Atacar's great-great-nephew and the Women's Museum director. People are still gossiping, wondering how a nice girl like you fell for a guy like him." Kiki flashed another playful grin. "But I know the real scoop."

"That he turned me into a Jared junkie?"

"Exactly." Kiki paused. "Does he know you're trying to find the journal? That you're hoping to acquire it for the museum?"

Mandy nodded. "Yes, but he doesn't think it exists."

"He's a nonbeliever?" Kiki sounded surprised.

"He tried to find it, too. A long time ago. But he never did, so he thinks it's a lost cause."

"Then I'll do my darnedest to prove him wrong."

The phone rang, and they quit talking as Mandy took the call. A few seconds later, she exhaled a quick breath and hung up.

"That was Gloria," she said, referring to the curatorial division secretary. "She wanted to know if she should accept my flowers or have the delivery boy bring them directly to me."

"Your flowers?"

Mandy struggled to keep her cool, to not make a fuss, even if her heart was heading toward a girlish patter. "Apparently someone sent me a bouquet."

Kiki reacted openly, her voice boosting a notch. "Do you think it was Jared?"

"I doubt it. It doesn't seem like something he would do. It's probably work related." Mandy reached into her bottom drawer for her purse, removing her wallet for some bills, preparing for the tip. "But I told Gloria that I'd take them. Just in case."

They waited, Kiki perched on the edge of her chair, and Mandy standing near the door, lying to herself, insisting it didn't matter who the flowers were from.

When the bouquet arrived, the women gazed at each other. A stunning spray of long-stemmed, deep red roses in a sleek crimson vase. Maybe it *was* something Jared would do.

Mandy asked the delivery boy if he knew what kind of roses they were since they were so dark, and he said they were a hybrid tea called Black Magic.

After he left, she snagged the miniature envelope that accompanied the bouquet. But there wasn't a traditional gift card inside. Instead, she discovered a business card of an adult store in Albuquerque. It was called Black Magic, too. She turned the card over. Jared had written a note for her to meet him there tomorrow at three o'clock.

"So?" Kiki asked. "Are they from him?"

"Yes." She couldn't think of anything to say except that one little word.

"Can I see?"

Mandy extended the Saturday-afternoon invitation, and the other woman studied both sides, her eyes going wide.

"He's full of surprises, isn't he?"

"Always." Mandy wet her lips and tasted the lingering pepper juice. "I wonder what he'll talk me into buying."

"Something that will make you want him even more?" Kiki asked without expecting an answer. "Black Magic is right. That man is casting a spell on you."

"I know." Heaven, how she knew. Without thinking, she leaned in to inhale the roses' sweet, light fragrance, to touch their bewitching petals.

Jared waited in the parking lot, leaning against his truck, a customized fifty-seven Chevy big block, Prussian blue with polished centerline wheels. It wasn't his ranch vehicle. He drove it for fun.

Life was supposed to be fun, wasn't it? Especially with Mandy. So here he was, keeping things light, telling himself not to feel guilty. He'd lied to Mandy from the start. He knew Catherine's journal existed because he had it. He'd searched for years and then had uncovered the book unexpectedly. But that wasn't something he could reveal. The journal was a secret he'd promised to keep.

He glanced up and saw that Mandy had arrived. She parked next to him and got out of her midsize sedan. He didn't start a conversation. He let her do the talking. She was fifteen minutes late.

"I didn't know what to wear to a place like this," she said. "I changed three times."

Was she kidding? He broke into a smile. "What you have on is fine." Slim-fitting jeans, a blouse that shimmered in the sun, jeweled sandals. She'd painted her fingernails red for the occasion. Her toenails, too. Normally she wore pink polish.

"I hope I don't see someone I know."

He tapped her chin. Her face was shaped like a heart, with a cute little point at the end. "If you see someone you know, you'll both pretend it never happened. You won't discuss it at the next stuffy fund-raiser."

"The last one wasn't stuffy. You were there."

He knew she was referring to the night their affair had begun. The charity dinner had been for a Native American cause, so Jared had bought a ticket and paid an astronomical price for his meal, hoping to do his part. He hadn't intended to get sidetracked by the museum director whose job included keeping his ancestor's portrait in her care. Her interest in Catherine and Atacar should have kept him away. But it had intrigued him instead.

He reached for her hand and led her toward the sex shop. She stalled for a moment, studying the shaded windows and shiny black door. He urged her forward. Black Magic wasn't a dungeon, even if it seemed dark and cavernous from the outside.

He escorted her into the building, and she made a pleasant sound.

"It smells good in here," she said. "Like cinnamon."

He didn't comment, but he'd heard that cinnamon produced heat within the body, increasing physical and sexual appetites.

The store was big and well-lit with an array of toys, BDSM gear, fetish clothes, lubes, lotions, books, and DVDs.

Sensual accoutrements, he thought. For all types. A group of young women who appeared to be planning a bachelorette party were waving rainbow dongs at each other and giggling about wedding colors.

Mandy glanced at Jared, and they both laughed. "Are you still nervous about seeing someone you know?" he asked.

"Not anymore." She walked over to a female-friendly display, a glass table showcasing massage oils and bath products.

"Try this." He reached for a tester on another display and pumped clear liquid onto her hands.

She rubbed her palms together, as if she were analyzing a department-store moisturizer. "That's nice. Silky." She spread the lingering wetness over the backs of her hands. "It's not drying very well, though."

He bent forward to whisper in her ear. "It's a silicone lube. For the toy I'm going to buy for you. To make it nice and slick."

She caught her blunder and grabbed ahold of his shirt, a basic white tee, keeping her body close to his. Their pelvises would've bumped if they'd been the same height, but he was taller.

"Are you getting a toy, too?" she asked.

"No." They separated, and he led her to the dildo section. The giggling girls were gone. He gestured to a wall of rubber phalluses. "Check them out. Touch them."

She blinked at him. "Is one of these going to be my toy?"

"No. But I want you to touch them anyway."

She stepped forward and examined the samples, weighing them in her hands, running her fingers along their sculpted shapes.

Jared stood back and watched. He'd created this game for her, and he thrived on every inch of it. "Do you like the realistic ones?"

"Yes. Like this." She fondled a model equipped with a thickly veined shaft, hefty balls, and a bulging head.

"Good. Because you're going to make one of me. When I'm big and hard."

She looked up. By now her cheeks were flushed, giving her a warm glow. "Make one?"

He led her to another shelf, where he showed her a dildo-making kit. Her cheeks turned pinker.

"It'll include anatomical details," he said, enjoying her reaction, the shyness that made seducing her exciting. "Veins, ridges, balls. Just like the one you said you liked."

"Only it'll be an exact replica of you." She picked up the kit. The box depicted a picture of an erect penis. "I can use it when I'm alone."

"Not the first time. You're going to use it when you're with me. I want to watch you slide it between your legs. In your bedroom, with the lights turned low and candles burning."

She clutched the box, pressing the cardboard against her chest. The good girl. The want-to-be-bad girl. "That sounds romantic. Sort of," she added softly.

Jared didn't respond. Sort of romantic was the best he could do. In the silence, they gazed at each other. Was she imagining him in her bedroom, instructing her how wide to spread her thighs, how deeply to insert her homemade toy? A copy of his cock. He knew it made him seem arrogant, but he didn't want her to use a device that was fashioned after another man. He wanted to be her lover in every way.

"Will you do this for me?" he asked. "Will you use it and let me watch?"

"Yes." The word came out in a sensual rush. "But we have to pierce it. It won't feel like you if it doesn't have your PA."

Damn, she was sweet. Multiorgasmic Mandy. "We can use one

of my barbells." He would be sure to go home and get one before they went to her place to make the mold.

"What about the candles?" She glanced around. "Can we get them here?"

"Sure. But the only kind they sell are shaped like body parts. Or full nudes. Like statues of people."

"I think I'd like to get some of those."

"Okay." He knew what area of the store they were in, so he pointed the way.

She chose two white candles, one shaped like a man, the other molded as a woman. She went for a red candle, too, where a couple was together in a Kama Sutra position called Flower in Bloom.

"This is beautiful," she said.

It was, he thought, wondering how it would look with a flame burning at the tip, making the lovers melt into each other.

She glided the wax creation under his nose. "It's scented."

He caught a fragile whiff of roses, like the bouquet he'd sent. Suddenly he worried about losing her, about their affair ending before he was ready to let her go.

"Don't ever say no to me," he said. "Don't ever not be there when I need you."

"I won't," she responded. "I swear I won't."

A naked man in her bathroom, Mandy thought. Tall and dark and waiting for her to make him hard.

She'd already read the directions on the kit and mixed the

molding powder with water. The specially designed container was ready. But Jared wasn't. He'd asked her to do the honors.

He sat on the closed lid of the commode and opened his thighs. He was so unabashed, so comfortable with his nudity. And why not? Between his gym routine and endless hours on horseback, he had the body of a modern-day god.

Mandy knelt on the contour rug at his feet. Her bathroom was decorated in dusty blue and sea-foam green, with a clear white shower curtain. She lived in a one-bedroom condo in a fast-growing urban area.

Jared skimmed her hair away from her face, and she darted out her tongue. He'd removed his piercing, so the cast would be smooth.

"That's my girl," he said.

She smiled against his growing erection. One lick, and he was half-hard. He leaned back against the commode and widened his legs.

She gripped the base of his shaft and lowered her mouth, stroking and sucking at the same time. He smoothed her hair again, keeping it from falling forward, from obstructing his view.

His testes were drawn tight. She cupped the tender sacs, and he pushed deeper into her mouth. He was cheating, she thought. By now he was hard enough for the negative mold. He just wanted to get sucked some more.

Mandy gave him what he wanted until he groaned and told her to stop.

Before he inserted his cock and balls into the container, she dabbed a little petroleum jelly onto his pubic hair to be sure the molding material didn't grab any of it.

Sixty seconds later, the negative casting portion was done. The next step was pouring the liquid rubber into the container.

"It'll take hours to set," she said. "It won't be done until later tonight."

"Then we'll hang out together and wait." He reached for a washcloth and dampened it with soap and warm water, cleaning himself, getting rid of the jelly. He slid his piercing back in, too.

They both stood beside the sink, their reflections in the vanity mirror. She wanted to spend the evening with him, to have dinner, to sit on the patio and watch the sun go down. But she wasn't fooling herself into believing that they were headed toward an emotionally committed relationship. Earlier when he asked her to never say no to him, to be there when he needed her, she was well aware that he meant sexually.

He tossed the washcloth into the hamper, and she glanced at his cock. He was still half-hard, hungry for more attention. Apparently she'd left a lasting impression.

"Do you want me to finish what I started?" she asked.

Jared looked down, then back up at her. "Is that a rhetorical question?"

Mandy smiled. "I think maybe it was."

She guided him back to the commode. The moment she knelt at his feet, he sat down and assumed the fellatio position, spreading his thighs the way he'd done before.

She stroked and sucked, and he went back to playing with her hair, running his fingers through it, keeping it away from her face so he could watch.

"You're getting good at this," he said.

Enjoying his praise, she relaxed her throat and took him as deeply as she could, the way he'd made her do at the museum.

Although he tasted clean and sexy, he tasted salty, too. Semen was already beading at the tip.

He scooted to the edge of the commode lid, getting as close to her as possible. His breathing hitched; his legs went taut. His stomach tightened, too.

He thrust forward, fucking her mouth. She couldn't think of another way to say it, not with the way he was moving in and out.

When he bucked his hips, she felt the pressure of his oncoming orgasm. He spilled into her, and she swallowed every drop.

Afterward, she returned to the sink to sip some water, and he came up behind her. Once again, they were standing in front of the mirror. He didn't say anything. Instead, he put his arms around her, then unzipped her jeans and wedged his hand between the denim and her skin.

Instantly aroused, she exhaled a quick breath, and he worked his way into her panties.

"Do you know what I was fantasizing about when you were sucking me?" he asked.

She pressed against his fingers. By now, he'd found her clit.

"What you're going to do to yourself later," he said, answering his own question. "I can't wait for the damn thing to set so I can watch you use it."

She shivered against his touch. She was getting slick and wet. "You were watching me go down on you, too."

"Can you blame me?" He grazed the side of her neck with his teeth. "You're my bad girl."

She had an insane urge to ask him to give her a hickey, to

brand her in a visible way. But she wasn't a smitten teenager letting her high school boyfriend get to second base. He'd already been to third and back. He'd scored at least a dozen home runs.

He trapped her gaze in the mirror. "I want a key to your condo. Will you give me one?"

"Yes." The tension between her thighs got thicker. He thrust two fingers inside of her, banging her in that dirty-boy way of his.

"Do you know why I want it?"

"To come over in the middle of the night when I'm asleep. To kiss me. To climb on top of me." But not to cuddle, she thought. He never did that.

"That's right. Spontaneous sex. I can't get enough of it with you."

"Me, neither. With you." She angled her hips to give him better access, to show him how wet she was. She was more than willing to let him steal into her bedroom at whatever ungodly hour he chose, to give her a fix, to feed her addiction.

Losing control, she climaxed, staring at her haunted image in the glass. All she wanted was Jared. Just him. Her lover. All the time.

The way Catherine had probably wanted Atacar.

Mandy pitched forward against the sink and closed her eyes. She didn't want to think about Jared's great-great-uncle or the woman who was rumored to love him.

Not now. Not while Jared was standing behind her, with his hand still wedged in her pants, working her into another frenzy.

And making her come again.

CHAPTER THREE

Atacar didn't take me. He didn't sweep me into frenzied passion. For what seemed like the longest minutes of my life, he continued to hold me at gunpoint.

Should I tell him my name? That I am Catherine Burke, a twenty-two-year-old virgin artist with a wanton reputation? That I want him to kiss me? That I long to feel his nakedness against mine?

What if he didn't speak English? Then what? My words would be lost on him. But my actions wouldn't. I repeated what I'd done earlier and looked at his cock. I could see his genitals in much greater detail now that I was standing only a gun barrel away from him. He grew bigger, aroused by my visual attention, and I got bolder.

I brought my gaze to his face and stared him down, biting my bottom lip, sucking it lustfully between my teeth. His granite-cut features didn't soften. They were as hard as his penis. I felt triumphant. His eyes burned for more. My boldness made them darker, pitched like a midnight fire.

At that point, I expected him to lower the rifle, to sweep me into the passion I craved. But he didn't. He appeared to be waiting for me, to see what I would do next. Nervous energy skittered through my blood.

What would I do next? I'd never seduced a man before. I couldn't just stand there like an inexperienced ninny and stare him into ejaculation.

So I did what I assumed a seductress would do. I curtailed my fear and removed my clothing. I got as far as my dress, petticoat, and corset cover and stopped, letting him look at me in my ribbon-trimmed corset, lace-hemmed drawers, and high-top boots. To heighten the image, I loosed my daytime coiffure, which was already messy from my nap, allowing my wheat-colored hair to fall in long, unbound waves.

Atacar finally lowered his gun, resting the butt of the weapon on the ground. He looked at me as if I were a divine delicacy, the best sweetmeat he would ever taste. My breasts tingled. The juncture between my thighs went moist.

He jutted his chin, telling me, without words, to complete my state of undress. I prepared to unfasten my corset, and a sudden noise caught both of our attentions.

The rustle of foliage, of riders approaching.

Atacar moved at a spinning pace, and so did I. We gathered our clothes and dashed for the cottonwoods. He latched on to my arm to speed me up, and I felt as if I were being dragged. He was much taller than I was, making quicker strides. His horse spooked and ran, too. The animal disappeared out of sight. The riders were still coming from the opposite direction.

Once we were hidden in the trees, Atacar pushed me down and thrust his water-damp body on top of mine. He was heavy, big and muscular, and the air whooshed out of me.

He lifted his head and arched his torso to see who would appear. All I could see was his naked chest, which bore varying scars. War wounds, I presumed. I knew he was clutching his rifle. If the riders threatened us, he would attack, living up to his name.

The strangers arrived. I heard them dismount. I heard them talking, too. They were cowboys, filling their canteens at the stream, discussing the stray cattle for which they were searching.

Atacar's posture relaxed a bit, and I realized that he understood what they were saying. I could have spoken to him after all. Either way, I suspected that he was relieved that the other men weren't associated with the army. Luckily, they didn't linger. They were gone soon enough.

Leaving Atacar and me alone once again.

This time I waited to see what he would do. Would he lift his body from mine and don his clothes so he could track his missing horse? Or would he stay where he was, pressed intimately against me?

He stayed.

Our gazes locked. My heart rapped in raw excitement. His hips bumped mine, creating friction. His arousal returned, stone-hard and insistent.

"I'm aware of who you are," I said.

"And I'm aware that you're bewitching me," he responded in

a strong, choppy accent I'd never heard before. But that was probably how Indians sounded when they spoke English.

Dangerous. Exotic.

"Soldiers came through this area last week," I told him. "I saw your picture."

"And now you want to lie with me?"

I nodded, feeling my pulse rise. "Yes."

After that, we quit talking. Our words no longer mattered. I battled my corset, and he tugged at my drawers. I didn't show him that the crotch seam was open. I let him pull them down instead.

I knew that women could have orgasms, and I was anxious to experience what my bohemian friends in Paris whispered so deliciously about. They'd told me that I could make it happen myself, but I'd wanted to wait for my first lover.

And here he was.

Atacar kissed me, his tongue fornicating with mine. He tasted wild and forbidden, and I hungered for more. Liquid heat, as powerful as the sun itself, rained down on us.

Experimenting, I rubbed his cock, circling the head. It was silkier than I'd imagined. I felt as wonderfully wanton as my reputation, sliding my hand up and down, enjoying the gliding sensation. He groaned and kissed me harder. Our teeth clashed, and I bit his lip. He pinned me down and told me do it again, and I made a drop of his blood spill into my mouth.

We rolled over in the dirt, the grass-patched, leaf-laden ground abrading the exposed portions of my skin. My corset, which laced in back and contained a front opening, was partially undone, and my drawers were halfway down my legs. A twig scratched my bare bottom.

Atacar used his fingers, parting the curls that covered my mound, and I spread my thighs for him. He looked down, aroused by how willing I was to expose myself, to let him see. I looked down at him, too. His cock was even more engorged. I imagined him spending his seed all over me.

He played with the secret folds of my flesh, making me sinfully wet, making me squirm. I didn't need to wonder if the nub he tended was my clitoris. I knew it was. My bohemian friends whispered deliciously about that, too. I finally understood why.

The world burst at my core. I shuddered and shook, lifting my hips in jerking motions. He dipped two fingers inside, spreading even more wetness, more of what I needed. I panted until there was barely breath left in my lungs.

Then I heard a familiar voice call my name. "Catherine!"

Atacar rolled away and grabbed his rifle.

"No!" I told him, scrambling to right my undergarments, pulling up my drawers and fastening my corset. "That's my nanny. I'm from England, and she came to America with me." I managed to put my petticoat in place, but I couldn't find my corset cover, so I climbed into my dress the way I was, nearly tripping over the fabric. Nanny kept calling out to me, expressing her concern. I'd been gone a long time.

Atacar shoved on his clothes, too. But he couldn't get his cock to behave. In spite of our predicament, he remained half-hard, the buttons on his pants straining. He still desired me.

For all the good it did. By now, he looked as if he wanted to rip my hair from my pretty little head, to make me suffer for his unresolved erection. I hoped that scalping one's enemies wasn't a practice in his tribe.

Nanny called my name again.

"Hurry," he snapped. "Go to her. Before she finds you here with me."

"I'm trying." I had leaves in my unscalped hair, and my hastily fastened corset was threatening to come undone. I was an abomination.

It was to no avail. Nanny discovered us. She came puffing through an opening in the trees, stopped in her tracks, her gaze darting from me to him, then back to me. Although my appearance was ravished, she didn't accuse Atacar of hurting me. She must have recognized a seductress when she saw one.

"Goodness, child." She shook her head, her double chin quivering. "What have you done?"

It was done.

Jared leaned against the sink while Mandy popped the dildo out of the cast. She traced the naughty phallus, and his cock went hard.

"It's you." Her fingers caressed the rubber form, moving from the head to the shaft to the testes. "Every sexy detail."

"You're making me excited." He leaned over to kiss her, the toy pressed against her blouse.

"Pierce it," she said.

He used a needle. Mandy seemed intrigued, studying the procedure. He put a circular barbell in the same location as his piercing to give her the familiarity she craved. He washed the dildo with an antibacterial solution, cleaning it for her.

Once it was dry, Mandy licked the newly decorated head. He

thought about the blow job she'd given him earlier and got even more excited. He wanted her to suck the dildo, too.

"Let's go." He took her hand, and they went into her bedroom.

Jared removed the quilt and top sheet from her bed, leaving the bottom sheet and two pillows. Her room was soft and feminine with whitewashed furniture, pastel prints, and hints of lace. It was perfect for tonight, ideal for a man's voyeuristic obsession. He angled a chair, positioning it at the footboard, where he intended to watch the show. He put the dildo in the center of the bed, along with the lubricant they'd brought.

She dimmed the lights and lit the candles, placing them on the dresser beside several ornate bottles of perfume. The stage was set, he thought.

Jared took his seat, and Mandy turned toward him. The Kama Sutra candle began scenting the air, the light rose fragrance enhancing the ambience.

"Take off your clothes," he said.

She stripped, removing her sandals first, then her blouse and jeans. Her flesh-colored bra and panties came next. She had small breasts with full, pink nipples. Her stomach was flat, and her hips flared. As always, her pussy was delicately waxed. She was so beautiful, she looked like a centerfold come to life.

"Give me your panties," he said.

She walked forward and handed him her daintily laced underwear. He tucked them in to the front right pocket of his jeans, taking them as a trophy, wanting to keep something that belonged to her close to him.

All pink and pretty, she blinked, seeming unsure of what to do next.

He motioned with his chin. "Get on the bed."

She did as he instructed, kneeling on the sheet, waiting to fulfill the rest of his needs.

He gave her another aroused order. "Lick the dildo. All of it. Every inch. And imagine it's me."

"It is you." She darted her tongue over the head and played lavishly with the piercing.

By the time she worked her way down, he scooted to the edge of his seat. She held the phallus high enough for him to see her scoop one of the balls into her mouth.

Damn, he thought. Hot fucking damn. "Do that to the other one. Then give it a really nasty blow job. Hot and dirty, the way I like it."

She didn't disappoint. Clutching the base, she wrapped her lips around the dildo and sucked, pumping the device as if it really were his dick. She tipped back her head, exposing the ladylike column of her neck.

Somehow, someway, Jared was going to get through this without jerking off. Looking but not touching her or himself was part of the fantasy.

Mandy made the dildo come. Or that was how it seemed in his mind. He imagined white-hot liquid spurting into her mouth. She even made a swallowing sound. When she released the dildo, she licked her lips.

This was the best fantasy he'd ever had, and it was just getting started. "Put the lube on it now. Make it as slick as you can."

She used a generous amount, gliding the silicone solution over the rubber form. He could almost feel her sleek, smooth strokes. She took her time, favoring her new toy.

"Lie back and spread your legs," he told her.

Mandy propped both pillows against the headboard and opened her thighs. But it wasn't enough.

"Wider," he said. "All the way."

She inched them open a bit more.

He didn't back down. It was part of the game, and they both knew it. "More. Show me how pretty you are. Show me what I want to see."

She did it. She went as wide as she could, exposing her inner folds. He didn't ask her to do anything else. He just sat there, staring at her cunt.

Mandy flexed her hips, offering him an even prettier view of her labia and the hood of her clit. She glistened in her own juices. He could only imagine how much wetter she was going to get.

He lifted his gaze to her face, and she gave him her best naughty-girl smile. He'd never met anyone like her. Good. Bad. Shy. Wild. He wanted to grab her panties out of his pocket and press them against his fly.

"Tell me to put it in," she said.

"Not yet." He needed a minute.

She clutched the dildo. "When?"

He took a steadying breath. "Now. But don't insert it very deep. Go slow so I can see it happen."

Mandy followed his direction, soft and easy, and he watched the pierced head disappear.

"A little more."

She gave the dildo another tender push, and he marveled at how sweet and sexy she was. She was looking down at herself, watching, too.

When she glanced up, they stared at each other. He unzipped his jeans to ease the pressure, to make his hard-on more bearable. His boxers tented through the opening.

"Go deeper," he said. "But not all the way. Just enough to hit your G-spot."

She made a curious expression, biting the inside of her cheek, looking girlish and womanly at the same time. "I don't know how far that is. I've never tried to find—"

"Try it halfway. At an angle." He knew it was difficult to reach during regular sex, but devices like dildos and vibrators were easier to maneuver. Some vibrators were made especially for that spot.

"Like this?" She repositioned the dildo, angling it with each stroke.

"Yeah. Like that." Jared spread his thighs. He wanted to give up the fight. He wanted to jerk off, as hard and fast as he could, but he gripped the underside of his chair instead.

Mandy stimulated her G-spot, using both hands to hold the tool, going at a watch-me pace that drove him half-mad. Her rhythm was steady: shallow, then hard, then shallow again.

She went faster, and her firm little tits bounced with each pumping stroke. Her nipples were as hard as rock candy. He wanted to dissolve them on his tongue.

"I like doing this for you." She arched her back against the pillows and thrust her hips. "Just for you." She thrust again, showing him how good it was.

He tightened the hold on his chair.

"Jared." She panted his name, making sure his gaze was locked on the point of impact.

He dragged a gust of rose-scented air into his lungs. He felt as if he were going to explode. He knew she was going to come.

Her orgasm ignited the bed, shooting imaginary sparks straight at him. He could have sworn that she'd made the flames on the candles dance. The Kama Sutra couple melted all over each other.

When it was over, Jared gave Mandy and himself time to recuperate.

Before he told her to do it again.

Atacar scowled at me. He'd planned to cross the hills and ride into Mexico, where he could escape the law. But he didn't recover his horse.

He blamed me for his dilemma, claiming his desire for me had affected his judgment. He should have tracked his horse before it had gotten so far away from him.

"I bewitched you," I bragged, making his scowl deepen. He wasn't amused, and neither was Nanny.

He formulated a new plan, pulling her and me into it. He assumed that we lived within walking distance of the stream, or else we wouldn't have traveled on foot. He questioned me, making sure we resided alone, just the two of us. We did. At a farmhouse I'd purchased from the bank. Up until last week, we had a farmhand, but he'd left our employment to marry the widow he'd been courting. Nanny and I had yet to replace him.

Rifle in hand, Atacar nudged us forward, insisting that we offer him food and lodging until he raided a neighboring ranch for another horse to steal.

I carried my stretching board and paint box, and Nanny trudged beside me, complaining that Atacar was forcing us to the farm so he could steal our *horse. We only had one, and we needed it to pull our buggy when we went into town for supplies.*

"That red Indian will leave us on the plains to starve," she said, even though I caught her darting wistful glances at him.

Nanny was rather plump, with graying brown hair and sagging bosoms. I'd heard that she was quite voluptuous in her youth. Long before she'd become my nursemaid, she'd been a fetching farm girl. She'd also been accused of having a forbidden tryst with a notorious London thief. She'd denied the allegation, but I always wondered if the story were true. Now, seeing the way she looked at Atacar, I suspected it was. My old nanny missed her thief.

Hours later, Nanny served supper. The three of us sat at a simple wooden table and ate in silence. Compared to the genteel dwelling in which I'd been raised, the farmhouse was primitive. But in this area, it was considered quite nice. Nanny and I each had our own bedroom, and I used the third for my studio.

I watched Atacar beneath my lashes, trying to get his attention. I caught Nanny's instead. She scolded me, squinting her eyes and pursing her lips. It wasn't unlike me to misbehave during a meal. I'd done so at society events, poking fun at my already soiled reputation. My parents were greatly relieved when I'd expressed an interest in moving to America. Father bestowed a portion of my own dowry upon me, providing means for my survival. He was certain I would never snare a respectable husband anyway.

Nanny pursed her sour-plum lips again. I ignored her and

resumed flirting with Atacar. He finally turned his frustrated gaze upon me.

"How long are you going to be uncivil?" I asked.

"When you stop bewitching me."

"I won't stop," I countered.

"Then I'll be civil," he said, leaning toward me and speaking directly in my ear, keeping his words from Nanny, "after I fuck you."

His harshness aroused me. But it frightened me, too. Had I taken my seductress game too far? Would he thrust hard and fast upon entering me? Would losing my maidenhead be more painful than it should be?

"You'll be the first," I whispered back, too stubborn to let my fear show.

His expression changed. He seemed confused. How could such a brazen girl be a virgin?

"I've been waiting for a man who makes me feel the way you do," I admitted.

Atacar didn't dispute my claim. He didn't say anything. He just looked at me as if I'd bewitched him even more. I relaxed, sensing that he would be gentle my first time.

The farmhouse had a sleeping loft in the barn. At bedtime, Atacar told me to meet him there. I knew it was because he wanted to lie with me where Nanny couldn't hear us. She knew it, too. She'd figured out that she'd interrupted us in the cottonwoods before he could deflower me.

I changed into my finest undergarments, a red corset and matching drawers that were fashionably called lingerie. I brushed my hair until it shined, pinning a portion of it up and allowing the remainder to fall freely. I removed a buttercup from the glass jar beside my bed and worked it into my coiffure.

Before I left for the barn, Nanny draped me in a blanket. She insisted that I drink a special blend of tea, too. She told me that it would help me relax. So I took a few sips of the brew she offered.

"While you were getting ready, I asked Atacar why he speaks English so well," she said. "And do you know what his response was?"

I shook my head. The blanket was soft and fluffy, providing the comfort she wanted me to have. The tea helped, as well.

"He scouted for the army," Nanny told me. "He translated for them, too."

"If he served the army, then why is he a prisoner of war?"

"After the Chiricahua hostiles surrendered, the entire tribe, including the scouts, were exiled to military installations. First to Florida, then to Alabama, and now Oklahoma Territory. It didn't matter that Atacar served the army; the government treated him and the other scouts as if they were hostiles, too."

"He's lived a complex life," I said.

"Yes, he has." She tucked the blanket tighter around my shoulders. "And if he doesn't steal our horse, he'll probably steal your heart."

"The way the London thief did to you?"

She didn't answer. She took my empty teacup and handed me a kerosene lamp. I turned away, slipping off for my rendezvous, the moon a silver crescent in the sky.

I entered the barn and climbed to the loft. Atacar waited for me. He was stripped to the waist. I held up the light to admire him and to let him appreciate me.

Neither of us spoke. I stepped forward and placed the brass lamp on a hook on the wall, then spread the blanket on a bed of straw.

We came together and kissed, standing on the fluffy floor covering. I showed him that my fancy silk drawers were slit between my legs, and he smiled. It was the first time I'd seen his lips curve. He looked wickedly handsome.

He knelt down and licked me there, right through the opening. I gasped and widened my stance. I knew this was called cunnilingus, and it elicited the warmest, wettest, most naughty sensation. I could scarcely wait to orgasm, to shake and shudder against his tongue.

Atacar gazed up at me, making sure I was watching. I was. Totally. Completely. How could I not? I felt like a wild-hearted bride on her secret wedding night.

He stopped pleasuring me, but only long enough to order me to lie down and remove my drawers. I did his bidding, and he knelt between my thighs and lifted my legs onto his shoulders, licking me some more.

He told me how womanly sweet I tasted, calling my private place my cunt. My bohemian friends had familiarized me with that word, and like all of the other definitions they'd taught me, they'd whispered it scandalously. From Atacar, it sounded rough and dangerously romantic.

I removed my corset so my breasts would spring free. He laved my clitoris and reached up to stimulate one of my nipples, to roll it between his thumb and forefinger.

I scooted even closer to his mouth. I was drenched with his saliva and my own honey-slick moisture. He stilled his tongue, and I rubbed against his face, teasing him the way he teased me.

Finally he resumed his skillful ministration, and I put I my fingers down there, encouraging him to lick them. He turned my boldness into a game and told me to do it, too. So I did. I tasted my own fingers after they'd been inside me.

Heat danced between us. I couldn't take my eyes off of him, and he couldn't stop looking at me. I'd aroused him, and myself, beyond reason.

I climaxed, even more powerfully than before, streams of fire bursting through my quaking body.

After it was over, Atacar wiped the wetness from his face and rose up to hold me. I clung to his neck, and he said something in Apache. I had no idea what it was, but I could tell it was an endearment. He removed his pants and slid between my legs, his rock-hard penis poised at my soft, slick entrance. My heartbeat quickened, and I exhaled a virginal breath.

Desperate for him to take me.

CHAPTER FOUR

Jared paid an unexpected visit to Mandy. He arrived at her office, dressed in his work clothes: a practical denim shirt, jeans, and durable boots. His hair, as always, was combed away from his face and plaited into a thick, shiny braid. A canvas satchel was slung over his shoulder.

A cowboy, she thought, with a bag of tricks. She didn't ask him what was inside of it. Silent, she waited for him to open the flap and release the zipper, to see what sort of magic he would produce.

They both stood with the barrier of her desk between them. From the moment he'd entered the room, they'd barely spoken, barely done anything but exchanged magnetic eye contact. Mandy and Jared hadn't seen each other in a week, since he'd sat at the foot of her bed and watched her play with the toy they'd made. She wanted to tell him that she'd been using it every night since, all alone, reliving the fantasy, but she kept quiet instead, focused on the satchel he'd yet to open.

Finally he got into the bag and removed swatches of silk, velvet, and lace, fanning them across her desk in a composition of color.

"Jared?" she queried, looking at the little squares of material, then back up at him.

"I'm having a Victorian gown made for you. For a costume ball. You'll be wearing a decorative mask, too. Jewels, feathers, that sort of thing."

Her heart skipped a thrilled beat. The sun shone through the window, making the swatches shimmer. She'd never been to a masque, at least not where she'd participated. She'd attended street fairs and carnivals, but not in costume. As a child she'd gone door to door on Halloween, but that didn't count, certainly not in a glamorous way.

"When and where is the party?" she asked. "Who's hosting it? Are—"

He held up his hand, halting her questions. "We'll discuss the details after you choose the fabrics for your gown."

Mandy's mind whirred. She wanted answers, but she wanted to browse the materials, too. The feminine finery intrigued her. She stepped around from the other side of her desk and stood beside Jared.

"Pick one of each," he told her. "Silk for the main part of the gown, velvet and lace for the trim."

She took her time, laboring over the luxury. She examined the silks first, zeroing in on different shades of pink. It was her favorite color.

Jared remained patient throughout the process. Finally she handed him a swatch that was labeled Cherry Blossom. "This one."

He studied it for a moment.

"Is something wrong?" she asked.

"No, it's a good choice. I like this, especially for you. In China, cherry blossom is the symbol of female dominance, beauty, and sexuality."

"It is?"

He nodded. "That's what I've heard." He smiled a little. "But I'm not an authority on female dominance."

No, but he was pretty damn good at male dominance, at controlling their affair. He was the aggressor, and she couldn't stop herself from craving him. He gripped the pink silk lightly between his fingers. The same fingers that stimulated her. Mandy shivered. She wanted him to touch her right now, to put his hands all over her.

"Keep going," he said.

She struggled to stay focused, but she could barely breathe. Sex had never mattered before she'd met Jared, not like this, not to the point of consuming the air that chopped in and out of her lungs.

"The swatches. Pick out the other two."

His voice cut into her thoughts, stealing more oxygen, making her more light-headed. Being addicted to him was a bitch. But it felt incredible, too.

"*Mandy.*"

"Oh, yes, of course." She returned to the fabrics on her desk.

For the velvet, a rich emerald caught her eye. As for the lace, all of it was white. Virginal, she thought. The needlepoint style she chose had an intricate floral pattern and finely scalloped edges.

Jared placed her selections on the corner of the desk. Then he reached into the satchel and removed a clear plastic container filled with decorative trim and faux jewels.

"Should I pick through those, too?" she asked.

He nodded. "As many as you want."

Mandy went for satin ribbon and an array of sparkling ornaments, assuming that some of these items were for her mask.

She glanced up, anxious to know more. "Will you give me the details now?"

He shook his head. "Not until I take your measurements."

She dropped the jewels into their container, and they scattered like stones in a fishbowl. "*You're* going to measure me?"

He made a macho expression, squinting his eyes and tightening his jaw. Tiny lines bracketed his mouth. "I can handle it. The seamstress showed me what to do."

"I'm sure you can. I just didn't expect . . ."

"What?" he pressed.

She searched for an explanation that would make sense to a man she'd masturbated for. It was odd, she knew. She'd fucked herself with a dildo for him, but this was different. This was like telling him how much she weighed. "My measurements won't be impressive. They—"

"Don't get shy. Not about this." He moved closer, and before she could collect her senses, he took her in his arms.

Transfixed, she breathed in his scent. He wasn't wearing cologne. He smelled faintly of the earth, of the ranch where he lived.

He kissed her, tugging her bottom lip, using his teeth in a soft, sexy fashion. She sighed into his mouth. Her skin turned explicitly warm; her nipples went hard.

When he released her, she blinked at him. She wanted to keep holding on, to rub against him, to get down and dirty.

"Are you going to be a good girl and let me pull out my tape measure?" he asked.

She couldn't stop the smile that ghosted around her lips. Her self-consciousness was gone. "Is it big?"

"Are you kidding? It's"—he stepped back and whipped out the article in question—"a hundred and twenty inches."

Playing along, she feigned a shocked expression. "I hope it doesn't hurt."

"It will if you don't hold still." He positioned her, making sure both of her feet were planted firmly on the floor. He told her not to inflate her lungs, expand her chest, or stretch her height.

Mandy obeyed his commands. She'd never had a dress made, but she recalled the day the wedding gown she'd chosen had been fitted.

Of course, this wasn't the same. She wasn't headed for an altar-bound mistake with her mother and sisters gathered in the bridal shop, exchanging fussy opinions. On this sunny afternoon, she was being measured for a glittering costume with her lover at the helm. This was far more compelling.

Jared went around her bust, shoulders, chest, back, waist. He took lengthwise measurements, too, pinning the tape measure when it was necessary, following the lines of her body, recording every inch. Instinctively she swayed toward him.

"You need to stand straight."

"Sorry." She corrected her posture.

By now he was doing a center-front measurement from her waist to the floor. The last time he was on his knees in her office, she'd removed her panties, lifted her dress, and straddled his gorgeous face.

She looked down at him, but he didn't offer to repeat the performance. He was too busy writing numbers on a sheet of paper in a spiral notebook.

"You're teasing me," she said.

"Am I?"

"You know you are."

He stood up. "I've got something planned."

Desire zinged through her blood and zapped into her pores. Was he going to flip up her skirt and bend her over the desk?

"For the night of the party," he added.

He took a side-front measurement, going down on his knees again. Then he got to his feet once more. Finally he finished, rolling up his big, bad tape measure and putting it away. It might as well have been his cock. He wasn't going to make her come. Not today.

"What size shoes do you wear?" he asked, keeping his notebook handy.

She scowled at him. Sexual frustration battered her like a rutting ram, defying her femininity, the silk, the velvet, the lace—the masque she'd been so eager to attend. "This party better be worth it."

"Don't worry, baby. It will be."

"Fine." She huffed out her shoe size, giving him several brands for reference. He jotted down the information.

Her phone rang, and he indicated that she was free to answer it. Mandy wasn't about to.

"You owe me details, Jared."

This time he didn't protest. He responded casually. "Pia Pontiero is hosting the ball."

The fashion designer? Mandy had heard that the aging blonde diva owned a mansion in Santa Fe, along with a villa in Rome, a town house in London, and beachfront property in Malibu. "You're friends with her?"

"I know her fairly well."

Of course he did, she thought. Or else Pia wouldn't have put him on the guest list. This was his social circle, his glamorous peers. Mandy wondered how many of his former girlfriends would be there. Not that she was about to ask. They didn't talk about old lovers. He'd never even questioned her about her ex-husband. Sometimes she wished that he would, and sometimes she was glad he hadn't brought it up.

Mandy crossed her arms, then uncrossed them, battling her body language. Was she afraid of sharing her emotions with Jared, of creating more than a sexual bond with him?

"It's a history-of-fashion theme," he said, watching her the way a hawk watched a field mouse. "Guests can wear a costume from any time period."

Another crossing. Another uncrossing. More vulnerable body language. Why couldn't she just stand still? "When is it?"

"A week from Saturday."

"Oh, my goodness." She couldn't help it; she gave him a startled look. He never failed to make her head spin. "You're having a dress made for me that soon?"

"Yes." Cool and calm, he cleared the swatches and jewels from her desk and put them away. "The gown and everything that goes with it will arrive on the day of the party. And at seven 'o clock that night, a limousine will pick you up."

"We're taking a limo?"

"Yes, but we're not riding together. I'm going earlier." His smile was slow, sinful, as smooth as a brandy-and-cigar salute. "By the time you get there, I'll already be at the mansion, and you'll have to figure out who I am."

Images of searching for him among the other guests twirled in her mind. She pictured a Spanish Colonial Revival mansion with wrought-iron window grilles, hundreds of colorful tiles, and a courtyard leading to a sprawling Southwestern garden. A house designed for gallant men and finely clothed women.

"Do you think you'll be able to recognize me?" he asked.

She refused to think otherwise. Surely she would know her own lover, even if he were cloaked and masked. His height, she thought. The width of his shoulders. The confident way in which way he carried himself.

"Yes," she told him. "I'll recognize you."

"You better. Because you're going to proposition me at the party." He latched on to her wrists and brought her, full-force, next to him. "You're going to get this close to me, then you're going to whisper in my ear."

Already her pulse was fluttering at her neck, eager for what came next, to participate in the carnality he'd created. "What am I going to say?"

"That you want me to fuck you. There. At the mansion. But if you don't choose the right man, if it isn't me, you'll be making a sexual advance to a stranger." He smoothed her hair away from her cheek, grazing her skin. "And he just might take you up on your offer."

She reacted to his touch, needing him, wanting him. "That won't happen."

"What won't? You choosing the wrong guy? Or him banging you breathless while both of you have your masks on?"

"It's going to be you, Jared. You're the only man who's going to do that to me."

He stepped back, but his gaze remained fixed on hers. Strong. Hard. Possessive. "Did you ever make me a key to your condo?"

She nodded. "It's in my purse. I'll get it for you."

"I don't want it now. Slip it into my pocket when we're at the party. When I'm making you come." He reached for the satchel and looped it over his shoulder, pausing at the door. "I'll see you at the masquerade."

"You, too." Caught up in his game, she watched him leave, her heart beating in her chest just as deeply as it pounded between her legs.

~

On the night of the masque, Mandy stood in front of the closet-door mirrors in her room, wearing her underwear. But it wasn't a bra and panties. She'd donned the undergarments that had arrived with her dress. So there she was in a lace-and-ribbon-trimmed corset, a decorative corset cover, embroidered stockings, and a pair of wide-legged drawers, also trimmed in ribbon and lace, with the crotch seam open.

She felt positively decadent.

She had expected a gown and mask, but she hadn't considered time-period undergarments, too. She hadn't realized that Jared would go this far.

"Look at you," Kiki said from behind her. The historian had come over to help her get ready.

Mandy reached for her petticoat and put it on. The stiff garment flounced and frilled at the bottom. "I'm being transformed."

"Yes, you are. The lady of the Victorian manor." The other woman pointed to a makeshift vanity table they'd set up. "Now let me do your hair."

Mandy took a seat, allowing herself to be pampered. Kiki dived right in, enjoying her self-appointed role in all of this. She'd researched hairdos that had been featured in *Harper's Bazaar* in the mid-1890s and wanted to try her hand at a fancy evening coiffure.

First she curled Mandy's hair, forming a profusion of ringlets in front and dividing the rest into three sections, where she created a soft, intricate bun. For the finishing touch, she used jeweled combs Jared had provided, working them into the design.

"Women were so elegant then," she said, seemingly pleased with her work.

Mandy was pleased, too. She gazed at her own reflection. She was becoming more and more Victorian. "You did an amazing job."

"So did Jared." Kiki walked over to where Mandy's dress was hanging. "This is an exquisite replica. It's sewn exactly the way it would have been in that era."

"Jared is a stickler for detail." Mandy thought about the dildo they'd made and got warm in the vicinity of her open-crotch drawers. "He likes things to seem real."

"He must really be into you." Kiki took a lingering look at the gown. "This must have cost him a fortune."

"He's a successful horseman. Rich clients and all that." Her heart went a little haywire, but she reined it back. "He's made a name for himself in this town."

"He's making one for you, too. Of course, tonight no one will know who you are."

Mandy nodded and glanced at the bed, where she'd placed the mask that accompanied her costume. She knew the history behind masked balls: to disguise oneself to create confusion or anonymity, to have bouts of harmless fun. But what Jared had in mind wasn't harmless. It was dangerously erotic.

Like him.

"I better finish getting ready," she said, butterflies winging their way to her stomach.

Kiki reached for the gown, offering to fasten the back closures.

The cherry blossom dress fit Mandy beautifully, with sleeves that puffed at her shoulders and a skirt that flowed into a bell, balancing her figure and creating a striking silhouette. The neckline was trimmed in velvet with a row of iridescent beads, as was the hem, which erupted into embroidered lace. A matching wrap, a capelet, went with it.

Kiki smoothed the back of the gown. "You look gorgeous. He's going to die when he sees you."

"Thank you." The butterflies went crazy. "I chose the colors."

Mandy stepped into her shoes, evening slippers that complemented her dress. The winged eye mask came next, adorning her face with glass jewels and ostrich feathers.

By the time Kiki left and the limousine arrived, Mandy had blotted and refreshed her lipstick three times. She kept imagining how Jared was going to taste. All she wanted to do was kiss him.

She rode in the back of the long, black car, fingering the drawstring on her small, beaded purse. It, too, had been fashioned after the Victorian era.

Although she considered pouring herself a drink, she refrained. She was already drunk on Jared. She kept thinking about his disguise, anxious to discover what type of costume he'd chosen.

Surely he would be in Victorian garb, as well.

As the vehicle traveled farther into the mountains, she gazed out the window, watching the nighttime landscape go by.

She refused to believe that she would falter at the party. She would recognize her lover, no matter what his masquerade.

Wouldn't she?

Now that the time grew near, her confidence wavered. What if he'd disguised himself beyond recognition? Mandy wet her mouth, tasting her pretty pink lipstick. What would happen if she propositioned the wrong man?

Nothing. Because Jared wouldn't let someone else touch her, not while they were involved, not while she belonged to him. He was possessive that way.

Wasn't he?

She shifted in her seat. If she weren't in jeopardy of wrinkling her dress, she would've bunched her skirts and touched herself through her slit drawers.

For Jared. For the excitement he'd created.

She actually wanted to come in the car, to close her eyes and imagine that Jared's cock was buried deep inside her.

Damn. She squeezed her thighs together.

Earlier, she'd closed the glass partition that separated her from the chauffeur. Now all she had to do was lower the electronically operated blind. Then she would have even more privacy.

Her clit throbbed, desperate for attention.

Should she do it?

No, she thought. She wasn't about to arrive at the party a rumpled mess, with her fingers creamy from her own come. Instead she would sit here like a good girl, squirming in her glittering gown, coiffed like the proper lady she was supposed to be.

The limo wound its way along a private road, finally taking her to a sprawling estate hidden in the hills.

The chauffeur opened her door, and she climbed out of the car, holding up the hem of her lavish dress, feeling like Cinderella exiting her coach.

She thanked the driver and presented her invitation to a tuxedoed man at an iron gate. He allowed her access, and she walked along a brightly lit path toward the front door, passing a tiered fountain and a spray of indigenous foliage.

The house was what she'd imagined: an enormous two-story Spanish Colonial Revival mansion with a clay roof, stuccoed archways, and prominent pillars.

Music spilled into the air. Voices echoed festively into the night. The moon was decidedly half-full, adding a bewitching ambience.

Another tuxedoed man was stationed at the door. He directed her to the coat check, where she left her wrap. From there, she was guided to a ballroom with stained-glass windows, malachite floors, and carved wood accents. It was breathtaking.

And so were the other guests.

Costumes varied. She noticed Renaissance, Regency, Romantic, Victorian, Edwardian, flapper, as well as trends from the 1940s to the 1990s. Power-dressing and haute couture were represented, too.

No fashion stone was left unturned, particularly with the women: flounced ruffles, ladylike fans, feather boas, vinyl, leather, pearls, diamonds, hats, bonnets, long, flowing scarves. It was endless.

Masks ranged from simple to extravagant, from swan shapes to butterflies to shiny stars and eclipsed moons. One curvy redhead could have been a panther on the prowl, with an exotic mask and a jet-black gown plunging to her navel.

The men were equally dashing. She scanned the crowd for Jared, but there were hundreds of guests in attendance, spilling into the buffet room and onto the dance floor. The patio was occupied, too.

Mandy didn't know where to begin.

She decided that she needed the drink she'd neglected to pour in the limo, so she twined her way through the fashion extravaganza and beelined to the nearest bar. She went for a Between the Sheets, a cocktail consisting of rum, cognac, passion fruit mixer, and lime juice. Jared had introduced her to Between the Sheets, in more ways than one.

Now she wished she would have strummed her clit in the car. The bartender handed her a rocks glass. He'd given her an extra cherry.

In case she lost one? She sipped the drink. It was too late for that. A woman couldn't get her cherry back. And this woman didn't want to. She just wanted to find Jared, to hold him close, to whisper naughty words in his ear. Her dirty-boy lover.

Where the hell was he?

Mandy took a deep breath and started her search, looking at every masked man she passed. Some of them looked back. But none of them had Jared's granite-cut jaw, six-foot-one frame, or cocky swagger.

No, that wasn't true. There were plenty of tall, square-jawed men with fuck-me attitudes, but she could tell that they weren't him.

Because they didn't make her hot or hungry or desperate to get laid. The eye contact she'd made with them didn't arouse her; it didn't ignite the fire in her veins.

She sipped more of her Between the Sheets, letting the liquid slide down her throat. Trying to conjure Jared, she imagined that she was tasting his come. That he was kneeling over her, spilling into her mouth.

"That's my favorite drink, too," a female voice said from behind her.

Mandy spun around.

An incredibly leggy blonde in a micro-miniskirt and plastic, peek-a-boo top clanked her glass against Mandy's. She was one of the most dazzling creatures at the party. Her hair, which could have easily been a wig, was long and thick and flatiron straight. But even if her hair was fake, the rest of her was real. Model-thin with perky breasts quite visible through her geometric-printed top, she embodied a 1960s mod girl. Her mask made her eyes look big and wide. It even had overly exaggerated, spiky eyelashes attached. The effect was stunning.

"Here's to Between the Sheets," she said.

"And to men who make women weep," Mandy added, knowing instinctively that the glossy girl with the fishnet stockings, flashy go-go boots, and killer legs was one of Jared's former lovers.

CHAPTER FIVE

"By the way," the mod girl said, her voice lilted with a unique accent. A bit British. A bit Italian. A bit American. A lot sexy. "We made your dress."

Mandy blinked beneath her mask. "We?"

"Our company. Pia Pontiero, Inc."

"You work for Pia?" Was she a showroom model? An assistant designer? An illustrator? Surely she wasn't the seamstress Jared had mentioned.

"I'm Amber. Pia's daughter."

Damn. It wasn't the designer who'd put Jared on the guest list. It was her young, gorgeous daughter.

"When I was little, Mama used to buy me things to make me behave," Amber said. "She still does." The announcement came on the heels of a pretty, if not self-indulgent, smile. "I'm what they call a spoiled heiress. I also fucked the twirling daylights out of Jared."

Mandy wasn't used to these kinds of situations. These kinds

of women. But she was in Jared's world now. Who fucked who was par for the course. The *inter*course, she thought, determined to keep her sense of humor. "I already figured out that you and Jared used to be lovers."

Amber brought her glass to her lips, leaving pearly pink marks on the rim. "We met at the club scene in London, then reconnected here when Mama bought this house."

Jared had been to England? He'd partied on another continent? Mandy frowned. There was so much she didn't know about him. So much he hadn't revealed.

Amber continued. "On our first Santa Fe date, we went to a local bar and discussed the appeal of erotic-named drinks."

"Like Between the Sheets?"

"And others. He enjoys watching women having Sex on the Beach, a Kiss in the Dark, or a Screaming Orgasm. Hand Jobs make him crazy, too. But Blow-Job Shooters are his favorite. Has he gotten you into those yet?"

Mandy tried to keep her voice neutral, to not sound as clipped as she felt. "No. Not yet."

"They're delightful. Bailey's Irish cream, Amaretto, and whipped cream. The correct way to shoot a Blow Job is to place your hands behind your back, pick up the glass with your mouth, tilt your head back, and drink."

Screw not sounding clipped. Mandy had just earned the right to act catty. "What about a Hand Job mixed with a Blow Job? Or haven't you ever tried that?"

"Mixing cocktails isn't a good idea. Or did you mean the real thing? I'm quite proficient at that."

"So am I." She didn't used to be, but she was now.

A beat of silence passed before Amber asked, "Did you know that I'm part of the game? Of what Jared arranged for you tonight?"

Damn him all to hell. Him and his go-go girl. "He told you to approach me?"

"No. I wanted to meet you on my own. To tell you who made your dress." Amber's accent softened. "Do you like it?"

"Yes." Mandy relaxed a little, glancing down at the front of the skirt. It was a gown Catherine could have worn. "I love it."

"Jared has been planning this for a while, but he didn't want to tell you until the time got closer. That's why we had to put a rush on your costume."

"My friend said it probably cost him a fortune."

"It did." The other woman angled her head, making her hair—or her wig—sweep her cheek and fall to one side. "But men should pay for sex. Girls like us shouldn't give it away."

Was Amber putting Mandy in the same sexy league as herself?

The designer's daughter smiled, and so did Mandy. Suddenly knowing that they'd fucked the same man seemed hot. Gloriously naughty. A secret between strangers.

They smiled at each other again, as "Masquerade," a song from *Phantom of the Opera*, vibrated from the DJ's sound system, receiving an instant response from the crowd.

"Paper faces on parade," Amber said, reciting a portion of the chorus.

"Hide your face," Mandy added, "so the world will never find you." She paused, thinking about her lover's disguise. "So exactly how are you part of Jared's game? Of what he arranged for me tonight?"

"Besides my involvement with your costume? I know what he's wearing, too. How he intends to trick you."

Intrigued, Mandy moved closer, catching a hint of Amber's perfume. She smelled as fresh as a new rain. "You could tell me."

"And spoil the fun? Not a chance." Amber finished her drink and placed it on the tray of a passing waiter. The bartender had given her two cherries, too. But she'd left both of them in the bottom of her glass.

"Not even a hint?" Mandy asked. She'd eaten her cherries. She'd sucked them right down to the stems.

"Sorry, no. But maybe you and I get can together sometime. We can do some Blow Jobs. The cocktail kind," the heiress clarified.

"That sounds good."

"To me, too." One last smile, and Amber was off, gliding through her mother's multimillion-dollar mansion.

As Mandy watched her go, she realized how unusual their encounter had been: polite, then bitchy, then strangely, sexually empowering.

Jared's former bedmate was gone, and Mandy's body tingled beneath yards of silk, velvet, ribbon, and lace.

She craved her dirty boy even more.

So she set out to find him. She wandered through the party, examining the men, but more carefully this time. She checked them out in every way. She even glanced down at their flies. It was crazy to think that she would recognize Jared's cock beneath a pair of pants, but it gave her wicked pleasure to try.

Then it happened. Mandy caught sight of a tall, broad-shouldered, slim-hipped man headed for the buffet who could be

Jared. His long, dark hair was banded into a ponytail, and he was dressed in Victorian formalwear: a Tombstone shirt, an elegant silk puff tie, a classic gray vest, black Highland pants, and a matching frock coat. On his lapel, he wore a pink rose.

The same shade as her dress.

Her heart went volcanic, nearly erupting on the spot. She dashed across the room to follow him, to get a closer look at his masked face.

She lucked out, managing to get directly behind him in the buffet line. He reached for a plate, and she noticed his hands were gloved. He glanced her way and gave her a gentlemanly nod. But that was it. He wasn't behaving as if he knew her. His attention returned to the food that awaited him.

Mandy picked up a plate and silverware, too. But her mind wasn't on their upcoming meal. She studied his profile. His black satin mask altered the contours of his face. It completely covered his forehead, reshaped his eyes, and molded around his cheeks and down his nose, leaving only his nostrils visible. His mouth was exposed, too. But she didn't know if he was Jared, not for certain.

Were those the lips she'd been kissing? Was he her lover? The man who'd been making her come?

He filled his plate, selecting various meat dishes, along with chipotle-spiced potatoes and herb-braised vegetables. For dessert he chose rice pudding. He'd skipped the salads altogether.

She'd seen Jared eat salads, hadn't she? He wasn't opposed to leafy greens. Or was he? Mandy furrowed her brow. She should know Jared better than she did.

Since his mannerisms gave nothing away, she focused on his

hair. It was the right color, the perfect length, the correct thickness. It was Jared's hair. Wasn't it?

Before he carried his meal to one of the many linen-draped tables in the dining room, she asked if she could join him.

"Yes, ma'am," he responded, his deep, rich timbre tinged with a slight Southern drawl. "You're more than welcome to dine with me."

For a moment, Mandy went still. She didn't move. She barely breathed. His slow, sensual drawl slid straight to her drawers, making her sweet and creamy. Could another man besides Jared do that to her?

"Where did you learn to talk like that?" she asked.

He guided her to a window-seat table. "I was raised in Oklahoma."

Was that a clue? Was that where Jared was originally from? As far she knew, most of the Chiricahua Apache hailed from a reservation in New Mexico, where their ancestors had gone after their incarceration at Fort Sill had ended. Of course, there was a small group who'd stayed behind and had become the Fort Sill Apache of Oklahoma.

She sat across from him. He didn't remove his gloves to eat. A waiter came by to take their drink orders. She decided to have another Between the Sheets. He asked for a Coca-Cola, using the formal name for Coke.

"It was invented in 1885," he said, after the waiter departed.

She spread her napkin on her lap, preparing to taste her meal, sparse as it was. She'd barely put any food on her plate. "What was?"

"Coca-Cola. It's Victorian, too."

"Like us?" She gazed into his eyes, but they didn't give him away. She wondered what he would do if she came over to his side of the table and put her hand on his thigh, if she rubbed his cock through his pants, if she made it swell.

He would love it if he were Jared, she thought. He would encourage her to play, to go through with their plan, to proposition him.

And if he was a stranger?

"Is something wrong?" he asked.

"No." Nothing but the hot and cold chill snaking her spine. When the waiter brought their drinks, she took a desperate swig.

Her Victorian-garbed partner smiled, and she went sweet and creamy again. She imagined him thrusting inside her. If he wasn't Jared, then she was in trouble. His masquerade, his similarity to Jared, aroused her.

"Who are you?" she finally asked.

"A guest at the party," he told her, keeping his identity to himself. "Who are you?"

She almost said her name, but she caught herself before it slipped out. What good would introducing herself do?

He turned away from her, noticed someone he knew, and motioned to whoever his acquaintance was. Mandy shifted in her chair, hoping to see Amber with a couple of Blow-Job Shooters. At least that would prove that her dinner companion was Jared.

But it wasn't Amber he'd solicited. He'd just invited two men to their table, and both of them looked *exactly* like him: the same mask, height, body type, hair, clothes. The only difference was the color of the roses on their lapels; one was red, and the other was blue. Both carried dinner plates brimming with Southwestern delicacies.

The red-rose man sat beside her, and the blue sat on the other side of the table next her original companion, the Coca-Cola drinker sporting the pink boutonniere.

So this was the game Amber had helped create. She'd found two men, probably models or actors, who resembled Jared enough to pull off this deception, especially with masks covering most of their faces. For all Mandy knew, a touch of Hollywood makeup had been added. Hair extensions. Whatever it took to clone them.

No one spoke. The waiter reappeared for more drink orders, did a triple take, and raised his eyebrows at Mandy, almost as if she were headed for an orgy. What the hell, she thought, as she shrugged back at him. At the moment, it seemed like a pretty good plan. She didn't have a clue who was who.

As the waiter darted off, she divided her gaze between the sexy trio. "I think I want all of you."

Pink Boutonniere smiled, Red speared a roasted pepper on his plate, and Blue sat back in his chair.

"You can't have all of us," Blue said, his voice slow and sinfully Southern, too. "You'll need to choose one."

"You?" she asked.

He didn't respond, and suddenly his hard-edged silence made him seem like the real Jared.

But that didn't mean he was. He could be as phony as the dyed flower on his lapel. Blue roses didn't exist.

She turned toward Red. He'd yet to speak. But at least his

rose embodied the Black Magic bouquet Jared had sent to her office, at least that was genuine.

"What do you think?" she asked him.

"I think you should dance with me," he responded. "After we finish our meal."

Another Southern boy. His voice mirrored the other candidates. She got goose bumps. "Are you from Oklahoma, too?"

"We all are. We're all Jared," he added, reminding her that she was caught in a carnal charade.

The waiter returned with Red and Blue's drinks, but this time he didn't raise his eyebrows at Mandy. He left her to her orgy.

Red leaned closer to her, close enough to cast a Black Magic spell. Mandy was tempted to kiss him, to taste the roasted peppers on his lips. He seemed to have Jared's mouth. But all of the men's mouths were shaped the same. Damn. Now Red was arousing her, the way Pink had done earlier.

She looked at Pink, getting his reaction. He liked watching her and Red. He seemed turned on by seeing her flirt with someone else. He dipped into his dessert and swallowed the frothy pudding on his spoon.

"Bad girl," he said.

"I'm always bad for Jared," she told him, casting a glance at Blue.

Blue returned her eye contact, but only for a stolen moment, an instant in time. Compared to the other men, Blue hadn't done anything to entice her. But his aloofness compelled her more than Pink's playfulness, more than Red's charisma.

Was he Jared?

Blue ignited her entire body, from the top of her intricately coiffed hair, to the hood of her swollen clit, to the tips of her satin-covered toes. She wanted to fuck every hard-edged inch of him. She even drew her thighs apart to ease the pressure.

"Dance with me," Red said, catching her attention. By now, they'd finished their meals.

"Yes, of course." She hesitated before she stood up, curious to see what Blue would do. But he didn't do anything except flag down the waiter for another beer.

"Be good," Pink told her. "Until we get our turns."

"You mean be *bad*," she corrected him, anxious for Blue's turn. But she had a feeling he was going to make her wait. He didn't seem to be in a hurry to dance with her, and that made her want him even more.

Stupid girl, she thought. She should have the sense to ignore him. But as she walked away with Red, she looked over her shoulder at Blue. He didn't return her interested glance. He'd made eye contact with another Victorian woman in the room. Mandy wanted to kill him.

She hoped he wasn't Jared.

"Screw Blue," she said out loud.

Red chuckled beneath his breath and swept her onto the dance floor. The song was soft and elegant, so she swayed in Red's arms. Throughout the night, the music had been changing, going from fast to slow to somewhere in between, accommodating all of the guests, all of the eras from which they were attired.

"This is an amazing party," she said.

"It is," he agreed. "Especially this part. We've never danced together before."

That was true, whether he was Jared or an imposter. Either

way, Red was an impeccable dancer. He was light on his feet, the way a society-schooled Victorian man should be. Mandy had learned to waltz for her wedding, but that was a lifetime ago. But at least she knew the basics.

"You're good," she said.

"I try." He embellished his next move and made her laugh. She wondered if he was as creative in bed.

"You're not Jared," she said suddenly.

He quit smiling. "Now why would you say that?"

Because if he were Jared, she wouldn't be wondering if he were a creative lover. She would already know. She would feel it. As well as she and Red moved together, their sexual rhythm was off.

"I've never danced with you before," she told him. "But I've never slept with you before, either."

"Dear lady." He kept the Southern drawl. He stayed in character. Or maybe it was his real voice. "We could remedy that. You could pick me anyway."

Her face went hot. Was she blushing? Were her cheeks turning rosy? Was she behaving like a Victorian miss with her skirts all aflutter? "You'd sleep with a girl you don't even know?"

His smile returned. "I'm trying to get to know you. I'm giving it my best shot."

Yes, she thought. He'd admitted that he wasn't Jared, but he wasn't succumbing to defeat. "What about the other man? Would he pursue me, too?"

"I don't know."

"Do you know who he is? What color of flower he's wearing?"

"No." Red glanced in the direction of the dining room. "We've had quite a few dress rehearsals that included the three of us, but we got ready separately this evening. We didn't see each other until our roses were in place."

"So you don't know who Jared is, either?"

"Not this evening, no." The song ended, and Red took her hand. "Shall I escort you back to the table?" He paused. "Unless you'd prefer to slip away for a tryst with me?"

Mandy smiled in spite of herself. He was quite the charmer. "It's tempting, but I came here to rendezvous with my lover."

"He's a lucky man."

"He better think so."

Red looped his arm through hers, and they walked side by side, probably looking as if they belonged together, as if they were a tight-knit couple.

As they passed beneath a hand-painted archway, Mandy glanced up at the Mayan symbols above her head. The mansion was adorned with ancient-style artwork.

Red stopped walking. "Which one do you think he is?"

"Pink or Blue? I honestly don't know. Pink isn't possessive enough, and Blue isn't attentive enough. They both confuse me."

"That's too bad." Red made a last-ditch effort to woo her. "Maybe you should just go for me."

"Maybe I should." She bumped his shoulder, and he laughed. He knew she didn't mean it.

He removed the rose from his lapel and handed it to her. "You might as well take this. Maybe keep it as a memento or something."

Mandy pinned his boutonniere to her purse. She thought him offering it to her was a nice gesture.

They returned to the table and found Pink sitting by himself. Blue was gone.

Mandy's heartbeat quickened. Her pulse went deliriously mad. The game kept twisting and turning, coiling her emotions with it. Deep down, she wanted a chance with Blue. She wanted to win his affection.

"Where's Blue?" she asked Pink.

"Who's Blue?" he responded.

"Your partner in crime."

He shook his head. "Good God, woman, if he's Blue, have you been calling me Pink?"

Behind her, Red burst into a chuckle, amused by Pink's reaction to his own nickname. She almost nudged Red to shut him up. Her sense of humor was wearing thin. The least Blue could have done was stay at the damned table.

"So where is he?" she asked Pink again.

"Hell if I know." Pink shrugged as if his partner in crime didn't matter. "He got up and walked away. I didn't see which direction he went."

Mandy snared his gaze. It seemed darker than before, less flirtatious, less playful than Pink's. Everything about him seemed different. Harder. Edgier. Sexier.

Something wasn't right.

"Did you switch flowers?" she asked, her nerves skittering to a halt. "Did you used to be Blue?"

"Who? Me? The Coca-Cola man? No, I've always been Pink." His lips twisted into a grimace. Red chuckled once more, but he quieted down when Pink told him to piss off.

"You're Blue," Mandy said. "You're him."

"Then prove it," he told her.

She accepted his challenge. "I will. But first you have to dance with me."

"If that's what you want." He stood up and moved toward her, pausing as if he were going to lean in to kiss her. But he didn't. He removed the pink rose and pinned it next to the red one on her purse.

"Now I'm Jared," he said.

"You're still Blue, and you're going to be Blue until *I* decide that you're Jared."

"She's a hellcat," Red interjected.

"I hope so." Blue was smiling now. The first time he'd smiled all night.

He offered her his arm, and they entered the dance floor. He was a better dancer than Red, and Mandy hadn't thought that was possible. But Blue moved with such masculine grace that even her heart followed his lead.

Her heart?

No, she thought. No. That wasn't part of the plan. She almost pulled away, lifted her skirts and dashed into the night, leaving him in her panicked wake.

But she stayed where she was, stumbling on her next step, inwardly cursing her discomposure.

"What's the matter?" He held her close. "Haven't you ever seduced a stranger?"

Mandy's breath rushed out. She went hot beneath her corset, her petticoat, her modesty-free drawers. "Are you a stranger?"

"I might be."

She looked into his eyes, searching for the man she knew. She wanted to prove that he was Blue and that Blue was Jared. But what if he wasn't? What if he was Pink playing a trick on her?

"You're not sure who I am," he said.

Once again, Mandy had trouble concentrating on the waltz. Other couples twirled around them, jeweled masks catching the light. The floor was filled with Renaissance, Regency, Romantic, Victorian, and Edwardian dancers.

Finally she snapped out of her shell. She refused to stumble again, to be as stiff as her petticoat. The music was sweet and melodic, wonderfully fluid. She wanted to be part of it.

"Kiss me," she told her partner.

"Not now. Not yet."

Damn. Whoever he was, he was following the rules of the game. Her hunger went unfed. He wasn't going to give himself away with a kiss, not unless she propositioned him for more.

"Maybe it would be better if you were Pink," she said.

His voice went a little more Southern. "And why is that?"

She wondered if Oklahoma had truly been his home, if he'd grown up there as a child. "Because there's no such thing as a blue rose."

"Isn't there?" Without missing a beat, he removed a blue boutonniere from inside his frock coat and gave it to her. The flower was identical to the one she'd seen him—or was it the other man?—wearing earlier.

"It's fake," she chided, trying not to be awed by him.

"That one is. But I heard that scientists have been working on making them real, and that someday they'll be available."

Without thinking, she pinned the boutonniere to his lapel,

moving to the music while she did it. "They'll never be this bright. This vivid."

"That's what scientists are working on. Getting the color just right." He rejoined their hands. "Did you know that in the Victorian era, they used flowers to communicate? Lovers weren't allowed to express their feelings for each other in public, so they sent coded messages through flowers." He paused, his mouth set in a serious line. "There were even dictionaries on the subject."

It was impossible not to be awed by him. "How do you know all of that?"

"I read about it."

The song ended, and she stepped back and gazed at the rose, studying its cobalt petals. It fit him beautifully. He'd been Blue all along.

But was he Jared?

"I saw you looking at another Victorian woman," she said, reminding him that he'd offended her earlier.

"Maybe I was envious of you and those other men."

"Then you shouldn't have created this charade. You shouldn't have put Red and Pink in my path."

"Maybe I did it to test you."

"To see if I would recognize my own lover?"

The music started again. Another classic song. Another gliding melody. Without the slightest hesitation, he reached for her. They were quarreling, but Blue still took what he wanted.

Silence tick-tocked between them. Sway, turn, promenade, chassé. She followed his every lead. She didn't stumble; she didn't falter. On the outside she was floating across the floor. But inside she felt as if she were being branded.

"I didn't look at her the way I'm looking at you," he said.

He was right. She couldn't deny his claim. Even with all of the people, with all of the festivities surrounding them, he was riveted to her, as she was to him.

Mandy couldn't stop herself if she tried. She wanted him inside her. Deep and wet. Hard and powerful. Her addiction was crying for relief. She needed a fix; she needed the man in her arms.

She moved closer, pressing her mouth to his ear. "Fuck me," she whispered. "Here. Tonight. At the mansion."

He nuzzled her delicately coiffed hair, and she envisioned him ravishing it, tugging at the pins, one by one.

"Are you sure?" he asked. "Are you sure I'm him?"

"Who else could you be?" She held him with all of her might. No one made her feel the way he did.

Good, bad, naughty, nice.

"I could still be a stranger," he told her.

She held him tighter. He was Jared. He was her lover. But she liked that he was offering to be a stranger. "Then fuck me," she said, heat spiraling through her core. "As if you've never fucked me before."

CHAPTER SIX

My heart wouldn't quit pounding. Atacar's body was so close to mine, I could smell the hunger on his skin. A male scent. Hard. Primitive. Animalistic.

"Are you ready?" he asked.

I nodded and looked up at him. He was on top of me, supporting his weight with his arms. I marveled at his face, just inches from mine. I still wanted to paint him, to immortalize him in a way only an artist could. I knew he would be my greatest work, my deepest challenge. He was dangerously handsome, as wild as the land that had borne and bred him.

The lantern flickered, and I caught my breath. Shadows danced like demons inside the barn, shifting across our bodies.

"Say it." His gaze pierced mine. "Tell me you're ready."

"I am," I insisted. To prove my point, I spread my legs wider. Tingling with anticipation, I glistened in my own juices. I was a

virgin, hungry to be had. But that wasn't enough for him. He wanted more from me.

He cuffed my wrists with his hands, holding me down, using the masculine power that compelled him. "Are you sure?"

Heat coiled in my belly. A girlish sheen of sweat broke out across my forehead. My nipples peaked like mountaintops.

"Yes," I whispered, my voice barely audible, barely recognizable. I couldn't imagine being more ready, more eager to lose my maidenhead.

He gentled his hold on me, lowering his mouth to mine, kissing me softly, making me sigh. I put my arms around him and prayed that he would stop teasing me. I needed him. I needed his hardened length thrusting inside me.

Concern edged his voice. "It's going to hurt."

I wet my lips, tasting the aftermath of his kiss. "I know."

He reached down, and I scooted closer. When he pushed the tip of his cock inside, I tensed. I didn't mean to, but suddenly he seemed too big for my tight passageway. He didn't stop. He kept pushing, going deeper, filling me, packing my body with his.

I curled my toes. It didn't hurt. Not yet. But I was bracing myself for the pain.

Boom. He thrust all the way, nearly shattering me in two. I gasped from the invasion, digging my fingernails into his back. Every time he moved, I clawed him. He told me to relax, but I didn't know if I could. We were immersed in shadows, fire demons licking our skin.

"Watch it go in and out," he said.

Needing a diversion, I glanced down at our joined genitals.

His penis was thick and heavily veined, and my vagina was soft and pink, the delicate folds stretching for him. His pubic hair bumped mine. He was as dark as I was blonde.

"We're beautiful," I said.

Atacar laughed, the sound rich and husky. Apparently beautiful wasn't the word he would have used. But I couldn't think of a more fitting description. He was all man, and I was all woman. What could be more beautiful than that?

I lifted my bottom in the air, experimenting with the position I was in. His penetration didn't hurt quite as badly. It still stung, but I decided that I liked it. Having him inside me, making me ache, gave me a vivid sense of being alive.

I was like a wolf, breathing in my mate. His scent, the male arousal I smelled earlier, got stronger, assailing my nostrils.

His stomach muscles rippled with every stroke. Deep. Shallow. He went forward, he withdrew, heightening the pleasure, intensifying the ache.

I hoped that Nanny was wrong. That he wouldn't steal my heart. Or worse . . . that he wouldn't break it. He was watching me now, analyzing the expression on my face. I tried to level my emotions. But it didn't work.

He touched my cheek with such tenderness he almost made me cry. I wasn't a girl prone to tears, but this was a monumental moment in my life. I turned my head and kissed his fingers.

"I had a wife," he said suddenly. "I was married."

His confession nearly knocked the wind out of me. I clutched his shoulders to sustain the blow and gouged his flesh so sharply I drew blood. He was still inside of me, still stretching my inner folds.

"Did she die?" I asked.

"No. I threw her away."

I assumed that was the Apache way of saying he'd divorced her. I didn't have the courage to ask him why he'd left his wife. Not now. Not while our slick, naked bodies were entwined.

We both went silent. The only sound was the meeting of our flesh, the hot, desperate sin between us.

He covered my mouth in a searing, scorching, soul-burning kiss, plundering me with his tongue, bewitching me as deeply as I'd bewitched him.

Unable to control my passion, I rasped a dirty word in his ear, encouraging him to pound me into the blanket. My body was like a wooden bow, arched and ready to snap. His cock was so hard and his balls so tight I feared he might explode.

His driving rhythm torched my womb, but I didn't care. I didn't want him to be gentle. I didn't want him to touch me in a way that might trigger tears. I was already getting too attached.

"Don't stop," I said.

"I won't." He kissed me again, wedging his fingers between us, strumming my clitoris.

He played me like the piano in my mother's gilded parlor. A thundering concerto filled my head, and I reached beyond the blanket and grasped handfuls of straw. By now, I'd locked my legs around his waist. He rocked my body, bouncing my breasts. His powerful chest heaved.

The music got louder, more demanding. I slammed my hips against his, meeting his generous strokes. My cunt was wet and sore; my clitoris was on fire. His callused fingers kept playing me.

He looked down, and so did I. Together we watched ourselves make forbidden love. Being with him was more scandalous than anything I could've imagined.

"You're beautiful," he said.

"We're *beautiful," I countered.*

He didn't expel a husky laugh, not this time. He accepted my opinion. He allowed me to speak my feminine mind. I wanted to tell my Paris friends about him, but how could I? The best I could do was document our affair within the pages of my leather-bound journal.

I dropped the straw in my hands, scattering prickly stalks. Desire flooded my core, bubbling beneath the surface of my mound. Atacar used his fingers like Merlin's magic, his cock like King Arthur's sword. We were both sticky with my juices.

An orgasm lashed my body, whipping me into a fevered cry. He followed with a raw growl, thrusting, pounding, until he soaked me with his seed.

Our breathing slowed to a hush. Sweat evaporated from our skin. He sat up and produced a canteen of water Nanny had given him. He offered me a drink, and I took it readily. He swigged after I did, putting his lips where mine had been. I was still feeling sexual. But I felt vulnerable, too. I hadn't forgotten about his wife. That there was a woman he'd thrown away.

Without speaking, he reached for his shirt and dampened the edges, cleaning the redness from my thighs and around the opening of my vagina. Some of the stickiness had been blood. How foolish of me to forget what losing my maidenhead meant.

Discomfort overcame me. I tried to close my legs, but he insisted on bathing me. I furrowed my brows. He was soiling his only shirt.

After he was done he cast the garment aside. Then he noticed that the buttercup I'd pinned into my hair had fallen onto the blanket sometime during our copulation. He retrieved it, tucking it back into my tousled coiffure.

I wondered if he knew about the language of flowers. If not, would I have time to teach him? Or was I dreaming of things that would never be? I wasn't sure how soon he intended to steal a horse and leave.

He took me in his arms, and I put my head on his chest and listened to the masculine patter of his heart.

For tonight, he was mine.

Mandy waited for Jared to lead her to one of the mansion's guest rooms, to make love with her in a richly draped bed. But he didn't.

"Let's go for a walk in the garden," he said.

"The . . . garden?" she parroted, unable to stall the confusion in her voice.

He lifted her chin, angling her face so her eyes met his. "Did you think I was going to take you upstairs? I can't do that. I don't have access to any of the rooms."

"I just assumed . . ." She stalled again. "Are you sure we can . . . in the garden . . . I mean . . . how can we . . . ?"

"Don't worry about it. We'll figure out a way."

She tried to quit fretting. But as they exited the ballroom and entered the flagstone patio leading to the garden, she took inventory of the guests enjoying the outdoors. They were everywhere, seated at wrought-iron tables, nestled on rustic benches in torch-lit corners, standing out in the open with cigarettes and/or cocktails in their hands.

"I told you not to worry about it," he said.

"I'm not," she lied.

"Yes, you are. I can feel your apprehension."

But he couldn't see it. Her expression was hidden behind her mask. Which was the beauty of a masquerade, she thought, of having your features concealed. No one but Jared knew how she was feeling, no one but the man who was going to fuck her senseless.

She looked around again. At a populated party.

As Mandy moved forward, she snagged a chip in the stone walkway, latching on to his arm to brace her unladylike stumble.

"Relax." He stopped to give her a chaste kiss, feathering his lips across hers. "I promise, it'll be fine."

Her heart tagged torridly after his, the way it had when she'd faltered on the dance floor. But she made an excuse. "My skirts are too long."

"You're nervous. You're afraid someone might come by and see us. And they might." They stood at the edge of the patio. "But trying not to get caught is part of the thrill."

She looked toward the garden. What properly reared woman wouldn't be nervous? "I've never done anything like this before."

"I have. I'm good at it."

She studied him. Moonlight cloaked his clothes and highlighted the inky darkness of his hair. "Now why doesn't that surprise me?"

"It's not supposed to." He took her right hand into his left hand and drew her closer. From there he cupped her shoulder blade with his other hand, placing his fingertips against her spine. "Dance with me again."

"Here? Now?"

"I can still hear the music. Can't you?"

"Yes." A Nat King Cole song drifted through the air. "Unforgettable."

He smiled, his lips curving softly, sensuously, devilishly. "You are, you know."

Mandy went breathless. The Jared she knew wouldn't have teased her with a love song. But he wasn't behaving like himself tonight. He was still talking like Blue, still using the Oklahoma accent. It was part of the game, the stranger fantasy. He swept her into an elegant waltz, and she swayed in his arms.

"The garden is terraced on three acres," he said. "With lots of paths, lots of trees, lots of areas to stop, to appreciate the elements."

"And each other?"

"Definitely each other," he whispered against her cheek, creating a relentless surge of warmth. "I can't wait to fuck you."

A deliberately romantic dance. Rough, carnal words. Mandy couldn't begin to describe the conflicting sensations.

After the song ended, they kissed, mouths questing, tongues tangling. The ostrich plumes on her disguise fluttered, but his mask didn't move. It remained securely molded to his face.

He released her, and they explored the garden, where scores of plants and flowers bloomed. Some areas were well lit, and others contained a sprinkle of light. A few tall, leafy corners were completely dark.

While on a brightly lit path, they approached a bentwood arbor and passed another costumed couple, decked out in 1940s fashions. The man's hat dipped in front, and the woman's gown presented an austere image.

Mandy's nerves kicked up again. How many guests were

strolling the grounds? How many people were shadowed in the shrubs? Quite a few, she suspected. But she doubted that any of them were looking for a place to have sex.

A sense of propriety told her what they were about to do was wrong. But a deeper sense of naughtiness made it seem right.

They kept walking, and she thought about the language of flowers he'd mentioned earlier. She noticed poppies, daisies, cosmos, marigolds, and petunias.

"Do you know what any of these mean?" she asked.

He pointed to the cosmos. "Those represent modesty. The pure love of a virgin. And those"—he indicated the daisies—"embody innocence."

"Really? Oh, my goodness. I don't we think we should mess around in this area."

He laughed and pulled her into a kiss. "Maybe we should find some snapdragons. They mean dazzling but dangerous."

"I'm impressed that you know all of this."

He shrugged. "I only know some of it. There are hundreds of flowers. Hundreds of meanings."

While on the snapdragon hunt, Mandy and Jared came upon a gazebo. It wasn't a private spot. A trio of Elizabethan ladies graced the hedge-flanked structure.

As they passed berries and currants, Jared said something about this being like an English garden. Mandy thought about him partying in London, but she didn't question him about it. For now, she wanted to retain the fantasy that she and Jared were strangers. That they didn't know anything about each other. She liked the romantic in Blue. Jared's alter ego fascinated her.

"There," he said. "Snapdragons."

She looked across a sloping field and saw their bounty. The ruffled, tubular flowers ignited in a range of colors: white, pink, red, purple, orange, and yellow.

He took her hand, and they crossed the field. A breeze caressed the air, stirring the snapdragon scent.

"They're beautiful," she said. "Dazzling but dangerous," she added, repeating what he'd told her.

He agreed, and when they got close enough to touch the magical flowers, he picked one, squeezing the top and bottom of the bloom to make the dragon roar. Mandy laughed, and he smiled, enchanting her even more.

"There are thirty to forty different species of snapdragons," he said. "Some of the hybrids are bicolored. Like those." He indicated a pastel mix. "They're called Peaches and Cream."

"Your knowledge of flowers really is impressive."

"Maybe I learned it for tonight. For you."

"Maybe you did." She looped her arms around his neck. "Some men will do whatever they can to get laid."

"Damn straight." He scooped her up and carried her through the snapdragons, taking dirt pathways that divided rows and rows of rainbow blooms. He didn't stop until he came to a weather-beaten chair, positioned next to a rustic little table.

She gazed at the cozy niche. "You knew this was here." And he'd known the exact location of the snapdragons, too.

He set her on her feet. "Does it matter if I did?" He unscrewed the bulbs in the nearby floodlights, making the area dark. Mandy's breath lodged in her throat. This was where they were going to make love, where he was going to fuck her.

He didn't remove one stitch of clothing. He didn't even loosen his tie. Mandy didn't adjust her costume, either. She remained the way she was, wearing an old-fashioned gown and clutching a delicately beaded purse, waiting for him to make the first move.

"Rub against me," he said.

She moved forward, pressing her pelvis against his. Although her heavily tiered dress hindered the intimate contact, he made an appreciative sound. She suspected that his cock had gone hard. That being surrounded by silk and lace was arousing him.

Their mouths came together, and he sucked on her tongue as if he were half-starved, as if she had the capacity to feed him. She kissed him back with the same hungry fervor, the same passionate need.

Finally he removed an article of clothing. His gloves came off. He bunched up her skirts and invaded her open-crotch drawers, teasing her with bared fingers. When he found her clit, she squirmed with honey-sweet pleasure.

"I was going to do this to myself in the limo," she said.

"Really?" His Southern accent went rough. "Why didn't you?"

"I didn't want to mess up my dress, to get wrinkled. To make my fingers sticky."

"Mine are getting that way. I'm going to have to lick them clean. Or maybe I'll make you do it."

"We can share them, can't we?" She impaled herself on his sticky digits, creaming them even more. She couldn't help her reaction to him. He made her nasty. He made her desperate to do dirty things.

"You first." He freed his fingers and offered them to her.

She took a ladylike lick, tasting the musky flavor of her own juices. She could barely see him in the dark, but she could tell that he was watching, gazing at her through slivers of moonlight.

"Your turn," she told him.

He didn't hesitate. He laved the sexual treat, roughly, diligently, like a mountain lion cleaning his paws. Mandy got wet again.

"Touch me some more," she said.

He gave her what she wanted, and she gripped the hem of her dress, holding the petticoat with it, allowing him better access.

"Do you like messing around with a stranger?" he asked, heightening the game.

She pitched forward a little. "Yes."

"Then stay there, and I'll put my mouth on you. I'll eat you until you come."

She wasn't about to refuse. She wanted him to taste her, to push his tongue through the slit in her drawers.

He knelt on the grass and put his face under her skirt. She lowered the hem of her dress and petticoat, letting the materials curtain him.

He ate her deep and slow. She sank onto the wetness, rocking back and forth. Her sex swelled, craving more and more.

Being completely clothed while a masked man lapped deliciously between her legs was almost more than she could bear. She told him to lick her clit, too.

He did, feverish, sucking the sensitive nub. Her dirty boy was doing his job, making her crazy for him.

Mandy widened her stance. The fabric around the opening of her Victorian drawers was soaked.

In the distance, she heard voices, other guests strolling the lush garden, talking in party-chipper tones. But she didn't care. Nothing mattered but her impending orgasm.

Finally she convulsed, jerking her hips, bucking forward, coating her lover with her juices. In her mind's eye, the moon burst in the sky, raining over the snapdragons, making their colors explode.

Voices sounded again, but she barely heard them. She was too dizzy from climaxing so hard. Jared climbed out from under her dress. Then he shifted his gaze and grabbed her, pulling her deeper into the darkness.

Suddenly she realized how close those voices were. Two sets of couples encroached the snapdragons. She could see the foursome clearly. The path they strode was generously lit.

"Shit," Jared said. He spoke barely above a whisper.

"I thought trying not to get caught was part of the thrill," she chided, keeping her tone as quiet as his.

"It is. But I'm hard as a goddamn rock, and I want to fuck."

"We're going to have to wait it out."

"Easy for you to say; you already came."

"I'm ready to come again." She watched the couples stop to chat. "I'm still wet."

"Yeah? Well, you have no idea how wet you're gonna be by the time I'm done with you." He put his arms around her, holding the back of her body tightly against the front of his.

She leaned back, enjoying his possessive touch. He hissed out a breath, giving her chills. The other people hadn't budged.

"What the hell are they doing?" Jared complained. His hold was getting tighter, more aggressive.

"I think they're tipsy." Mandy focused on their overly jovial voices. "They probably drank too much moonshine." The foursome was dressed from the speakeasy era, the women wearing flapper fringe and long pearls.

"I don't care if they've been chugging turpentine. They need to get their asses moving."

She turned in his arms, smiled, teased him. "You're impatient."

"I'm tired of waiting."

But wait they did, standing together, pressed against some scratchy shrubbery. One of the speakeasy men cracked what appeared to be a silly joke, and his companions chortled.

"Screw this," Jared said.

Mandy nibbled the inside of her lip to keep from giggling, until her lover shocked her into silence. Within the span of a heartbeat, he lunged for the chair, sat down, and plunked her on top of him, so she was straddling his lap, hip to hip, face-to-face.

She held her breath, waiting for the other couples to notice them, to hear the rustle they'd created. But nothing happened. She and Jared remained in the dark, and the partiers kept talking and laughing.

Jared reached down and undid his pants. Mandy did her damnedest not to gasp. He freed his cock, spread her skirts to cover them, and pulled her onto his erection, determined to have his wicked way with her.

No matter who was around.

CHAPTER SEVEN

Jared pushed deeper, and Mandy reveled in the familiarity of his touch. His passion. His piercing. Sometimes he wore only slightly curved barbells, and sometimes he wore circular jewelry. Tonight he was in a circular mood. And so was she. For her, the circular barbells created stronger sensations.

He kissed her, possessing her mouth and making the moment even more intense. His rhythm was smooth and sexy, hot and hard. Her purse fell from her lap and dropped onto the ground.

"I like this position," he whispered. "I like how your skirts drape over me."

"Me, too." The entire scenario felt like a color-hazed dream: their timeless costumes, the mansion in the clouds, the half-moon, the aroma of plants and flowers, the other people's voices buzzing like bees.

"This isn't going to be enough for me," he told her. "After I come, I'm going to want to come again. And again. I don't think I'll ever get enough of you."

She looked into the darkness of his mask. He seemed like a shadow, a flesh-and-blood mist. But he was real. She shaped her hands over the breadth of his shoulders and onto his lapels. On his left side, she encountered his boutonniere.

"What do blue roses mean?" she asked.

"Mystery."

She touched the petals. Now she understood why he'd chosen it. Blue, the man he'd personified this evening, created a mysterious effect. He nuzzled her neck, gently, roughly, kissing and nipping.

She sank onto his lap and made her skirts rustle. "Are you going to come home with me later? Are you going to spend the night?"

"Yes." He'd stopped using the Oklahoma accent. He was no longer talking like a stranger. He was completely himself. Or was he? He'd never been this romantic.

"Will you hold me when we're in bed?"

"Yes," he said again.

Her skin tingled. Her heart sparkled. While he was still inside of her, she reached for her fallen purse.

He circled her waist, keeping her balanced, keeping his sweeping rhythm. "What are you doing, baby?"

Her desire spiraled higher. She loved it when he called her baby, when he used endearments during sex. "Getting the extra key to my condo. The one I had made for you." She pressed her lips to his satin-covered cheek and rasped his name, sending chills up and down her own spine.

Suddenly he stopped moving. She almost complained. She almost told him to keep going, to quit teasing her, until she realized why he'd gone motionless.

The other people's jovial voices grew louder.

Mandy held her breath. She didn't know exactly how close the intruders were. Her back was to them. So she waited, knowing Jared was watching the foursome, tracking their garden-strolling path. She tried to gauge his reaction, but between his mask and the lack of the light, she could barely see him.

A second later, his face seemed to disappear completely. She glanced up at the sky. The moon was the culprit, peeking in and out of trees, sending nighttime shadows across Jared's face.

She waited, and so did he. Finally, the other voices faded, along with shuffling sounds that she assumed were retreating footsteps.

"They're gone," he said, affirming her assumption.

Mandy's breathing returned to normal. She opened her purse and dug around for the key. *There.* She ran her fingers along the metal teeth. Leaning forward, she kissed Jared, dropping the key into his coat pocket.

He resumed their activity, thrusting his cock again, filling her with rapture. The chair beneath them creaked, rebelling from his aggressive motion, from their combined weight. Beneath her lace-trimmed corset and the equally decorative corset cover, her nipples went sweetly, sensitively hard.

"I'm going to go down on you in the limo," she said.

He thrust harder. "So I can fantasize that I'm a lord and you're a naughty Victorian lady?"

"Yes." His imagination stirred hers. "The limo can be our

carriage." She wanted to give him a blow job while he destroyed her properly coiffed hair. She wanted to suck every engorged inch of him.

In the distance, birds sang a nighttime song, and suddenly this place seemed like the Garden of Eden. Breathtaking. Beautiful. Dangerous.

"Do the Apache believe in Heaven and Hell?" she asked.

"Why? Am I tempting you into Hell?"

"I think maybe you are. But it's like Heaven, too." She was wet and creamy, and it was all for him. He was an angel. He was a demon. He was everything good, everything bad.

She climaxed with her breath panting and her pulse skittering. He came at the same time, shooting his essence into the very core of who she was, of who she'd become.

She put her head on his shoulder. The birds were still singing. Crickets chirped, too. She didn't want to let go, but she knew they couldn't stay there forever. He lifted her up, setting her on her feet, and his semen trickled between her legs. She clenched her inner muscles, trying to keep the sticky warmth inside.

He stood up and adjusted his pants and buttoned his coat. From there, he screwed the floodlight bulbs back into their sockets. Within seconds, the area was illuminated again.

Mandy smoothed her skirts. Some of his come was still leaking out of her, but between her lacy drawers, silk hose, and stiff petticoat, there was plenty of fabric to absorb the moisture.

"You don't need those anymore," he said.

She blinked. "What?"

"The other flowers."

He pointed to the roses pinned to her purse. Some of the

petals were missing, and the leaves were slightly bent, but the boutonnieres remained attached to her bag.

"Who were Pink and Red?" she asked, curious about the men who'd participated in the charade. "What are their real names?"

"It isn't important." He snagged the other roses and flung them, destroying the symbolism. "I'm the only guy who matters. I'm the one you're going to be waking up with tomorrow. Me, and me alone."

I awakened alone in the barn. Dawn had barely broken. Only a sliver of light streamed through the breezeway.

Had Atacar left me after our night of lovemaking? Was he gone for good? Or had he stayed and breakfasted with Nanny? I imagined her preparing a hearty-size platter for him. Nanny was an accomplished cook, and she believed that the first meal of the day was the most beneficial.

I searched for my undergarments and put them on. I suspected that I looked quite wanton in rumpled red silk with my hair mussed and my lips swollen from a man's lustful kisses. Needing to feel closer to my lover, I picked up the blanket we'd slept on and draped it over my shoulders. It smelled of moonlit sex and summer straw.

The lone horse on the other side of the barn whinnied, capturing my attention. I descended the loft ladder to visit with her.

She was a sturdy mare with varied colors, a breed that had gained popularity in Buffalo Bill's Wild West. I'd seen the smashingly successful show when it had toured Europe. I'd been young at the time, but still mature enough to appreciate the striking beauty of the painted horses they'd used.

And to be fascinated by the Indians.

They'd looked so grand in their feathers and breechcloths while they'd re-created historical battles for the crowd.

Was it any wonder I'd been instantly attracted to Atacar? I touched a finger to my lips. How I longed to kiss him again, to press my body against his.

I wanted to know more about him, to learn of his youth, his battles, his escape from the fort. There was the matter of his wife, too. That weighed heavily on my mind.

I headed into the daylight. My feet were bare, but I often went barefoot. Nanny said it was the bohemian in me.

I walked toward the house, a frame structure with a porch across the front. The kitchen served as a place to cook, but it was our conservatory, as well, with a hothouse arrangement so vegetables grew year-round. We had an outdoor garden, too.

At one time, there had been a sod house on this property, but that was before the railroad had arrived in this area, bringing lumber, brick, and other materials.

I entered the house, hoping to find Atacar, but he wasn't there. I approached Nanny. She was scrubbing the kitchen. She looked up and saw me.

"You slept late," she said. "You neglected your chores."

I defended my position. "It's barely dawn."

"Farm life starts early," she countered.

Nanny had been reared on a farm, and she had the annoying habit of touting her authority. Of course, our Texas settlement wasn't a crop-producing farm. Everything we did was for our own consumption, but there was still a lot of work, especially since our farmhand had quit.

Yesterday I'd neglected my chores, too. I'd gone off to paint and had met Atacar. And now I wondered where he was, but I was too fearful to ask. I didn't want to hear that he was gone.

"I'll tend to my chores," I said.

"Atacar already milked the cow, fed the chickens, and gathered the eggs. He's familiar with farming. When he was in Alabama, he and some of the other men in his tribe labored at farms near the military post."

My pulse spiked. I'd barely heard what she'd said about his work experience. I was too excited to think beyond his presence at my *farm. "He's still here? Where is he now?"*

"Making repairs to the wagon shed."

I turned on my heel to leave, to dash off, to be with my lover, and Nanny grabbed my arm. I tried to pull away from her, but she held tight.

"You shouldn't flitter about like that. You should wash the sex from your skin and don some modest clothes." She removed the blanket from around my shoulders and placed it on top of her laundry pile. "I'll heat the water for your bath."

"Did Atacar bathe?" I asked, wondering if he'd washed the sex from his skin.

"As soon as he arose this morning, he went down to the stream."

"Mmm." I made an appreciative sound. "He was bathing in the stream when I first met him."

Nanny shot me an exasperated glare, warning me not to discuss his nakedness any further. I focused on my nakedness instead.

She helped me haul the tub into my room, and I soaked in the water she'd heated. I was impatient to see Atacar, but Nanny had been right. Not only did I need to bathe, I needed to soothe the lingering soreness that came with losing my maidenhead.

After I dried off, I pinned my hair neatly to my head and put on a practical daytime dress fashioned from pastel-printed cotton and decorated with a row of simple buttons.

I returned to the kitchen, and Nanny fixed me a cup of tea, the same special blend from last night. I wasn't hungry, but she insisted that I eat some bread and jam. As I'd suspected, she'd fed Atacar a big, scrumptious meal, and according to her, he'd devoured every bite. She seemed to like that he had a strong appetite. So did I, but I was thinking of his appetite for me.

I couldn't sit at the table any longer. I left my bread half-eaten and my tea half-sipped. Eager to greet Atacar, I walked briskly to the wagon shed. The property was littered with outbuildings. The family who'd built the farm had returned to the East, allowing me the opportunity to finance a ready-made home and make payments to the bank.

I entered the shed and found Atacar engaged in the repairs Nanny had mentioned. He heard me approach and turned to face me. Our gazes met and held, but no words were spoken.

We didn't exchange a proprietary "Hello." We didn't say, "Good morning." We did nothing except look at each other.

Finally I broke the silence, stunning him, and myself, with an emotional question. "Why did you throw away your wife?"

He tensed. He frowned. But he responded just the same. "She had sex with another man."

I gaped at him, then closed my mouth before I swallowed a flying insect. "Why did she do that?"

"Because I didn't love her."

I doubted that many men loved their wives the way they should. Papa barely tolerated Mama. But Atacar seemed plagued by his distant feelings toward his wife. So I asked, "Why did you marry her?"

"It was arranged by our families."

"Is that common in your culture?"

"It can be. Some of the old people think it's foolish to marry for love. Our families were close, so her parents perceived me as a good match for her."

"But you weren't?"

"No. She was congenial. She tried to be a good wife, but I felt nothing when I was near her." He made an empty gesture. "I should have refused the match."

"How long ago was this?" I needed to see the time line in my head, to picture him as he was then. He looked to be in his mid-thirties now.

"Twelve years have passed." He paused, as if he were gathering his thoughts. "I touched her at night, but my passion for her was forced." He repeated the empty gesture. "She didn't please me, in or out of bed. I kept hoping that she would, but she never did."

Another question. More curiosity. Atacar was a mystery that had just begun to unfold. "Did the other man love her?"

He nodded. "I threw her away so she could be with him. They're still together. But what I did was considered unmanly." He frowned again, tiny lines creasing his eyes. "I didn't punish my wife for being unfaithful. I didn't beat her or cut her nose to make her look ugly. I didn't go after her lover, either. I would've had the right to kill him."

I frowned, too. How could anyone consider Atacar unmanly? He was strong and fierce. He emitted power. "Why didn't you do those things?"

"It didn't seem right to destroy her. Or the man who cared for her."

I was impressed by the mercy he'd bestowed upon his wife and her lover. "I think what you did was noble. Compassionate."

He disagreed. "I should have tried harder to love her, to make her feel special. But mostly I ignored her. I made the marriage bad."

"Sometimes a person can't help who they love." I stepped closer to him. His gaze was nailed to mine. "But if you'd been my husband, I wouldn't have gone to another man. I would've waited for you to favor me, no matter how long it took."

He responded in kind. "If you'd been my wife, you wouldn't have needed to wait. I would have favored you from the start."

Silence engulfed us once more. We weren't saying that we loved each other. How could we? We were scarcely acquainted. But our physical attraction seemed strong enough to sustain us.

"Will you stay?" I asked.

"For how long?" he wanted to know.

I wanted to say "Forever," but instead I said, "Until I can find a permanent farmhand. Maybe a month or so? I can give you room and board and a modest wage."

He accepted my offer, deciding that having currency to take to Mexico would enhance his trip. "But if someone discovers that I'm here and who I am, you and Nanny must say that I forced you into giving me a job and hiding me from the authorities."

I was touched that he was trying to protect us, but I knew he was right. Aiding a prisoner of war was dangerous business. I accepted his terms.

He leaned in to kiss me, lightly, briefly, and I sighed and put my arms around his neck.

I'd found a way to keep him. If only for a while.

At nightfall while Nanny slept in her room, I led Atacar to mine, and he glanced around. Most of the furnishings were basic, items I'd purchased locally. My journal sat on a simply constructed desk, the pages burning with my writings. As for my bed, it was far more luxurious than it should have been. I'd ordered it from a catalog and had it shipped to Texas. It didn't fit the farmhouse, but I didn't care. The wooden frame was ornately carved with fabric draped over the top and front of it. The mattress was a soft, feather-stuffed luxury to which I'd become accustomed.

"My family has these kinds of beds at home," I told Atacar. "They're called testers. This one has been reduced in size. It's not as big as they normally are."

"It's still big," he commented.

"I suppose it is, considering the size of the room. It takes up a lot of space."

He gazed at the bed once more, then asked me to remove my clothing and lie upon it, with my legs spread for him. His request was bold and erotic, and I tingled, eager to do his bidding.

I took my time, lingering for his benefit. He watched me with keen interest. I suspected that he'd gotten used to my fancy undergarments since he'd seen me in them several times by now, but I could tell that he enjoyed how I looked in my corset and drawers.

When I was bare, I climbed on the mattress. He stared at my pink-crested breasts, my quivering stomach, the exposed juncture between my thighs. He studied my face too, watching my expression.

Did he know how excited I was? How nervous?

"Turn over," he said. "On all fours."

I stalled. That wasn't what I had expected to hear. He gestured for me to follow his command, and I nibbled my bottom lip, tugging it between my teeth. But I didn't refuse him. I rolled over and got into position. I realized that he was going to mate me this way. It made me feel like a mare that was about to be mounted by the biggest, roughest stallion in the herd.

I heard Atacar getting undressed. He would need some new clothes, especially since he'd stained his shirt with my maiden's blood. But that was last night. Tonight I was no longer a virgin.

I wondered if he would lick me, the way a stallion tasted a mare's vulva before they copulated. I hoped he would. I wanted his tongue inside me.

He got onto the mattress. I could feel his weight shifting the soft feather stuffing. I didn't twist my body or try to look at him. I faced forward and let him crawl up behind me.

He placed his hands on either side of my hips, smoothing them across my bottom, tracing the rounded shape. After he admired my derriere, he moved on to my vagina, using his fingers, spreading me like the folds of a flower. He spoke in Apache, and I went desperately wet. I had no idea what he was saying, but the guttural sound of his language, coupled with his touch, aroused me. I could tell he was preparing to taste me. By now, he was lowering his head, putting his mouth in place.

I gazed at the burgundy and gold fabric on the front of the bed, the colors swirling before my eyes. He darted his tongue, tasting my juices. But he couldn't get enough of me that way, so he positioned himself below me and pulled me down. I gulped the air in my lungs. He'd seated me right on his face.

He licked; he kissed; he rubbed saliva all over me. He inhaled my scent, too, savoring it. I couldn't see what he was doing, but I felt every primitive sensation.

I climaxed in undulating waves, rocking back and forth. I undid the pins in my hair and let the loose waves fall over my shoulders and down my back. I wanted to look like a palomino for him, to allow my blonde mane to entice him.

When my orgasm ended, I raised my hips so I was on all fours again. He crawled out from beneath my legs and got behind me, fitting his cock against my cunt.

He entered me so hard, I gasped. But I loved it, too. He buried his face in my hair. He seemed pleased that I'd freed it from its ladylike confinement.

His heavy testes slapped against me as we fucked. Or made love. Or copulated. I wasn't quite sure what word to use to describe our second encounter.

He plowed through the silkiness of my hair so he could nibble, quite roughly, on the back of my neck. This kind of mating seemed to come naturally to him. He penetrated me with powerful thrusts.

In my mind's eye, I imagined how we looked, kneeling on a tester bed, naked as the days we were born, his big, dark hands wrapped about my small, fair waist, his penis sliding in and out of me. I wanted to paint us, to relive this moment forever. But I knew I couldn't. A painting of that nature would be far too scandalous, so

I decided that I would do a small sketch in my journal. I might even draw a heart around it. I realized how girlish of me that would be, but I couldn't seem to control my strangely romantic thoughts.

Atacar plunged even harder, taking what he wanted, what we both seemed to need. He impaled me, he stretched me, his body claiming mine. My breasts bounced with each rough movement. He reached around to cup them, to make me whimper. Fire spread from my nipples to my clitoris, then burned deep and low in my belly.

I was going to climax again.

My lover was going to orgasm, too. I heard the rumbling in his breathing and felt the thick, driving pressure in his loins. He growled in my ear, and I turned, trying to kiss him, but I couldn't reach his mouth.

Spasms shook my core. I grabbed a pillow and clutched its downy softness, digging my fingers into it. Atacar shot his seed, filling me with white-hot fluid.

He collapsed on top of me, and I hit the mattress with a thud, the pillow wedged beneath me.

He said something, but I didn't comprehend him. He was speaking Apache again. A second later, he caught his mistake and switched languages.

"Am I too heavy for you?" he asked.

"No." He was, but I didn't want him to move. He was still hard, and he was still inside of me.

"I think I am. This can't be comfortable for you."

He withdrew, leaving me naked and exposed. I rolled over to look at him. He touched my cheek, and I concluded that drawing an image of us with a heart looped around it made perfect sense.

"I'm glad I'm you're first," he said. "That you're exploring sex with me."

"So am I." I wondered how many positions he would encourage me to try, how many different ways he would shape and bend my body.

He lay down next to me, and we faced each other. I loved how he looked in the kerosene-lit glow. The light illuminated his deeply hollowed features.

"I want to paint a portrait of you," I said. "Will you sit for me?"

He shook his head.

"I don't mean right now. In the daytime. When you're fully clothed. You can pose with your rifle," I added, hoping that would tempt him.

"I won't let you seize my soul."

Was that some sort of Apache superstition? Or was he speaking metaphorically? "My painting wouldn't do that to you."

"Yes, it would. You would capture me for all time. Even after I was gone, I would belong to you."

I looked into his eyes. He wasn't being superstitious. He was worried about falling in love with me. I went fluttery inside. I was happy it had crossed his mind.

"That could happen even if I don't paint you," I said.

"It would be worse if I allowed you to create a portrait of me. It would be like leaving a part of myself behind. I can't do that. I won't."

Mortally wounded, I frowned at him. "You might have already left a part of yourself behind. You filled me with your seed. Last night and tonight." I glanced down at my stomach. "You could have made me pregnant already."

"I told Nanny about a tea you should use. I've heard medicine men speak of it."

My frown turned to surprise. The tea Nanny had been brewing for me was a preventative? I wondered how effective it was. Nonetheless, I was grateful that he'd considered me in that regard. In Europe, sometimes men used penile sheaths as implements of protection, but widespread use of them was rare.

"So, are you going to sit for me?" I asked, pressing him about the portrait.

"No." He remained firm in his conviction. "We shouldn't get too close." But even as he said it, he gathered me in his arms, holding me close.

So very, very close.

CHAPTER EIGHT

After the party ended, the limo picked Mandy and Jared up at the mansion's front gate, and the driver got out and opened the door. Jared helped Mandy inside and told the chauffeur to take them farther into the hills, to keep driving and not disturb them. They weren't ready to go to Mandy's house yet.

As the car pulled away, Jared closed the glass panel and lowered the privacy blinds. He removed his mask, and so did Mandy. They gazed at each other, and the moment turned hot and emotional.

She'd offered to give him oral pleasure, and he couldn't wait for her to nurse his cock. Earlier, she'd refreshed her lipstick, and he noticed that the glossy cosmetic complemented the cherry blossom color of her gown. Female dominance, beauty, and sexuality, he thought.

"I want to see you in your underwear," he said.

"Right now?"

He nodded. "Yes, right now. I want to push the envelope with the fantasy you inspired. The lord, the lady, the Victorian carriage."

She agreed, but he knew that she wouldn't deny his request. Whatever he craved, she gave to him. He couldn't ask for a more thrilling lover. She was dominant in a submissive way, the perfect partner for his lustful games.

"Turn around, and I'll help you remove your dress," he said.

She obliged, presenting him with her back. He went after the hooks and stripped her to her corset and drawers, tossing the rest of her garments aside. The petticoat had a life of its own, sitting stiffly by itself. The gown took a lot of room, too. But being surrounded by her feminine finery made him more aroused.

"My Mandy," he said, as she faced him once again. The tops of her breasts spilled out from her corset, but he'd had it designed that way. "My *multiorgasmic* Mandy."

Her voice went soft, sexy. "Is that what you've been calling me?"

"It's what you are." She was also a woman who'd asked him to hold her later. A woman who needed sex, but who needed affection, too. But he didn't want to think too deeply about that. Not now. Not while she was going to get him off.

"Have I told you how beautiful you look tonight?" he asked.

"No. But thank you."

She leaned forward to kiss him, and he plundered her mouth, practically swallowing her tongue and bruising her lips. Nothing had ever felt so right. When they separated, he could barely breathe. She amazed him, the way she sat on the seat with her thighs pressed demurely together and her breasts partially bared.

The good-bad girl.

Anxious for more, he removed his tie, unbuttoned his shirt, and opened his pants. Making his intentions known, he pushed his pants down his hips, exposing his cock and balls. He wanted her to lick and suck his testes, too. He wanted the package deal.

Mandy got onto the limo floor and knelt in front of him. He glanced down at her. He'd meant what he'd said about how beautiful she was.

She reached out and circled the head of his cock, running the tips of her fingers over his piercing. He went shivery. She was teasing him, making him wait for her mouth.

"Why is this called a Prince Albert?" she asked.

"No one knows the true origin, but it's alleged that Queen Victoria's consort, Prince Albert, wore a ring attached to his penis, which was then strapped to his thigh."

She played with the barbell. "Why would he do that?"

Damn. Jared went shivery again. "To maintain the smooth line of the tight trousers that were fashionable at the time. In the nineteenth century, this kind of piercing was referred to as a dressing ring. Or that's one of the theories. As I said, no one knows for sure."

"You dress on the left. That's the side you keep your cock on."

He skimmed her cheek. "I'm glad you noticed."

"I notice everything about you." She paused and licked the skin around his jewelry. "And I like that your piercing has Victorian roots. That makes it even sexier, even if it's a myth."

He delved into her hair, dislodging the decorative combs and unearthing pins. If she didn't hurry up and suck him, he was going to fucking die.

She finally lowered her head all the way and took him in her mouth. He lifted his ass off the seat and pushed deeper. She cupped his balls, gently abrading the sacs.

He continued to ravage her hair. Curls tumbled and fell, draping her heart-shaped face. She sucked him harder, bobbing her head.

She did everything he wanted her to do. She alternated his balls, licking and sucking each one, until she returned to his cock, taking his granite length all the way to the back of her throat. He groaned, deep and rich and guttural. Her eyes drifted closed; her cheeks went hollow.

The limo slid along a mountain road, and he watched Mandy make love to him. She paid special attention to the circular barbell, flicking her tongue along its horseshoe shape. He'd worn it especially for her. He knew it was her favorite.

"I'm so into you," he said.

She stopped to nuzzle his thigh, to think about what he'd said, to look up at him with depth in her pretty blue eyes. "I've been calling my attraction to you an addiction."

"Really?"

She kept nuzzling his thigh, tickling the tiny hairs on his legs. "I'm going to need a twelve-step program to get you out of my system. You and all of the things you tempt me into doing. You're corrupting me, Jared."

"I know, baby. But I can't help it. You tempt me, too." He liked sweeping Mandy into his world. He liked having control of their affair. But even more than that, he liked how she responded to him, how much she enjoyed being corrupted.

Beyond aroused, he pushed her down, making her suck him

again. Thinking about the sexual side of their relationship made him hot as hell. All he wanted to do was come.

She gave him the blow job of his life. His modern Victorian lady. His lover. The woman driving him to agonizing distraction.

He tugged at her gorgeous hair, rocking back and forth, fucking her cherry blossom mouth. When it happened, when he ejaculated, she tipped her head back so he could watch. She swallowed every milky drop, then licked him clean. She even mewled like a cat, a feral little kitten, mink-soft and dirty-sweet.

Adrenaline shot through Jared's veins. His heart beat rapidly in his chest. Every nerve ending in his body burst into flames. He waited for the feeling to end, but it didn't go away. Not until she sat back on her haunches, not until she quit touching him.

As air chopped through his lungs, he yanked up his pants and adjusted the rest of his clothes. She blotted her mouth with a delicate handkerchief from her purse. Always the lady, he thought. She put on her corset cover and petticoat. Jared helped her with her gown, fastening the hooks in back.

She turned around to face him once more. "I used to hate the taste of come."

He lifted his eyebrows. "But you like it now?"

"I like knowing it's yours. That it's part of you. I even fantasized about it earlier, when I was drinking a Between the Sheets." She angled her chin. "That's when I got acquainted with Amber."

He started. "She approached you? She told you who she was?"

Mandy nodded. "We agreed to get together, do some Blow-Job Shooters sometime."

That was just what he needed, his current lover partying with his ex, or whatever the hell Amber was to him. "Sometimes she's a bitch. And sometimes she can be a good friend."

"That's the impression I got of her. She said that you met in London."

He didn't want to talk about England, but if he avoided it, Mandy would wonder why he was being evasive. "It was just a couple of trips I took."

"A couple? You've been there more than once?"

"The first time, it seemed like an interesting place to see, to do the tourist thing. The second time, I enjoyed it enough to go back." A lie, if he'd ever told one. The weeks he'd spent in England were more than a vacation, more than a holiday dalliance.

"I'd love to go there someday."

"I'm sure you'd like it." On his second trip, he'd met Amber, but he hadn't been honest with her, either. She didn't know real reason he'd ventured onto British soil. He'd told her the same bullshit story he'd just told Mandy. Jared switched subjects. "Are you ready to head home? Should I tell the driver to take us to your condo?"

"Okay." Mandy removed the stray pins that remained in her hair and shook the rest of her curls free. "He's going to know we messed around."

"I imagine he's to used it. People mess around in limos all the time."

"This has been the most erotic night of my life," she said. "The party, the charade, the garden, and now what I just did to you."

"For me, too." He kissed her softly, preparing himself for the promise he'd made: to hold her while they were in bed.

He just hoped that he didn't disappoint her. Jared did erotic well. But being warm and romantic made him uncomfortable. Suddenly he wanted to put his mask back on, to hide behind the man she called Blue.

~

The sky was a brilliant shade of blue. I stood on the porch, gazing at the horizon and waiting for Atacar. But he was still completing his chores. As our new farmhand, he'd taken on most of the outdoor work, leaving Nanny more time for domestic duties and me for my art. Of course, my art was done for the afternoon. Mostly because I'd worked on secret sketches in my journal. For the past two days, since Atacar had agreed to stay, I'd been drawing us in various states of arousal. And, yes, I included those girlish hearts, too.

"Catherine!" Nanny called from the kitchen. "Come inside and fetch the food."

I turned and entered the house. As soon as Atacar finished his work, he and I were going on a late-day picnic. Nanny had prepared roast chicken. She'd even baked a gingerbread cake.

She handed me a carefully packed basket with a blanket folded on top, and I thanked her. It hadn't taken Nanny long to grow extremely fond of Atacar. She fussed over him like a cackling hen, making sure that he was well fed and well cared for. Tomorrow, she and I were going into town to purchase fabrics for his new clothes.

"It'll be a shame to lose that man," she said. "He's a good worker."

I nodded, a lump forming in my throat. I didn't want to think about Atacar leaving in a month. "I could implore him to stay a bit longer. But I don't think he will."

"Maybe he'll change his mind later." She heaved a laden breath. "Or maybe it's best if he moves on before you two get too close. Before what you feel for each other gets too deep."

"I'm trying not to fall in love with him."

"I know, child. He's trying not to fall in love with you, too."

I put down the basket and reached for my old nanny, hugging her, needing her comfort. She wrapped me in her ample arms. Finally, I stepped back and rubbed my eyes. They'd begun to water, and I didn't want Atacar to see me this way.

Nanny righted her appearance, as well. She smoothed the wisps of hair escaping her gray-streaked bun and flattened her apron. Then she shooed me back onto the porch, picnic supplies in tow.

My lover arrived with his hands and face freshly washed. I could tell that he'd cleaned up at the pump. He smiled at me, and I warned my heart to be still. He was wearing a Western hat Nanny had given him. When I first bought the farm, she'd found a few cowboy items the previous tenants had left behind in the barn: a torn neckerchief, holey gloves, a battered hat marked by John. B Stetson Co. She'd kept everything, fascinated by their rugged appeal. And now she'd put those articles to good use. Not only had she given Atacar the hat, she'd repaired the gloves and neckerchief for him.

I stepped forward. I was ready for our picnic. I'd already decided that we would eat at the cottonwoods near the stream. As always, Atacar had his rifle with him. He was never far from his gun.

As we headed to our destination, I fantasized that he was court-

ing me. That he'd come calling, and I'd invited him on an outing. Of course, if I were living with my parents, Mama would've insisted on a chaperone. She never would've allowed me to be alone with him. I smiled to myself. I was grateful to be living with Nanny. She'd permitted me to have sex with him.

"If someone crosses our path, we should try to hide," he said, interrupting my thoughts. "But if we can't and they recognize me, I'll have to raise my rifle, and you'll have to tell them what we agreed upon."

"That you're forcing your company on me." I wondered how that would fare in a picnic setting. I paused to look more closely at him. "With the hat, you could pass for Mexican. Especially if you keep your head down and shield most of your features." I created a story. "If we are seen, I could say that your name is Juan, and you're my new farmhand." At least the farmhand part was true, I thought. "I could tell them that you showed up at my door, looking for work. You speak Spanish, don't you?"

"As well as I speak English." He considered my plan, then sent me a cheeky grin. "You could say that you brought Juan along on your picnic to keep you safe from renegade Indians."

I scolded him. "That's not funny."

"Yes, it is." His grin broadened, and we both laughed.

Silence befell us for a moment after that. Everything we did was a risk. In the quiet, I studied him. His skin was dark, but sometimes he behaved the way a white man would. Atacar knew Anglo customs well. I imagined he knew how to behave in a Mexican manner, too. At one time, the Apache had warred with the Mexicans, just as they'd warred with the whites. But those battles were over now.

"My plan has merit," I said.

"It does," he agreed. "But we still need to be cautious."

We arrived at the cottonwoods and spread the blanket in the copse where we'd first touched and kissed. I set up the picnic, and we settled in to eat.

"Why did you enlist as a scout?" I asked, handing him some chicken.

"In the beginning, we helped the army fight our enemies. It elevated my status as a warrior." He bit into the meat, chewed, and swallowed. "It allowed me to have a horse and a gun. We didn't have those things anymore."

"Because you were confined on a reservation?"

"Yes. Later, when the army started using us to track our own people, we were sometimes called traitors."

By his own people, I knew he meant the Chiricahua Apache who'd been considered hostiles.

He continued. "I was loyal to the army. But in the end, it was futile. They held all of us accountable for Goyathlay and his followers. Geronimo," he clarified when I gave him a blank stare.

Ah, I thought. The infamous Geronimo. I noticed that Atacar spoke his name with respect. Maybe it was because Geronimo had eluded capture for so long. Or maybe because he'd fought so hard for what he believed in.

"We've been prisoners of war for nine years," Atacar said. "The government continues to make promises they don't keep."

"Nine years?" I shook my head, understanding why he'd chosen to escape and wondering how much longer his tribe would remain in military custody.

He changed the subject, clearly uncomfortable with his memories, with the choices he'd made. "Tell me about your life. Before you came to America."

"It was difficult," I admitted. "I'm from an upper-class family, and they put a lot of restrictions on me."

"You misbehaved?"

"Every chance I got." I nibbled playfully on my chicken, lightening his mood and making him smile. He knew how easily I misbehaved. "I convinced my parents to send me to Paris to study art, and then I took up with a bohemian crowd. That mortified them."

"What is bohemian?" he asked.

"Impoverished and marginalized artists who live nontraditional lifestyles."

"They are improper?"

"Yes. Quite so. I learned about sex from my bohemian friends."

Like the man he was, Atacar disputed my claim. He wanted responsibility for my lustful ways. "You learned about sex from me."

"True. But I already knew what was what." I gestured to my skirt. "When you lick me down there, it's called cunnilingus." I paused, making sure he was watching every move I made. "And if I were to suck you . . ." I let my words drift, right along with my gaze. By now, I was looking at the front of his pants. "It would be called fellatio."

He stopped eating. I'd actually shocked him. As bold as I was, he hadn't expected me to talk about sucking cock, at least not at a picnic.

I continued. "I've heard the taste of man's seed is salty." I steadied my gaze. "I like salty flavors."

"Don't tempt me," he said. "Not here."

"Why not here? We're surrounded by trees." I popped some cake into my mouth. "I want to learn how to do it."

Atacar made a strangled sound. "Not here," he reiterated.

"You put your fingers inside me here. We rolled around in the leaves." I pointed. "Right over there."

He cursed in English. He didn't repeat the vulgarity in the other languages he spoke, but he didn't need to. His arousal was evident.

"You're wicked," he said.

"I'm trying to be." I was teasing him, playing a game. He was right about not having oral copulation at this location. We needed to stay on guard, to be aware of our surroundings. But it was fun to fantasize.

He caught on to my game. He bit back a smile and handed me more cake. I refused to eat it. I drank some water instead, pretending to cleanse my palate, to prepare for the taste of his cock. "I want something salty."

He rifled through the basket, searching for the right food to satisfy me. He found pretzels Nanny had baked and salted, using a recipe she'd acquired from an neighbor. She enjoyed knotting the dough, and they kept well as a snack or meal accompaniment. But nonetheless, I shook my head no.

He continued looking and came up with a pair of pickles. He analyzed them.

"Those aren't salty," I said.

"No, but you can suck on them." He extended the largest of the two. Its length and girth was impressive—for a pickle. "Try this one."

I burst out laughing. He had a diabolical sense of humor. He laughed with me for the second time that day. I would miss him terribly when he was gone.

I stopped laughing. I missed him already.

"What's wrong?" he asked.

"Nothing," I lied.

"We can be together later," he told me.

"You'll teach me to perform fellatio tonight?" I asked, focusing on sex, even though we both knew there was more between us than carnal urges. "When we're in bed?"

He drew a rough breath. "Yes."

"Will you hold me afterward?"

"Always," he responded. "For as long as I can."

CHAPTER NINE

At our sleeping hour, I donned a white nightgown with an eyelet collar and ruffled hem, and Atacar stripped down to his skin. I longed for the sensation of being clothed while he was naked, and he didn't deny my request.

My heart thudded wildly. His penis was already hard, and I hadn't even touched him. We smiled at each other, and he moved forward to kiss me, to put his lips softly against mine.

Anxious to begin my fellatio lesson, I ended our kiss and got to my knees. I was close enough to inhale his musky scent, so I breathed him in. He didn't indicate that I should suck him right away. Instead, he allowed me a visual exploration, where I studied the bulbous head, the slit at the tip, and the heavily veined shaft that comprised his cock. I gazed at his testicles, as well. To me, they were a powerful testimony to his manhood, the place where his seed was stored.

Curious, I darted my tongue and tasted each sac. Growing

bolder, I got far enough below him to lick the seam of skin between his genitals and his buttocks. He shivered when I did that, and I knew I'd struck a highly sensitive spot. Finally, I lapped at his cock, swirling my tongue over the head.

He put his hands in my unbound hair, twining the long strands between his fingers. Then he ordered me onto the bed so he could kneel over my face. I followed his lead, aroused by his aggressiveness, by his desire to control me.

Once we were in bed, I did what I always did when we were together. I imagined how we looked, me in my flowing nightgown and him completely naked, wielding his erection over me.

I opened my mouth and took him inch by inch. I was careful not to graze him with my teeth. He watched me with divine interest and told me to take more. I gripped the base to give myself better leverage and took as much as I could.

But it wasn't enough for him. He pushed deeper. I actually felt him jabbing the back of my throat.

For an instant, I was stunned. I hadn't expected to fit all of him into my mouth, but he'd just proved that it was possible. His lesson was rough and sensual, and it aroused me.

I sucked him in earnest, sliding my lips up and down. I worked hard, bobbing my head with each motion.

After I gave myself a moment's rest, Atacar rolled over onto his back and opened his legs, encouraging me to pleasure him in that position, too.

Flushed with excitement, I crawled between his thighs and resumed his oral stimulation. He moved with me, pumping his hips in a steady rhythm.

He leaned forward and caressed my face. His touch was warm and tender, but it was carnal, too. He withdrew so I could lick his testicles and the sensitive seam I'd tasted earlier. He admitted that I was the first woman who'd dared put her mouth there.

Feeling deliciously decadent, I returned my attention to his cock. I used my hands, stroking while I sucked. He groaned his hunger, and I triumphed even more. I wanted to bring him to completion. Already I could taste a few beads of ejaculate seeping from the tip. It was as salty as I'd imagined. I had no idea how much would spill out when he climaxed, but I was prepared to take what he gave me.

Reveling in my own wickedness, I squirmed naughtily against the bed. If a pillow had been handy, I would've tucked it beneath my legs and pressed down on it. I was bare beneath my nightgown.

Atacar groaned again, deeper this time. His entire chest rumbled, making me keenly aware of his pending orgasm. As his body continued to tighten, as his stomach muscles clenched, I did my best to keep my jaw and throat relaxed. His hands were in my hair again, tunneling hard and fast.

His groan turned to a growl. He lifted his buttocks and fisted my scalp. Within seconds, his seed shot out like lava issuing from a volcano.

Atacar watched me, his gaze fixed on my semen-filled mouth. I swallowed as quickly as I could. I didn't want to miss a drop. I was thrilled that he couldn't seem to take his eyes off me.

I waited, giving him time to breathe. Then I sat up and smiled. He smiled, too.

"You're a fast learner," he said.

I ran my tongue across my lips. I could still taste him. "I've always been a good student."

He pulled me down on top of him, and we rolled over the bed. He tickled me, and I laughed.

"The man who marries you will be lucky," he said.

We were still playing, still wrestling like children. "Because I enjoy sex?"

"And because you're smart and witty and beautiful."

His words made me dreamy, but I didn't want to give myself away. "I'm a deplorable cook. And I can barely sew a straight stitch."

He winged his eyebrows. "Then why did you offer to make me new clothes?"

"Nanny is going to help me. Without her, I couldn't have made the offer."

"A man will still be lucky to have you." He tickled me again. "As long as Nanny is part of the bargain."

I pinched him, and he grinned. He had the most dashing smile. It made the expression in his eyes dance.

The lamp flickered, shadowing the room in a ghostly fashion, and we stopped teasing each other. Our emotions turned serious.

He looped his arms around my waist, bringing me close to his chest, where his heart pattered next to mine.

A few raven black strands of his hair fell across his forehead. His hair wasn't long, but it wasn't short, either. He wore it chopped to a medium length. I reached up to run my hands through it.

"Tell me about the status of your family," I said, wondering if he'd left anyone behind at Fort Sill. "Are your parents still living?"

"No. But I have a sister. She is married with a baby daughter. I love my niece dearly. My sister and brother-in-law, too. But I couldn't stay at the fort."

Because he needed to be free, I thought. "What's it like?"

"It's far better than what we endured in Florida. Many became ill and died there. My parents were among them." He paused a moment before he continued. "It's better than the post in Alabama, too. At Fort Sill, there are mountains, not as big as our homeland, but the soil is good. The first winter was harsh, but sod has been broken for planting now, and a cattle herd is under way."

"To help your people become self-sufficient?"

"Yes. But we're still at the mercy of the War Department." Atacar kept his arms around me. "I tried to escape once before."

My pulse jumped. "When?"

"Toward the end of our stay in Alabama, when I labored at a farm outside the post. But I was captured and brought back."

I inhaled a sharp breath. Had he been punished for running away? If so, it hadn't deterred him from making another attempt.

"My sister begged me not to escape again," he said. "She wanted me to remain in Oklahoma Territory. To comply with our new life there."

But he didn't, and now he was here with me. "I have a brother." I pictured my tall, trim, fair-haired sibling, impeccably groomed and gallantly spoken. "He begged me to comply, too. With the rules of society."

"But you turned bohemian instead."

"Yes." Seductress that I was, I rubbed against my lover. "I most certainly did."

"Maybe I am bohemian, too." His voice went rough. "From your bewitching."

"Maybe you are."

"And maybe you are in need of your turn."

I shuddered. I understood what he meant. I'd sucked him, and now he was going to lick me.

He raised my nightgown and bunched the fabric around my waist. I watched him lower his head, captivated by his exploration. I parted my thighs, letting him play sweet havoc with my clitoris. He kissed me down there, circling the bud of my womanhood with his tongue.

I asked him if he liked my cunt, if he thought it was pretty. I knew that he did, but I wanted to say something provocative.

He responded in an erotic whisper, the words warm against my skin. Yes, yes, he liked it. He liked my yellow curls, my delicate pink folds, my creamy moisture.

He behaved as if I were his favorite dessert, devouring me with his entire mouth. He laved my juices, and I nearly flew off the bed. He knew how much I loved cunnilingus. He knew it drove me mad.

I couldn't hold still. I rocked back and forth, clenching my bottom and thrusting my hips toward him. He continued to ravish me, making my slit wetter than it already was.

With my hair strewn across a pillow and my nightgown twisting beneath me, I climaxed.

In the moments that followed, he gave me one last, lingering lick, then righted my ruffled hem, smoothing it over my legs and down my ankles. I sighed my sheer and utter contentment.

"Next time we'll do it at the same time," he said.

I knew he was talking about mutual oral copulation, where the pleasure was simultaneous. I'd heard of it, of course. Intrigued, I envisioned us in that highly naughty position, certain I would like it. "I'm eager to do everything with you."

"Me, too. With you. But for now, we should sleep."

I agreed. I was sated, and so was he.

He extinguished the lamp, and we snuggled, the front of his body pressed against the back of mine. I closed my eyes, and he slipped his arms around my waist, holding me for the rest of the night.

~

Jared didn't know how long he was supposed to hold Mandy. Were they supposed to sleep in each other's arms? That wasn't his style. When he spent the night with a woman, he banged her brains out, then rolled over onto his side of the bed. Of course, he and Mandy had already had sex tonight. They'd gotten hot and heavy in the garden, and she'd given him head in the limo. This wasn't a booty call. Yet here they were at her front door.

After they entered the condo, he analyzed himself. What the hell was wrong with him that he couldn't hold a woman without panicking? That he didn't know how to give or receive affection? That he was so damned detached?

What indeed? How about an abusive father? And a mother he barely remembered? That was classic Freud, right? Psych 101 all the way.

"Do you want a nightcap?" Mandy asked, as they stood awkwardly in her living room.

"Okay." He figured a drink might help. Maybe she figured that, too. "What do you have?"

"How about some brandy?"

"That sounds good."

She went into the kitchen and opened a cabinet, where she

kept her liquor. He could see her from his vantage point. Her condo had an open floor plan.

She returned with two snifters of brandy. He thanked her and took a sip. She lifted her glass to her lips, too. Neither of them could think of anything to say, but at least the brandy hit the spot.

She finally spoke. "Are you tired?"

"Are you?" he responded.

She nodded. "Yes, but I probably won't fall asleep right away."

Which meant what? That they were going to lie in bed, cozy as you please, stumbling through a conversation? Freud be damned. He wished he'd never agreed to do this.

They finished their brandy, and she put their glasses in the sink.

"I'm going to take a bath," she said.

He noticed that she didn't invite him to join her, but it was just as well. He assumed that she wanted to do the girly thing and use the scented products she kept on the side of her tub.

"Will you undo me?" she asked.

"No problem."

He helped with the hooks on her dress, and she left him in the living room. Uncertain of what else to do, he sat on the sofa, turned on the TV, and flipped the remote control. If he thought he could bail out on his promise without hurting Mandy's feelings, he would head straight out the door. But he couldn't, so he watched a late-night talk show and waited for her.

Twenty minutes later, she reappeared, looking soft and clean and fresh. Her face was scrubbed free of cosmetics, and she wore a lace-trimmed nightshirt in an angelic shade of blue.

"The bathroom is free if you need it," she said.

"Thanks." Jared turned off the TV. He kept extra toiletries at her house. He had a few extra clothes hanging in her closet, too. He'd stayed over plenty of times. But tonight was different, and they both knew it.

He washed his face and brushed his teeth. When he entered Mandy's bedroom, he stripped down to his boxers. She was already in bed and had left a night-light burning.

He got under the covers. She moved closer, and they faced each other, but he didn't reach for her. It was too soon to cuddle. He needed time to ease into it.

He complimented her instead. "You smell good."

"It's a Hawaiian orchid body wash. I used the same lotion, too." She angled her head, making her pretty brown hair sweep the side of her face. "Do you know what orchids mean?"

"In Hawaiian? I have no idea."

"I meant in the Victorian language of flowers."

"Oh, that." He wondered if he should admit that he knew the answer, that he'd studied the language of flowers far more than he'd let on.

She waited for his response, gazing directly at him, and he realized that he couldn't avoid her question.

"There are different meanings," he said.

"Like what?"

"Luxury. Beauty. Lust." He gave a pause. "Love." He hesitated again. "It depends on what source you use."

Her gaze remained riveted to his. "I'm going to have to learn that language. It's fascinating."

"It is." He hedged, thinking about Catherine and Atacar, about the couple who'd lived and loved and lost. "Not that I'm an expert."

"You seem pretty good at it to me." She waited a beat, as if she were gathering her thoughts, her emotions. "You really are a blue rose, Jared. Full of mystery." She studied him with affection, with tenderness, with awe. "So, are you from Oklahoma?"

"Yes." Her attention made him uncomfortable. He wasn't used to this kind of intimacy. The Freud factor, he thought. In the past he'd avoided women like her, women who cared, who made men weak, who stripped them of their machismo.

"What about the accent?" she asked, questioning him further.

"I used to talk like that." But over the years he'd purposely rid his voice of the Southern inflection, determined to become someone new. He'd only incorporated it into the party charade to fool Mandy. "I moved here when I was eighteen."

"With your family or by yourself?"

"By myself." He gave her a condensed version. It was the best he could do. "My parents were divorced when I was a baby, but my mom died when I was seven, so I don't remember her very well. After that, I went to live with my dad."

She seemed to sense what was coming. "Did he treat you badly?"

"He used to push me around and tell me how worthless I was. But he quit doing that when I got big enough to fight back." Jared glanced at his hands. How many times during his teenage years had he balled them into knuckle-scraping fists, had he stood toe-to-toe with his dad?

Mandy looked as if she was going to wrap her arms around him, but he tensed his shoulders, letting her know that he didn't want that kind of solace. When they cuddled, it would be for her, not for him.

She didn't do it, so he relaxed a little and continued. "Dad resented having to raise a kid by himself. It didn't matter that I was *his* kid. That I looked like him. That I fell into his footsteps and started working with horses. That I was really good at it."

"Does your mom have any family left?" she asked. "Is there anyone from her side that you're close to?"

"No. She was an only child, and her parents were already gone before I was born."

"Was Atacar her ancestor? Are you related to him through her?"

"Yes." Jared blew out the breath he'd been holding. "And that was always a point of contention with my old man. A jealousy thing, I guess. He said Atacar's portrait didn't mean anything. That it wasn't important. But it was to me."

"So you moved here when you were eighteen, got embraced by the art world, and found success in the horse industry."

"All of that didn't happen overnight, but yes, that about sums it up."

She leaned on her side, watching him in that tender way of hers. Apparently she wasn't ready for their conversation to end. "How did your mother die?"

"It was a car accident." Most of his memories were vague, but he recalled that day vividly, as if it were a video that looped in his mind. "She was supposed to pick me up from school, but she never made it. I waited in the principal's office. They gave me crayons or a puzzle or something to play with, but it didn't help. I was scared, and I wanted my mommy. She'd never been late before. The administration didn't know what was going on, either. Not until the hospital called."

Mandy didn't keep her gentle hands to herself. She tried to console him, skimming her fingers along his cheek, his jaw, the tendons in his neck. "Do you have anything of your mother's? Any kind of keepsake?"

His throat went tight, and he pulled back, making her drop her hand.

Finally he responded, "I used to have this trinket-type box that belonged to her, but I broke it about six months ago."

"Was it made of glass?"

"No. It was made of wood, but it was really old. It had been in her family for generations. After she died, Dad gave it to me." Another vivid memory, Jared thought. Funny how the painful ones were the most clear. "He was packing up Mom's stuff for the Goodwill, and I was crying. He turned around and thrust the box at me. Then he explained that it was special to her, and she probably would've wanted me to have it. After that, he told me to shut up, to never cry again. I stopped bawling and clutched the box like my life depended on it."

Mandy made a troubled face, as if she wanted to console him again.

He kept talking. "When I was little, I kept my favorite Hot Wheels in it. When I got older, I used it as a men's valet, for my wallet, keys, extra coin."

"How did you break it?"

"I was reaching for something on my nightstand and knocked it over. The box hit the floor, and the bottom of it splintered and cracked."

"Did you try to repair it?"

"No."

"Why not?"

"I just didn't."

"Maybe it was subconscious. Your way of telling yourself that you couldn't bring your mother back."

The tightness in his throat returned. It was more than that. Breaking the box had changed his life, but he couldn't reveal that part of the story. Because that was how he'd found Catherine's journal.

By chance. By accident.

Or had it been fate? The journal had been sealed into a secret compartment, and there was no way to open that portion, short of breaking it.

Apparently his mom hadn't known of its existence, either. Once he'd read the journal, he'd discovered that the book had been there since the nineteenth century, since friends of Catherine's had put it there.

"I wish for your sake that your mother hadn't passed away," Mandy said. "That things would have turned out differently for you."

He didn't respond, and she added, "I understand why you moved to Santa Fe. Why you needed to be near Atacar."

Jared frowned. "You make him sound as if he's still alive."

"Sometimes when I look into his eyes, it seems as if he's looking back at me, as if he's inside Catherine's painting. Sometimes he gives me chills."

Jared was getting chilled right now. Atacar had been worried about Catherine capturing his soul.

"I hope I can find her journal," Mandy said. "That it's out there somewhere."

He protected his lie, repeating what he'd been telling her all along. "I don't think it exists."

She disagreed. "Look how the painting was found. Hidden inside the walls of the farmhouse where Catherine lived."

"That doesn't mean the journal was hidden, too." Jared had read it hundreds of times since he'd found it. He knew almost every word by heart. But he wasn't keeping it a secret for himself. Someone in England had asked him not to make Catherine's writings public.

"I'd rather cling to the hope that it was hidden. That it's in a spot no one has discovered yet."

Too late, he thought. "You should stop looking."

"I'm not giving up until I know for sure. Until Kiki exhausts her research. I've got her working on it. You know how important Catherine and Atacar are to me, to the museum."

They were important to him, too. More than he could possibly say. He changed the subject. "It's getting late. We should get some sleep."

Before she could protest, he turned out the light, and as darkness pitched the room, he realized that he still hadn't snuggled with her. That he hadn't kept his promise.

Shit.

His anxiety kicked up again. He could tell that Mandy was waiting, hoping he would come through.

So he sucked in a shallow breath and did it. He pressed the front of his body to the back of hers and put his arms around her waist.

An instant smile sounded in her voice. She even sighed. "This is nice."

He nuzzled her hair. It smelled as good as the rest of her. But that didn't calm his nerves. "I'm glad you think so, but don't get used to it. I'm not doing this every time I spend the night with you."

She got sweetly bossy. "Yes, you are."

"Listen to you. The dominant woman."

She laughed and nudged him in the ribs. He laughed, too. At the absurdity of his situation. Of being afraid of a little affection.

He breathed her in again, all warm and scented, all floral and soft. "It's not that bad," he heard himself say. "But it'd be better if I was inside you. Cuddle fucking. That sounds good, doesn't it?"

Another nudge. Another laugh. "Not on your life, buster. You're not using sex to get out of this."

"Buster?" He pinned her arms, teasing her right back. Sex was what he knew, what he did.

She wiggled. She squirmed. She played his silly game. But within minutes, they quit goofing around. So he did the best he could, mimicking what he'd read in Catherine's journal. He closed his eyes and held Mandy as close as he possibly could.

The way Atacar used to hold Catherine.

CHAPTER TEN

Mandy awakened to the aroma of fried food, then sat up and hugged her knees to her chest. She needed to give herself a moment to get her bearings. Jared was cooking for her? On a Sunday morning after they'd cuddled all night?

Before she got too giddy, she went into the bathroom and freshened up. Still in her nightshirt, she padded to the kitchen and stood in the entryway.

Yep. There he was, looking like a hunk-of-burning-Elvis-song love. Chest bare, jeans slung low on his hips, and hair in a ponytail, he manned a pan at the stove.

He noticed her right off. He turned and smiled. She told her runaway heart to behave. So he'd held her tenderly in the dark. So he was fixing her something to eat in the light. That didn't mean she should fall at his feet.

"What are you making?" she asked.

"Fry bread. I figured the smell would wake you."

"It did." She came forward. She was familiar with fry bread. She'd eaten it on a couple of occasions and had loved it. You couldn't live in the Southwest and not know that it was an American Indian staple served at powwows and selective restaurants. "I had the ingredients?"

He turned the disk-shaped dough, frying the other side to a golden brown. "It's a simple recipe. Flour, baking powder, salt, water, oil." He teased her with a playful wink. "Lots of calories. From me to you."

"Please, fatten me all you want." Mandy gazed at the greasy treat, and he removed it from the fire and put it on a paper-towel-lined plate to absorb the oil. Traditionally fry bread was topped with honey, powdered sugar, or taco fixings.

"I'll get the honey." She rummaged through the cabinet. "I might even have a box of powdered sugar that's been gathering dust."

She found both items, and he finished frying the rest of the dough. By the time he was done, he'd made enough to feed a tribe.

Unable to help herself, she grabbed him and kissed him. But not lightly. She planted a hard, head-spinning lip-lock right on him.

"Damn." He caught his breath. "What was that for?"

"The food." The kiss was for holding her last night, too. But she wasn't about to admit it. Her heart was misbehaving again.

She stepped back and noticed that he'd made a pot of coffee. She could've kissed him for that, as well. She poured a cup and doctored it with her favorite creamer.

"Ready?" he asked.

"Absolutely." For her this was like eating donuts in the morning, something she rarely did.

Jared set the glass-topped table, and they sat down to scarf. He sprinkled powdered sugar on his fry bread, then drizzled honey over it.

She watched him. "You're using both toppings?"

"Damn straight. The sweeter, the messier, the gooier, the better."

What the heck. Mandy tried it that way too, moaning when she took her first bite. The flavor melted in her mouth. "Can you cook anything else?"

"I grill a mean steak."

"We'll have to barbecue sometime."

He lifted his eyebrows. "Like a real couple?"

"Why not?" She let herself dream. "We could do it tonight. On my patio with citronella candles and a bottle of sparkling wine."

"I think maybe we should concentrate on one meal at a time, especially since I'm going to jump your bones after we're done with breakfast."

She met his calculating gaze. He wasn't kidding. He had a hungry look in his eyes that had nothing to do with food.

"To make up for not getting cuddle fucked last night?" she asked.

"Yep. Sweet, sticky, oral sex." He let her know exactly what he had in mind. "Right here in your kitchen."

The promise of decadent pleasure blasted through her body. This time she wasn't about to deny him. Or herself. She shifted in her chair, her pulse beating between her legs. "Can I pour honey down the front of your pants?"

He sent her a lethal smile. "As long as I can do it to you. Inside your pretty little panties," he added, reminding her that she was sitting there in a lace-trimmed nightshirt and matching underwear.

Eager, Mandy reached for another piece of fry bread and drenched it with the substance in question. "Do real couples have sex as much as we do?"

"How would I know? I've never been in a real relationship." He went for seconds, too. "You're the one who was married."

Mandy stopped eating. He was looking at her as if he expected her to discuss her marriage and divorce, to give him the lousy details before he dragged her onto the floor and oral sexed her to death.

"Fair is fair," he said.

She fought to stay focused. "What?"

"I sold my soul to you last night. It's only right that you sell yours to me today. Do you know how difficult it was for me to tell you that crap about myself?"

She nodded. The pain was still there, deep and dark within his psyche. She couldn't imagine losing your mother at such a young age, only to have your bastard of a father resent you for it.

"So?" he said, pressing her to open up to him.

She did, knowing that she had little choice. "My husband should have been my best friend, but he wasn't. We were married for fifteen years and got nothing out of it. Meals in front of the TV, average sex, work-related conversations." She fussed with her coffee, clanking the cup against the table. "We took vacations when we could arrange our schedules accordingly, but even that was dull. Empty," she clarified, using a more fitting description.

Jared squinted at her. "Was it more exciting when you were dating?"

"Not really."

"Then why did you marry him?"

"Because that's what good girls from Iowa do. They marry their college sweethearts and tell themselves that a diamond ring and a big church wedding will make a difference."

He ignored the ring and vow. "You're from Iowa?" The lethal smile returned, brimming with mischief. "I'm banging a farm girl?"

"I wasn't raised on a farm." She balled up a paper napkin and tossed it at him, hitting him square in the chest and making his grin widen.

"Damn. Spoil my fantasy, why don't you? I was picturing you as a milkmaid. All cute and corn-fed, with your boobs spilling out of a gingham dress and your hair in pigtails."

She sent another balled-up napkin flying. He laughed, and she broke down and laughed, too.

"I used to shop at the Piggly Wiggly," she said. "Does that count?"

"Sure. Why not?" He sat back in his chair, serious again. "What's your ex-husband's name?"

"Ken. Kenny, when we first got together."

"What does he do?"

"He's an audit manager. He has a degree in finance. And his career always came first. Every time we relocated, it was for him. Not that I couldn't find curator positions in the cities he chose, but do you know how many years I wanted to move to Santa Fe? This is my dream town, where I wanted to be."

"Did you come here after you got divorced?"

"Yes. Ken is still in Seattle. That's the last place we lived." Mandy looked across the table at her lover. The sun shone through the window, highlighting the bluish black streaks in his hair. "I'm not saying that I was a perfect wife. When a relationship fails, it's rarely one-sided."

"Did either of you cheat?"

"No. But I don't know why we hung on to our marriage for so long. Maybe it was the nonquitters in us. Or maybe we just got used to the rut we were in."

"Did you ever want to pour something sweet and sticky down the front of his pants? Did you ever fantasize about anything like that?"

Her heart struck her chest. Trust Jared to throw her off-kilter, to shift gears without warning. "No."

"But you want to do it to me?"

"Yes." Just like that, she got blatantly aroused. She even spread her thighs to combat the heat.

He left his chair and stood beside hers. "Because I turned you into a bad girl?"

"Yes," she said again, as he unbuttoned his jeans.

She got up, and with a snap of his wrist, he tugged the waistband of his boxers away from his skin, giving her the opportunity to seize the honey. Like a woman possessed, she gripped the plastic bottle and squirted the syrupy liquid into the opening he'd provided. She aimed for his cock and balls, but some of it clung to his pubic hair.

Whatever the case, he seemed to thrive on the sensation, on watching her do it. He sucked in his breath, and the ripple of muscle along his abs vibrated. She decided to blast some honey there, too. And all over his chest, coating his flat brown nipples.

"Damn." He inhaled another shuddering breath. "You're a girl on a mission."

"Yes, I am." She reached for the powdered sugar box.

"Shit," he said, even though he seemed more than willing to be her dessert, as long she was going to be his. "You're next, Multiorgasmic Mandy."

"I know." She dusted his chest and stomach with sugar, and it stuck to the honey. He was still wearing his jeans and boxers. "Take those off."

He peeled them down. His pierced cock sprang free, fully aroused and scrumptiously sticky. She sprinkled a light coating of sugar on it.

She glanced up at his face, and he went full-bore, dragging her nightshirt over her head. She held her panties open for him, and he grabbed the honey. Because she was waxed and her Brazilian only left a landing strip of hair, he was able to hit his mark easily, drenching her nether lips.

"Feel good?" he asked.

She nodded, dizzy on her feet, the sticky sensation ratcheting higher. By now, he was aiming a stream of the gooey substance toward the hood of her clit. She pulled open the waistband of her panties even wider, giving him as much room as he needed.

"We're going to sixty-nine," he said. "Then we're going to fuck in the shower."

He lifted the container and shot some honey across her nipples and down her stomach. The powdered sugar came next, and she relished every tantalizing second of their insane foreplay.

He removed her panties and tugged her down. He stretched onto the cool, tiled floor, and she straddled his face and lowered her head.

Their bodies stuck together like glue. He laved the sweetness between her legs, and she sucked him. He tasted like the topping on the fry bread, only better. Her Jared. Her addiction. She couldn't take all of him from this position, but she took enough to make him moan, right against her clit.

No matter how hard they tried, they couldn't eat each other clean. A warm, slick residue remained.

Mandy rubbed against him, glorifying in the swirl of his tongue. There was hunger in his touch, but reverence, too. Jared kissed and licked her silken folds, sweeping her into a delicious frenzy.

She couldn't imagine a more erotic setting. Here they were on her kitchen floor, painted in honey and dusted in sugar. Lovers without boundaries, she thought.

Animalistic. Beautifully wild.

With her senses spinning in prismatic colors, she climaxed, rocking back and forth. In the midst of her spasms, she did her damnedest to stroke him, to bring him to fruition, but he didn't come. He pulled away before it happened, saving his release for the shower.

He scooped her up and carried her to the bathroom. Thoroughly enthralled with their affair, with the way he made everything so passionate, she clung to him.

He put her on her feet, turned the spigot, and adjusted the nozzle. They stepped into the tub, water falling like rain. He kissed her, long and slow, then stepped back, preparing to shower, to get rid of the gooiness so he could fuck her nice and clean. She noticed that his big, gorgeous cock was still hard. She handed him a bottle of body wash.

"This isn't the orchid stuff, is it?" he asked.

She smiled, shook her head. "It's ginseng."

He took a whiff, then decided it smelled okay for a guy to use. She watched him pour a dollop into his hand and lather his long, muscular body.

She washed, too. But she couldn't look away from her lover. He consumed her. "Why haven't you ever touched yourself for me?"

He rubbed liquid soap over his chest and down his stomach. "Because you've never asked me to."

"You'd do it if I asked?"

"Yes, but not right now." He scrubbed his pubic hair and moved on to his cock and balls, then took her hand and made her wash him.

She pumped his soapy penis, and they kissed again. Steam filled the tub and floated over the shower curtain. Sharing the spray of water, they rinsed their hot, naked bodies.

He spun her around and pressed her against the wall. She widened her stance, knowing he was going to enter her this way. He cupped her breasts and caressed them, tweaking her nipples and making them ache. She moaned and waited for his cock, her sex soft and slick and swollen.

He went for the kill, swooping like a predator and thrusting so hard, so deep, rough, she gasped and begged for more. She even rasped, "Please, please . . ."

"Please, please . . . what?" he echoed in her ear.

"Do it harder."

He worked her like a jackhammer, and the power-tool motion was nearly her undoing. Her hips vibrated. Her boobs bounced. Her teeth rattled. She put her hands flat against the wall to hold herself up.

"Think about something dirty," he said. "Fantasize while I'm fucking you."

"I—"

"Do it," he commanded. "Use that naughty imagination of yours."

She closed her eyes and felt a rush of excitement.

"Are you doing it?"

"Yes."

"That's my girl," he praised, feeding the fire. "Now tell me what it is."

The excitement spiraled, hurtled, broke free. "I'm asleep in bed and you come into my room. You whisper my name, and I wake up. You turn on the light. It's bright, and I squint at you, my heart pounding in my chest. You start undressing me, taking off my pajamas and my panties. You strip me bare, and I lie there, wondering what you're going to do to me."

He thrust deeper, waiting for her to continue.

"You take off your clothes, too," she said, picturing the scenario in her head. "And then you kneel over my face."

"Damn." Jared pushed her harder against the wall. "Am I going to jack off?"

"Yes, but you don't use any lubricant. Nothing except saliva. You lick the palm of your hand."

"Then what?"

"You grip your cock and stroke yourself. From shaft to tip. Up and down, strong and hard. No man has ever masturbated for me before, and watching you fascinates me. I like that you're doing it so close to my face. But it's not enough. I want more. I want to put my mouth on you while you're doing it."

His voice all but vibrated. "Do I move closer?"

"You move close enough for me to lick whatever part of you I can reach. My tongue is everywhere. All over you."

"Fuck."

He sounded so aroused, so excited by her story, he could barely breathe. But he didn't come. He slowed his thrusts, pacing himself inside her. She could feel him, making her inner walls contract.

"While I'm licking you, you keep stroking yourself, getting off on what I'm doing." She paused to absorb the details. She didn't know that this was her naughty-girl fantasy, but it was. Heaven help her, it was. "You taste so hot and sexy, I can't get enough."

"How long do you lick me?"

"Long enough to drive you crazy."

"I'm already crazy. Fucking certifiable. You've got to tell me more."

"I will. Just give me a minute." She held on to the shower wall, hands fanned, fingers spread. She was getting certifiable, too.

Impatient, he withdrew and spun her around so they were face-to-face.

Suddenly Mandy went horribly, terribly shy. She didn't want him looking at her while she spun her sexual tale, while her imagination clawed its way to her cunt.

"Tell me the rest. I want to know how it ends."

Her face flushed, but there was so much steam, so much moisture, her skin was probably pink already. "I don't know. I—"

"You know, damn it. It's your fantasy."

She tried to think, to concentrate. His gaze was locked directly on hers.

He dragged her onto the tub floor and thrust into her again. "Come on, baby, tell me what I want to hear. Tell me what happens next."

She gripped the sides of the tub. The water was still running, and her bottom was sliding against the surface as he fucked her.

"By now your cock is leaking," she said, her shyness fading, her hunger burgeoning. "With beads of pre-come. So you rub it against my mouth and let me taste it."

He rocked back and forth, sloshing the water, intensifying the sex. "Am I close to coming for real?"

"Yes, and so am I. I reach down and stroke my clit. I can't help it. I need some relief."

His breathing went labored.

Mandy wrapped her legs around him, making him plunge deeper. "We masturbate together. Then you move down and position yourself over my tits."

"So I can splash your nipples?"

"Yes. And when it happens, it feels so good, so milky and warm that I rub it all over, across my breasts, down my stomach, and deep between my thighs. I use it like lotion."

Jared gave up the fight. He grabbed a handful of her wet hair, tangled it around his fingers, and kissed her. As their tongues collided, he spilled into her. The force of his orgasm triggered hers, and she shuddered through an equally desperate climax.

Seconds ticked by. Then minutes. But neither of them moved. He was still inside her, and she was still clutched around his waist.

Finally he helped her up, and they turned off the water. He wrapped her in a towel, and she nearly stumbled in his arms, reeling from the erotic aftermath. He held her a little tighter, promising that on one of these long, hot summer nights, he would mirror her imagination.

And make her fantasy come true.

CHAPTER ELEVEN

Mandy sat at one of the brightly colored patio tables in front of the museum, where a food vendor sold snacks and sodas. She sipped an Orange Crush and waited for Kiki to join her so they could discuss Kiki's research.

Alone with her briefcase at her feet, Mandy reflected on her surroundings. The Santa Fe Women's Art Museum was located within walking distance of the Plaza, a downtown area that served tourists with hundreds of gift shops and a host of restaurants and galleries.

In spite of its commercialism, Mandy loved the Plaza. Santa Fe meant "Holy Faith" in Spanish, and for her that epitomized the depth and beauty of this city. After her divorce, she'd come here to start a new life, to find faith in herself. In that regard, she and Jared were the same. He'd come here to start over, too.

She hadn't seen him since the morning after the masquerade. But it had only been a week. Besides, he'd invited her to have dinner at his house tomorrow. He'd offered to grill one of his mean steaks for her. Nothing could have pleased her more. Not that she wasn't anxious for him to fulfill her other fantasy, but she figured he was building the sexual tension, keeping her busy until he slipped into her room one unsuspecting night and made it happen.

Mandy glanced up and saw Kiki headed toward her. The historian's wavy red hair shimmered in the sun, and her gauzy dress billowed. She was a Santa Fe transplant, too.

"Sorry I'm late." Kiki sat beside her. As always, she'd accessorized with Southwestern jewelry. Today she wore a collection of coral, turquoise, and spiny oyster. "I got caught up at a last-minute meeting."

"That's okay. I was little late myself." Their workdays rarely ended on time, but they both loved what they did. They never complained. As for Kiki's research, Mandy made a pleading face. "Please, tell me you found the journal."

Kiki laughed. "Don't we wish it could be that easy? Still, I thought you might be interested in what I compiled on Catherine's nanny. Other historians have created files on her, but I'm hoping to make mine more complete. It might help us find the journal."

Mandy sat a little more upright. It was common knowledge that Catherine's nanny had moved to America with her, and that the other woman had probably been with her when she'd hidden Atacar's portrait and abandoned the farmhouse. But whatever had become of them after that was anybody's guess.

"In England she was known as Nanny Perkins," Kiki said. "But Catherine just called her Nanny."

"What was her full name?"

"Hattie Grace Perkins. Most nannies were from the lower classes, and she was no exception. She was a country girl who'd gone to London to seek employment. Staying on the family farm wasn't an option. Her family had too many mouths to feed."

Mandy tried to picture Hattie, to imagine what she looked like, but she couldn't get past Jared's lusty fantasy of a farm girl. Somehow she doubted that Hattie wore pigtails and too-tight gingham dresses. "Was Catherine her first charge?"

"No. She worked for other families before the Burkes hired her to look after their children. She was Catherine's older brother's nanny, too. But it was Catherine who captured her heart."

Mandy smiled. All of this made Catherine seem more real, more tangible. Mandy had seen pictures of Catherine in the museum's archives, and the artist always seemed to have an undeniable gleam in her eye, much like the mischief Jared sometimes got in his eyes. Who wouldn't be drawn to that type of charm?

Kiki continued. "No one else could handle Catherine, certainly not her parents, and not the string of governesses who came and went. Nanny was it for Catherine. They shared a special bond. I think it was because Nanny understood Catherine's wild streak."

Mandy could tell there was more to the story, so she sipped her soda and waited for Kiki to tell it.

"There were rumors that when Nanny was fresh off the farm, she'd had an affair with Thomas Boydell, a notorious London thief. Not only was he a thief, he was a social activist. Thomas robbed from the rich and gave generously to the poor, determined to improve the conditions of the city, to combat the poverty and filth."

Intrigued, Mandy leaned forward. "A nineteenth-century Robin Hood. He sounds sexy."

"Supposedly he was. Tall, dark, and dashing."

"What ever became of him?"

"He was killed in a mob riot. Nanny denied the allegation that they were involved, but supposedly she was never the same after he died. Part of her spirit floated away. Right into the muddy water of the Thames," Kiki added, putting her own spin on the British tale.

"Now I feel sad for her," Mandy said.

"I know. It's like Catherine and Atacar. What ever happened to happily ever after?"

"You're asking me?" Mandy pictured the wedding dress she'd preserved, then shucked; the ring she'd removed; the vows she shouldn't have recited.

Kiki had a ready answer. "At least you're dating a gorgeous guy who takes you to sex shops and masquerade parties."

"That's not synonymous with happily ever after."

"Who says Prince Charming can't buy his ladylove a dildo-making kit, wear a black mask, and bang her in someone else's garden?"

"I shouldn't have told you that stuff. Now you're being cynical."

"No, I'm not. I think he's turning out to be just what you need. Exciting, sensual, obscurely romantic."

The mere suggestion sent Mandy's pulse reeling. "He wasn't romantic in the beginning."

"Maybe not. But apparently he's trying to tap into that part of himself. And he's doing it for you."

Yes, Mandy thought, like the upcoming dinner at his house. But nonetheless, she countered Kiki's assessment of him. If she didn't, she was afraid she'd get too attached, that she'd let herself feel too much. Wanting him to hold her every night was bad enough. "You have no idea how emotionally guarded he is."

"Sounds like a match made in dysfunctional Heaven to me. You're guarded, too."

"Not like him." She thought about what his father had done to him. The damage that had been caused. "He hasn't been loved since he was seven, since the day his mother died."

"That pretty much says it all, doesn't it? The reason he turned into a bad boy. Bad boys are always tortured. If they weren't, they'd be corporate assholes like our ex-husbands."

"Now you really are being cynical."

"Sorry." Kiki flashed her signature grin. "I couldn't resist."

Caught in a gal-pal moment, they laughed. A moment later, they went reverently quiet, the city of Holy Faith shimmering around them. Soon the sun would be setting, painting desert hues across the sky.

"I won't give up," Kiki said, revisiting their original conversation. "I'll keep researching the journal."

Grateful for her friend's determination, Mandy asked, "Are you going try to locate Nanny's ancestors?"

The redhead nodded. "I'm working on that now."

"What about Catherine's family? Are you going to contact them, too?"

"I already did. Catherine only has one significant heir, and I knew she would refuse my calls. She won't discuss Catherine with anyone."

"Who is she?"

"Catherine's grandniece, and she's a reclusive old bird. Proper, prestigious, powerfully rich."

"What's her name?"

"Minerva. She's Paul Burke's granddaughter. Paul was Catherine's brother, and he had one son, who in turn had one daughter."

"Making her the matriarch," Mandy concluded. "Of a dwindling family."

"Yep. She's in her eighties now. But you want to know the ironic part? When she was young, she favored Catherine. Long, wavy blonde hair, blue eyes, fragile complexion."

"Really?" Mandy's interest in the old bird piqued. "That must have been a curse, to look like the black sheep of the family. Not that Catherine wasn't beautiful. She was stunning. But you know what I mean."

"I surely do. Minerva's lineage to the Burke dynasty runs deep. And so does her refined breeding. She married an equally proper man, but she's widowed now, and they never had any children. She lives in a country estate, but she still owns the house where Catherine grew up, too."

Mandy tried to envision it. "I wonder if it has one of those winding stairways with austere portraits, and if there's a missing spot where Catherine's picture should be."

"I don't know." Kiki glanced up at the predusk sky, but she didn't prepare to leave. She remained seated. "But as I said, I'm not giving up on Catherine or her nanny. Not until we know what happened to them."

~

Nanny drove our buggy, and I sat next to her. We were on our way to town to get the materials for Atacar's new clothes.

The ride was bumpy, but it wasn't Nanny's fault, as she couldn't control the condition of the roads. Our carriage, known as a runabout, was built for two with room in the back for supplies, and Nanny was good with the reins. We also had an old, broken-down wagon that had been left by the previous tenants, but we had no reason to repair or use it.

I gazed out at the land, searching for prairie dogs peeking out of their holes. In spite of their names, they weren't wild dogs. They were robust rodents, grizzled and fat, and they never failed to make me smile.

I spotted a mother with her young and thought about what Atacar had said. That a man would be lucky to have me as his wife. Marriage had never appealed to me before, but I was getting swayed by it.

Unable to quell my romantic notions, I turned to Nanny and said, "Do you think I'd make a good wife?"

She kept quiet, staring straight in front of her. A moment later she gazed at me and asked, "Why? Did Atacar propose marriage?"

"No. But he thinks a man would be lucky to have me."

"He's already having you."

I made a priggish face at her, and she laughed at how silly I looked. She never told me whether she thought I would make a good wife, but she probably didn't want to encourage me. I glanced back to catch another glimpse of the prairie dog and her pups, but they were no longer visible.

A deep sense of longing overcame me. If I found a kind-hearted husband, if I bore him rosy-cheeked children, if I lived to be a hundred, I would never forget Atacar.

Nanny frowned, as if she sensed what was on my mind. Because of her thief, I surmised. I opened my mouth to ask her about him, but I clamped it shut just as swiftly. I knew how protective she was of her memories.

We hit another pocket in the road, and the runabout wobbled. After that, we rode in silence without incident.

The town we frequented was the county seat. A courthouse dominated the community, along with a bank, a livery stable, a hotel, a post office, a general store, and a few smaller enterprises. On the edge of town was a railroad depot, a Methodist church, and a newly constructed school.

Nanny secured the horse and buggy to a hitching post, and we gathered our skirts, took to the walkway, and headed for the general store. The proprietors, Mr. and Mrs. Mayes, were some of the first to settle in this area and had watched their business grow.

The Mayeses were friendly and helpful. They were especially helpful to me because I was a spendthrift. I'd purchased my bed from a catalog they'd provided, and my extravagance had both staggered and pleased them.

Mrs. Mayes rushed forward to greet us. Although she wasn't a comely woman, she carried herself as if she were.

"Miss Burke," she said. "And Miss Nanny."

We responded to her in the same gracious manner, and she asked if there was anything special we needed.

I told her that we were interested in fabrics and sewing sundries. As we made our selections, it didn't take her long to conclude that the articles of clothing we intended to make were for a man. But Nanny and I were prepared for Mrs. Mayes's assumption. We'd discussed it ahead of time and decided that we should admit that we'd replaced our old farmhand, adhering to the story that Atacar was Juan.

I said to the lady proprietor, "He only has one set of clothes, and they're threadbare and permanently soiled. I believe that a man should look presentable, no matter what the nature of his work."

Mrs. Mayes seemed to appreciate my standards, citing that cleanliness was next to godliness. Then she suggested that I browse the store clothes, garments that were ready-made. "That way, you can outfit him right quick," she said. "We're nicely stocked. We received a shipment just yesterday."

Naturally I was compelled to shop. Nanny gave me a warning glare, but I ignored her. Some of the items were practical, and others were a bit smarter, garments Mrs. Mayes called go-to-meeting clothes. I chose a sturdy work shirt and a pair of denim blue jeans for Atacar. For the sizes, I used measurements Nanny had taken of him.

Mrs. Mayes draped my selections over her arm and proceeded to show me some dresses I might fancy. A two-piece ensemble caught my eye, along with some matching ribbon for my hair.

On our way home, Nanny scolded me. "You shouldn't draw that kind of attention to yourself."

"The dress I chose was simple." Not that I have could have done otherwise. The general store didn't stock Paris fashions.

"You know full well I was talking about what you purchased for Atacar. Store clothes for a farmhand? It's enough that we're sewing for him."

"Mrs. Mayes didn't seem to think I did anything wrong. It was her idea."

"That woman just wants your money. There were other patrons nosing about. You need to be more cautious."

I told Nanny to quit fretting. Atacar would be gone in a month, and no one would be the wiser. But even as I said it, I felt ill inside. Not about his clothes, but about losing him.

Before the sun went down that day, I invited Atacar into my studio. He was wearing his new shirt and jeans, and I thought he looked crisp and handsome.

"This room has many windows," he said.

"George, our previous farmhand, installed them for me. When I paint, I need extra light."

Atacar turned away from the windows. "Why doesn't George work for you anymore?"

"He moved to town. He got a job at the livery stable and married the young widow he'd been courting. She has two little boys, and George seems quite fond of them. I suspect that factored into her accepting his proposal. George is a simple man, but he's kind." I waited a moment before I asked, "Why didn't you and your wife have children?"

"Because she didn't conceive."

"Was she drinking the tea Nanny has been giving me?"

"No. It just didn't happen. I think she is barren. She has no children with her new husband, either."

"Do you hope to have a family someday?" I asked, pressing him further.

A frown furrowed his brow. "Not now. Not while my life is so unsettled."

I tried to seem unaffected by his words, by his future without me. "Maybe you'll meet a woman in Mexico, a pretty senorita who will help you settle your life."

"Catherine." He whispered my name, almost as if he shouldn't have said it at all. Then he moved closer, the light surrounding him like a sun-sparked halo.

I got teary-eyed. I didn't mean to. I so hated to cry. I blinked the wateriness away. I could see him watching me, wanting to take me in his arms.

I stepped out of reach, and his breathing went rough.

He continued to speak. "I wish you could come to Mexico with me. But I could never ask that of you. As long as my people are prisoners, as long as soldiers continue to search for me, no one can help me settle my life."

Whose heart was I trying to fool? His or mine? I walked toward him like the lovesick girl I was.

He embraced me, and I nestled against his new shirt. It was rough and scratchy, and I relished the masculine texture. He caressed my back, gliding his hand along my spine, and I looked up at him. I'd only known him for a short time, but I'd already begun to memorize his features. The corded muscles in his body, too. I even knew the placement of his scars.

"I want to teach you a new language," I said.

He regarded me with a curious expression: a quirk of one eyebrow, the slightest angle of his head. "I don't speak enough languages already?"

"This one is for lovers," I told him.

He didn't hesitate. "Then I am ready to learn."

Although my heart wrenched, I began his lesson, refusing to let the tightness in my chest stop us from having this moment.

I sifted through my botanical paintings and showed them to him, explaining that each flower, herb, tree, and shrub had been assigned a meaning.

"Lovers send each other nosegays," I said. "They used to be round tussie-mussies. Mostly they're corsage bouquets now, where the flowers are bunched loosely with longer stems. But no matter what the style, lovers must know the definition of each botanical so they can decipher their messages to each other."

He listened with rapt attention, so I proceeded. "My paintings aren't a complete study. But this is." I offered Atacar my floral dictionary, a book Mama had passed on to me. She, too, had studied this language. Some of the sentiments had changed over the years, but I knew the definitions from her time, as well as what was considered current.

Mama and I despaired over each other, but we shared the love of flowers. She was proud of my botanical paintings, and I cherished her dictionary.

Atacar examined the book and returned it to me. He didn't know how to read or write English, but he seemed fascinated by the concept of florigraphy.

"To express a thought, you must present a flower upright,"

I told him. "To express the opposite of that thought, you must allow the flower to hang in a reverse position. Otherwise the sentiment won't be clear, and your lover will misinterpret your message."

"Do you have a favorite flower?" he asked.

I considered his question. "I have many."

"Then which one speaks of us? What would you send to me? Here and now. On this day."

Something came to mind. But I hesitated.

"Tell me," he said.

I took a swift breath, preparing to respond. "I would give you flowers from a spindle tree. In England, they bloom in May and June, followed by an abundance of fruit."

"What is their meaning?" He motioned to the dictionary in my hand. "What do they represent in your book?"

"Leaves, flowers, or fruit from a spindle tree would say, 'Your image is engraved on my heart.'"

Atacar's gaze locked deeply onto mine. "What would I send to you to say that I share your sentiment?"

My response nearly stuck in my throat. We were admitting that we were falling in love, even if our words were coded. "Double-flowered asters."

He glanced at my paintings. "Do you have a picture?"

"No. But they're shaped like stars, and they mean precisely what you said."

He wanted to know more. "Do they grow in Texas? Can I pick them from the plains?"

The tightness in my chest returned. "I think so, but they don't bloom until late summer or early fall, and you'll be gone by then."

"What could I pick in Mexico that would have a similar sentiment?"

"A dahlia. The type with variegating colors." I sorted through my paintings. "Like this." I tried to sound light of spirit, to let him know I appreciated his romantic gesture, but I was still heavy inside. "Dahlias are indigenous to Mexico. They grow splendidly there."

Atacar queried me further. "What is their precise meaning?"

"They say, 'I think of you constantly.'"

"Then envision me in Mexico, gathering them for you. Imagine that my arms are filled with them."

In the silence that followed, my heart—the heart in which his image was engraved—collapsed. I didn't want to envision him so far away. I didn't want to reach out and not be able to touch him.

If Atacar felt the same crushing ache, he was doing a keener job of hiding his discomfort beneath the darkness of his eyes. I probably looked as if I'd been flayed.

"Maybe you should stop teaching me this language," he said.

"No." I gathered my wits. "I want us to create conversations this way. To use the plants and flowers available to us, as well as imagining using those which are not."

"So do I." He stroked my cheek. "What were you wearing in your hair on the first night we made love?"

"A buttercup. It means 'rich of charms.'"

He smiled. "You are *rich of charms. Dangerously so."*

Ah, yes, my bewitchment of him. I smiled, too. "I'll wear one tonight for you. I'll wear one every night."

Until my lover was gone.

CHAPTER TWELVE

Jared waited in his front yard for Mandy to arrive. His house was an adobe structure surrounded by sagebrush, trees, and towering mesas. It was his sanctuary, a place that made him feel spiritual, as if he truly belonged to the earth.

His dogs, two active Border collies, were off somewhere, romping the grounds. Probably zigzagging through the barn, with its rows of stalls and treasured occupants. Jared's horses were his life.

Suddenly Mandy's car appeared, turning onto the private road that led to his graveled driveway. He hooked his thumbs in his pockets and wondered what compelled him to want her so badly, to keep going out of his way to seduce her.

She parked and exited her vehicle. He moved forward to greet her.

"Hey," he said, sounding like he was in middle school again.

"Hey," she echoed, sounding like a pubescent kid, too. Sometimes he forgot that she was nearly ten years older than he was, and sometimes their age difference was part of the allure. It depended on his sexual state of mind.

He gave her a French kiss to break the ice, and she got breathy and flushed. Was it any wonder he got off on seducing her? If he slipped his hand down the front of her summer skirt and into her panties, she would probably be wet.

They went inside, and she put her purse beside a battered end table. He knew Mandy liked his flea-market style, the eclectic Southwestern furnishings he'd chosen. She hadn't been to his house as often as he'd been to hers, but they'd been known to fuck up a storm in his barn. In his big wrought-iron bed, too.

"Let's get the barbecue started." He escorted her onto a patio designed for entertaining.

"Wow. Look at this."

She seemed impressed that he'd dressed the table with flowers and candles and already had a trio of salads ready. He'd tossed the mixed greens, but the pasta combo and coleslaw had come from the deli.

He offered her a drink, and she accepted a raspberry-flavored malt liquor. He went for a Corona with salt and lime.

"We're having filet mignon and vegetable kebobs." He fired up the gas grill. "Corn on the cob, too."

She smiled. "You're planning on getting laid tonight, aren't you?"

He laughed and swigged his beer. "Do I ever plan on *not* getting laid?"

"Nope. You're a hot-blooded guy."

"Who's having an affair with a hot-blooded girl." He clanked their alcohol bottles, toasting their tryst. He was still focused on fucking Mandy, only now he was learning to hold her, to give her the tenderness she craved to go with it. That seemed like a fair trade.

She sat at the table, and he went into the kitchen to get the steak and vegetables. When he returned with a platter, she peered at the raw food. He'd already marinated everything.

"How do you want your steak?" he asked.

"Medium."

"Me, too." He manned the grill, glancing up to study her. "I like your hair that way." She'd banded it into a low ponytail with loose strands falling around her face. It made her look soft and breezy.

"Thank you." She motioned to the floral arrangement on the table. "That's a gorgeous centerpiece."

"They're variegated dahlias." He couldn't help using the flowers from Catherine's journal. He wanted to make them part of his and Mandy's affair, too. Part of the tenderness, he thought. "Dahlias were first cultivated by ancient Aztecs, but there's an interesting story about how they were introduced to England in the early nineteenth century."

She scooted forward on her chair, prepared for him to enlighten her. She seemed captivated already.

"Lady Holland is responsible for sending dahlias to England," he said. "She'd seen them in Spain, where they'd originated from Mexico."

"Who's Lady Holland?"

"She was a divorcée who was unwelcome at court. She used to be married to Sir Godfrey Webster until she ran off with Lord

Holland and had a scandalous affair. Holland was younger than she was. Just by a few a years, but he was considered a young lord."

"They sound like a sexy couple."

"They were, I suppose. Oddly enough, their affair blossomed into a long and happy marriage. When they lived in Spain, she saw the dahlias and sent them home to England. Lord Holland even wrote her a dahlia poem."

Mandy glanced at the centerpiece, then back at him. "That's a beautiful story. Did you hear it when you were in England?"

"No. I picked it up on the Internet when I researched dahlias. You know, the language of flowers thing. Dahlias have a few different meanings, but the variegated variety says, 'I think of you constantly.' "

"You still need to teach me all of those meanings."

"I will." He turned the filets and rotated the vegetables. "In fact, I bought you a book about it. It's in my room. On my bed."

Her eyebrows shot up. "We're going to read in bed?"

"Yes, ma'am." He wasn't giving her the dictionary Catherine had mentioned in her journal. Catherine had never specified the title, and even if she had, those old editions were difficult to find. But there were plenty of modern books about Victorian floriography. "We're going to have a little flower fun."

"I'll bet." She laughed, making him laugh, too.

He hoped she liked his upcoming surprise. He'd gotten her more than a book, more than words on a page. He'd spent all day preparing for her lesson.

They lingered over dinner, enjoying the night air. She complimented him on how good the meal was, and he had to agree. The steak was thick and juicy.

For dessert they sliced into a strawberry pie that had come from a restaurant bakery. The berries were big and ripe, the glaze sweet and gooey. Like the sugar gluttons they were, they topped it with whipped cream from a can.

"In the language of flowers, strawberries mean 'You are delicious,' " he said.

"Really? Fruits have meanings, too?"

"Some do, as well as herbs. All sorts of plants."

"I'm anxious to get my book."

"Then finish your pie."

She didn't finish, not completely. She left some of the crust. But he figured that she'd had plenty to eat.

A short while later, after they'd taken a breather from stuffing themselves, she helped him clear the dishes. He kissed her when they were in the kitchen.

"You taste like strawberries," he said.

"So do you. We're both delicious."

"Yes, we are." Another kiss. Another taste. "Let's go to my room."

She agreed, and he took her hand and led her down the hall. He paused at his doorway. "Close your eyes."

"Why?"

"Just do it."

"This better be good." She got a kid-at-Christmas expression on her face and squeezed her eyes shut.

He wondered if she used to shake her packages before she tore into them. He swung open the door. "You can look now."

She gasped, and he smiled. He'd filled the room with potted plants and flowers tagged with their common and scientific names. But more important, the bed was dusted with soft, silken petals. Mostly they were rose petals, but he'd included petals from other flowers that either mattered to him and Mandy or to Catherine and Atacar. The delicately dismantled blooms looked like big, rainbow-colored confetti. The book he'd promised sat on top.

"Oh, my God. This is so beautiful, Jared. I don't know what to say."

He slipped his arms around her waist. They were still standing in the doorway. "I told you we were going to have a little flower fun."

"I know. But I didn't expect anything like this." He released her, and she walked into the room and gazed at all of the botanicals. "I'm overwhelmed."

"The potted plants are from a nursery, and the petals are from a florist. I ordered everything last week, and it was delivered today."

"I would've died if Ken had done something like this for our wedding night. Or for one of our anniversaries. Or for any occasion."

Jared shrugged off her comment. He figured it was natural for her to compare him to her ex, considering how long she'd been married.

She picked up the book, making the petals surrounding it flutter. She didn't ask him why he'd chosen to combine those particular flowers, and for that he was grateful. He'd been prepared to lie about the ones associated with Catherine and Atacar.

"Kiki said that you've been trying to be romantic for me, and she was right. You are." Mandy clutched the publication to her chest. "You totally deserve to get laid for this."

"Damn." He grinned, glanced down at his fly. "Now you're giving me a hard-on."

She came forward and kissed him, tongue to luscious tongue. "I might even give you one my famous blow jobs."

He pulled her tight against him. "They're famous?" He couldn't stop from teasing her. She had a sparkle in her eye, and he knew he'd put it there. "Should I start calling you Mandy *BJ* Cooper in front of your friends and work associates?"

She teased him right back. "Not unless you want to get smacked."

To make her point, she swatted him with the book. Then she looked through it, connecting the plants in the room to their definitions. She was taking her lesson seriously.

She laughed that there was a succulent called hen and chickens and that it meant "welcome home, husband, however drunk ye be."

Jared chuckled, too. He hadn't realized that the nursery had sent that along. That he'd included it on the list. "I guess that's the kind of husband I'd be."

"Your wife would be happy to see you even if you were wasted? Somehow I don't think it works that way."

Mandy continued to thumb through the book and scan the plants in the room. She took her time, but he didn't mind. He appreciated her attention to detail.

Finally she started plucking flowers, leaves, and stems. When she was done, she handed her compilation to Jared.

"Let's see." He worked on deciphering its messages. He knew the language well. He'd been studying it since he'd found Catherine's journal. "The daylily is 'coquettish,' the azalea is 'romance,' the African marigold means 'vulgar-minded,' and the chickweed represents a rendezvous." He put it all together. "You're flirting with me so we can have a romantic, vulgar-minded rendezvous. In other words, my sweet, noble lady, you're telling me that you're ready to fuck."

She flung her arms around his neck. "You're good at this."

He scooped her up, and they landed on the bed. As they rolled around, kissing and touching, the petals stuck to their hair and created a snowflake effect on their clothes. Jared couldn't get over how radiant Mandy looked, and she was just as fixated on him.

They took turns getting undressed and watching each other strip. She went first, unbuttoning her blouse. The eyelet fabric had embroidered holes in it, too small to see through, but pretty enough to notice. Her bra was even prettier, but she didn't unhook it. She waited for him to take off his shirt.

He dragged the casual cotton tee over his head. Just for good measure, he unbuttoned the top of his jeans, too.

She undid her bra and exposed her breasts. Jared leaned forward and tossed some petals there. He loved her small tits and big, pink nipples.

Joining in his game, she tossed some petals at him, and they landed on his bulging fly. He pinned her down and kissed her. She still tasted like strawberry pie, but he supposed he did, too.

They finished removing the rest of their clothes. Steeped in flowers, they rubbed their nakedness all over each other, and the heady aroma of botanicals mingled with the scent of human lust.

She went down on him, making good on her "famous" blowjob offer, and he thanked the day he'd met her. She fondled his balls and sucked sensuously on his cock, flicking her tongue over the piercing.

While he toyed with loose strands of her hair, he told her that he was going to eat her, too. That he was going to dive between her legs and lap her up.

He could tell that his zealous admission turned her on. She swallowed him deeper, and the sensation of getting sucked off so thoroughly blasted through his veins. But when it got too deep, too aggressive, too flat-out torturous, he stopped her.

He switched positions with Mandy, but he didn't go directly for her pussy, even if it was the flower he craved. He kissed his way down, licking her nipples and trailing a damp path to her navel. He slid lower, and she moaned and spread her thighs to accommodate him.

As he absorbed the delicate warmth of her sex, he encouraged her to fantasize, to think about the night he was going to slip into her room and come all over her.

"I have been thinking about it." She ran her hands over her breasts and down her stomach, as if it were happening right now.

"You're so beautiful. So fucking sexy." He laved her clit, and the sensitive nub tightened.

She went breathy. "We're both beautiful, Jared. When we do things to each other, we're the most beautiful people on earth."

Familiarity seized him. Catherine had said something similar to Atacar. On the night he'd taken her virginity, she'd talked about how beautiful a man and woman could be when they were together. Atacar had been inside her at the time, but the sentiment had been the same.

Jared teased Mandy's clit, over and over, desperate to make

her come. He couldn't help it. He needed to feel that beauty against his tongue, to draw it toward him and back to her.

She caressed his face, and he looked up. Their gazes met and held. The intimacy struck him straight in the chest. It grabbed hold of his dick, too. Especially when she came, when her juices flowed like nectar into his all-too-willing mouth.

He waited for her spasms to subside before he reared up to fuck, to fornicate, to copulate, to have sexual intercourse, to bang, to boff, to screw, to mate, to make love. He didn't know which words to choose. He just knew that he needed to join his body with hers.

Jared entered her hard and deep. She wrapped her legs around him, and he couldn't remember the missionary position ever feeling this good, this right.

He didn't know why their affair mattered so damn much, but now he wished it didn't. There was a part of him that wanted to walk away, to quit seducing her, to quit creating parallels between their relationship and Catherine and Atacar's. But some of it wasn't his fault. Some of the parallels seemed to be happening without his intervention.

Confused, he drove himself into her. She held him while he pounded his way to relief. He couldn't have slowed his pace if he tried. He needed to come inside her, to spill every pulsing drop.

His heart hammered. His brain fogged. His vision blurred. At that explosive moment, he wasn't even sure of his own name. All he wanted was his release.

Locked good and tight, he thrust back his head, shuddering, until there was nothing left.

Afterward, he collapsed on top of Mandy. He tried to move, but he couldn't. Finally he asked, "Am I too heavy?"

But before Mandy could respond, déjà vu blasted him like a bullet. Atacar had asked Catherine the same thing. Shit, Jared thought. Had he done that subconsciously to see what Mandy would say?

She kept her arms around him. "You're fine."

Jared recalled that Atacar had been too heavy for Catherine, even if she'd liked his bulk.

He rose on his elbows, lifting most of his weight from Mandy's body. But he didn't disengage their hips. He was still inside her. "Did you come?"

She laughed a little. "Couldn't you tell? I clawed your back. I gasped your name."

"You did?" He hadn't heard her voice; he hadn't felt the sting of her nails. He'd never blanked out like that before. He'd never had an orgasm that intense.

She tried to hug him, but he wasn't up for cuddling, not while his mind was befuddled. He withdrew and rolled away from her, scattering flower petals onto the floor.

So much for being tender.

Silence befell them until she said, "I told Kiki you were guarded."

His frustration flared. He rolled back over to look at her. "Why do women have to tell each other everything? How would you like it if I told my friends personal stuff about you? That you used to have crummy sex with your husband? Or that you—"

She cut him off. "It was *average* sex."

"Crummy. Average. It's the same damn thing." Annoyed that she'd defended her ex, he sat up and thrust his hand through his hair, tugging his braid.

She sat up, too. Just as edgy, just as snappy. "What's wrong with you? Why did you do all of this if it's pissing you off?"

"It's not the flowers." He glanced around, assessing the jungle he'd made of his room. Tomorrow he and his gardeners were hauling everything outside to be planted. "It's just me."

She didn't respond, and he cursed himself for destroying the sparkle he'd seen in her eyes earlier.

"Say something, Mandy."

She sighed. "I'm sorry for talking to Kiki about you, but she's the only friend I have who I can confide in."

"It's okay. I don't care. You can tell her whatever you want." He zeroed in on his problem, his frustration. He was guilty for keeping secrets, for using Catherine and Atacar to seduce her. "But I wish you and Kiki would give up on the journal. That you'd quit fooling yourselves into believing it's real."

"What can I say?" Her voice went soft. "We're die-hard romantics. Women who look at Atacar and see what he felt for Catherine."

Jared pushed his secret to the limit, trying to dispel the truth, even if he knew how much Atacar had loved Catherine. "What if it's bullshit? What if he didn't care about her?"

Mandy got stubborn. "He did. I can feel it. And you should, too. He's your ancestor. You should have more faith in him than that."

Jared frowned. He had plenty of faith in Atacar. It was himself that he didn't trust. His own feelings. His own emotions. "Fine. Whatever."

She swung her feet to the edge of the bed. "I should go."

"No." He grabbed her before she could leave. "No fucking way. I'm not done with you yet."

"Done with me?" She tried to jerk free of his hold. "I'm not your property."

"I didn't mean it like that." He rained gentle kisses along her shoulder, doing what he should have done after they'd fucked. Or made love. Or whatever the hell it had been. "Stay with me, baby. Let me fix this. Let me hold you."

She fought her vulnerability, her addiction to him. He could hear the struggle in her voice. "You're maddening, Jared."

"I know. I'm an ass." He tucked her against him. What else could he do? He was addicted to her, too. "A shitty boyfriend."

She turned to face him. "You're not that bad. Girls like me dream about this kind of stuff."

He knew she meant the plants and flowers. "I owe you an apology bouquet. I'll pick one tonight."

She smiled and settled into his arms. "If I had any sense, I'd find a nice white-picket-fence guy and teach him how to have sex like you."

"That can't be taught." He paused, grinned, tapped her chin. "No one has sex like I do."

She laughed and cuddled closer, and he realized they'd just weathered their first fight. He held her, making the best of what they had.

Even if it wasn't meant to last.

CHAPTER THIRTEEN

I paced my studio, the wooden floors creaking beneath my feet. Whenever I attempted to create a new art study, I thought about Atacar. I couldn't focus on anything except him. He was the ever-present subject on my mind, the portrait I longed to paint. But he still refused to sit for me.

He was outside tending to his chores, and Nanny was in the kitchen preparing dinner, which in Texas was our midday meal, served hot and hearty. A light midday meal or picnic would have been considered lunch. Supper, whether hot or cold, came later.

"Catherine!" Nanny screeched my name.

I poked my head outside the studio door and acknowledged her. She rarely disturbed me while I was painting. Not that I had been painting, but she couldn't have known otherwise.

"Hurry!" Her voice screeched again. "Someone is coming."

My heart skipped a frantic beat, and my thoughts spun back to Atacar. Was it soldiers? Were they coming for him?

I dashed into the kitchen. Nanny was at the window. I peered out, as well. A carriage approached, not uniformed riders.

"I thought—" My voice nearly broke.

"What, child?"

"It was the army."

Although Nanny patted my shoulder, quieting my fears, she looked as frazzled as I felt. Wisps of gray hair escaped her bun, and perspiration dotted her brow. But she'd been tending a hot stove. She probably would've looked that way even if company hadn't besieged us.

The carriage moved closer, and I recognized its occupants: George, our former farmhand, his wife, and her two small children. The youngest squirmed on her lap.

George had promised to bring his new family around, but I hadn't expected a visit so soon after his nuptials.

"We'll have to invite them to stay for dinner," Nanny said.

"Yes, of course." It was the proper thing to do.

Nanny and I walked onto the porch to greet our guests. By now, they'd climbed out of the carriage, and George was hitching the horse.

He gave us a crooked smile. Even at thirty, he seemed boyish: tall and gangly with feet that were forever shuffling.

His wife, attired in a simple blue dress, was petite and commonly pretty. Although I'd met her during their courtship, this visit would give us the opportunity to get further acquainted. I just wished it wasn't happening while I was hiding my Apache lover at the farm.

"Mrs. Horn," I said, greeting her formally.

She smoothed the front of her hair. The light brown strands puffed into a delicate pompadour, then narrowed into a ribbon-garnished braid in back. "Please, call me Alice."

"Then call me Catherine."

The children were Jack and Peter. They did their best to behave, as their mother corrected them often. But they were only two and fours years old.

The Horns accepted our dinner invitation, and Nanny returned to the kitchen to continue the meal preparation. I sat in the parlor with George and his family.

George was as fidgety as the boys. "Maybe I should leave you ladies alone till you call me to the table."

"Your company is perfectly acceptable," I told him, trying to ease his obvious discomfort.

"I appreciate that, ma'am, but I don't cotton much to sitting still. I'd prefer to head on down to the wagon shed. Maybe pick up a hammer and get some work done. I should have fixed those broken boards before I quit on ya."

I tried to appear poised. "The wagon shed has already been repaired. Didn't you hear that we hired a new farmhand?"

"Who was I supposed to hear it from?"

"I told Mrs. Mayes when we were in town."

"She don't discuss other people's business with me." He scooted to the edge of his chair. He'd removed his hat when he'd come inside, and his ears were sticking out the sides of his head. "I'd still prefer to leave you ladies alone. How about if I go for that stroll anyhow? Maybe seek out your new hire?"

I wanted to exclaim, "No!" but I knew better than to overreact. "That would be for naught. Juan doesn't speak English."

"Juan? He's Mexican, then?" George wasn't deterred. "I can talk Spanish. Not much, but some."

Now what was I supposed to say? I looked toward the kitchen at Nanny, but she seemed unaware of my dilemma. "How about this?" I managed. "Before you stroll the farm, I'll invite Juan to dinner. I wouldn't want him to think that he isn't welcome at our table when we have guests."

It was the best I could do, the only solution I could fathom: Dash off to warn Atacar that George wanted to meet him.

"How'd you learn Spanish good enough to converse with Juan?" George asked. "You being from England."

"My family holidayed in Spain." Although that was true, my use of the language was sorely limited. I was embellishing my skills.

George didn't query me further, so I excused myself and entered the kitchen, telling Nanny what I was about to do. She gave me an anxious look.

I searched the farm and found Atacar working in the garden. He wore his hat dipped low, and his face was smudged with dirt.

"We have visitors," I said.

"I know. I saw the carriage."

Apparently he'd sullied his face purposely, hoping to mask his features. I explained the situation, and we discussed our options. We agreed that he should refuse to dine at the table, claiming that he preferred to eat alone in the barn. But allowing George an introduction seemed unavoidable.

"I'll send him out to meet you," I said.

Atacar nodded, and I was tempted to kiss him. But I knew I couldn't. This wasn't the time to promote our romance, to transfer the dirt from his person onto mine.

I returned to the parlor and relayed the message to George. He hopped out of his seat, eager to get his shuffling feet moving, and my nervous wait began.

I chatted with Alice and gave her children paper and pencils with which to scribble, but my pulse pounded the entire time.

George wasn't gone for long, and he reappeared seeming flustered. I hoped it was because his Spanish had given him more trouble than he'd assumed it would. That he'd fumbled between "Hola" and "Adios."

While Alice helped Nanny set the table for our meal, George motioned to get my private attention.

"Ma'am," he whispered. "I don't mean to scare you, but something don't feel right about Juan."

Heaven help me, I thought. "I don't know what you mean."

"He barely lifted his face to mine. I don't trust a man who won't look ya in the eye."

"He's reserved."

"I don't think that's it. I think he was trying to hide his appearance from me."

My knees threatened to buckle. Since when had George become so observant? "That's nonsense."

"Have you looked at him clearly?"

"Most certainly. He works for me."

"Then I want to look upon him clearly, too. Without his face being smudged up. Without him keeping his head lowered. I ain't even sure he's Mexican."

I kept my expression stern, my attitude unyielding. "Juan doesn't owe you anything, George."

"Don't he? He could be that Apache them soldiers was hunting. Don't you remember them showing us his picture?"

I folded my hands together, squeezing them tight. "Of course I remember, and Juan isn't him."

"I think he could be. But until I get a clearer look, I can't be sure."

"He isn't," I reiterated.

"No disrespect, ma'am, but—"

I interrupted. "His name is Juan, and he's from Mexico."

"You need to listen to what I'm saying—"

"No, you need to listen," I interrupted again, more adamantly this time. "If I say he's Juan, then that's who he is."

George gaped at me, the truth dawning in his eyes. By defending Juan so diligently, I'd just revealed Atacar's identity. I wanted to fall to the floor and weep my remorse, to curse the day I was born.

"Lordy," George said. "Oh, Lordy."

I resorted to begging. "He's a good man, and you have to promise to keep my secret. Please. He'll be leaving in less than a month."

George glanced at his wife. She was boosting her youngest boy onto a dining chair. "Alice says that all men have the right to be free. Her family is dead now. But they was abolitionists."

"Then Alice should understand. She might even want to help an Apache prisoner of war. The army wronged him. They wronged his people."

"Yes. But I—"

"Please," I implored once more, drawing George and his family into my plight.

A moment later, George spoke to Alice about Atacar, and she convinced her husband to take up my cause, to keep my secret. I wanted to wrap my arms around her, to thank her in a way words of gratitude never could. But I kept a proper distance.

Alice requested to meet Atacar, so I fetched him to dine with us. He washed up at the pump, gazing at me as if I'd betrayed him.

"How do you know you can trust them?" he asked.

I explained that Alice's family had helped free slaves during the American Civil War. And that she sympathized with Indians, too.

"And George?"

"I think his heart will keep him pure. That he's a man of honor."

"And if he isn't?" Atacar dried his face with a clean rag, his mouth taut, the frown lines near his eyes stark against his skin. "Promises have been broken to me before."

I didn't debate his point. How could I? What he'd said was true. I'd even told George that Atacar had been wronged. "If you're concerned about him contacting the army, then you should leave for Mexico tonight. You're welcome to my horse. You can take her on your journey."

"I won't take your horse from you." He reached out to touch my cheek. "Nor am I ready to leave. Not without spending more time in your arms."

I touched his cheek, too. I would never love anyone the way I loved him.

We went inside and gathered at the table. Everyone addressed Atacar as Juan. The children were too young to comprehend the situation, but not too young to learn Juan's name, to repeat it on other occasions.

Nanny had prepared stewed chicken with dumplings, accompanied by peas and potatoes. For dessert, we had coffee, tea, and cake.

I made fast friends with Alice, and she suggested that we continue to socialize. "George and I can stop by next week. He can play his fiddle, and the rest of us can dance." She smiled at her children. "The boys, too."

"That's a glorious idea," I responded, truly meaning it.

Nanny was pleased, as well. The men neither disagreed nor reacted favorably. But they did speak a few cordial words to each other.

It seemed like a good start.

~

As I lay in the dark with Atacar, moonlight drifted into the room, dusting the bed in silvery hues.

"Do you regret your decision?" I asked.

"To stay? To trust your friends?" He rolled sideways to face me. "No."

"Then why are you sullen?"

"Because when the time comes for me to leave, I will miss everything about you."

"Then invite me to go with you. Me and Nanny."

"I can't."

My chest turned tight, aching for more. "Can't or won't?"

"Won't," he admitted.

I considered turning away from him, but I didn't. He touched the buttercup in my hair, treating it with fragile care. The tightness in my chest deepened.

"I need to steal a horse soon," he said. "To have a mount available if I have to leave in a hurry."

"I'll purchase a horse from the man who owns the livery stable. He trades and sells. George can help me fetch a good price."

He lowered his hand. "You'll do no such thing. I've taken enough charity from you already."

I addressed the flaw in his plan. "You can't raid one of my neighbors and keep a stolen mount in my barn."

He frowned at me, his moonlit features partially shadowed. "Then you can purchase a horse and deduct the cost from my wages."

"You need that money for Mexico."

"Do not tell me how to spend my earnings."

"You're a stubborn man."

He tugged me into his arms. "And you're a stubborn woman."

I remained frustrated. "You're going to remedy our argument with a kiss?"

"No." He removed my nightgown, baring my body for his pleasure. He was already naked. "With more than that."

I cursed him for sliding his hand between my thighs. But I couldn't control my erotic reaction. I tingled from his touch.

He pressed his fingers against my clitoris. I sighed my acquiescence and opened my legs, giving him permission to make me climax. Not that it would have made a difference. He would have done it regardless.

He rubbed me until I shuddered, but that wasn't enough for him. He wanted to have mutual oral copulation, too.

Shivers slid up and down my spine. We hadn't performed that act yet. We'd spoken about it, but we hadn't brought it to fruition.

He told me to straddle his mouth, backwards, so I was facing his cock. I did his bidding, feeling quite naughty from atop his face.

From my vantage point, I admired the outline of his penis, big and hard against his stomach. The foreskin was already pushed back, exposing the bulbous tip.

He put his tongue inside me, and I lowered my head. I inhaled his musky scent, using my hands and mouth to stimulate him.

Doubled-edged hunger assailed my senses: him licking me while I sucked him. I took as much of him as I could, and he helped me set the rhythm, thrusting his hips.

But even as he moved, as he fornicated with my mouth, he didn't break his other stride. He continued to lave my vagina, to make it wet and slick.

I rocked back and forth, enjoying our wantonness. His cock was leaking ejaculate, pearly drops dissolving on my tongue.

We moaned our pleasure. The moonlight faded, and I could no longer see him. The room was pitched in inky darkness, and the sensation of being so close to him intensified. I could feel every vein, every ridge in his cock.

Nerve endings fluttered inside me, and I verged on another orgasm. My second that night. I wondered how many a woman could experience without pooling like candle wax.

Atacar laved ruthlessly, spearing my silken folds, and I relinquished the battle and climaxed, my juices warm and sticky. I pressed down on him, wanting him to savor my moisture, and he obliged, giving me the wickedness I craved.

As I shuddered and shook, he had an orgasm, too. His hot seed filled my mouth, and I swallowed, allowing the milky wetness to slide down my throat.

After it was over, we stayed like that, letting the intimacy of what we'd just done settle softly between us.

Finally we shifted, getting face-to-face so we could kiss. I tasted myself on his lips, and I suspected that he tasted himself on mine.

"This makes me want to fuck," he whispered.

"It does?"

He nodded in the dark. Or I thought he did. I couldn't be sure. "A warm fuck. Later tonight. After we rest. I don't want it to be over. I want as much of you as I can get."

I wrapped my arms around him. "Me, too. With you."

He kissed me again, and we stayed silent for a while. The moonlight reappeared, the glittering rays bathing our skin.

I thought about the dinner conversation that had transpired earlier. "Do you dance, Atacar?"

"Not white man's dances."

"You don't waltz, polka, gallop, or mazurka?"

"No."

"Then I shall have to teach you."

"The way you're teaching me to speak with flowers?"

"Yes." I wanted to share all of my favorite things with him. "When Alice and George return to socialize with us, we'll dance to his fiddle like the grand couple we are."

"How will I learn before then? Without music?"

"I can hum the songs for you. We'll practice every night beneath the stars, with crickets chirping and fireflies glowing." I smiled to myself. "Scientists say that they illuminate when they're courting."

"We're courting," he said.

"Yes, we are."

He moved closer. "We're illuminating, too. Inside."

I sighed, thinking how roughly romantic he was. His nakedness teased mine, creating sweet shivers. We kissed and rolled over the bed, locked in each other's arms.

He slid between my legs, and I felt his hardness nudging me. He was fully aroused and ready to mate. A warm fuck, I thought, enjoying the adjective he'd used. I clutched his buttocks, encouraging him to join with me.

We moved in perfect unison, our tempo slow, then dreamy, then swift. Changing positions, I landed on top, riding him the way a cowgirl would straddle a stallion. He gripped my waist and moved me up and down in a sleek and sensual manner.

I felt his cock so deeply, I wondered if he were stroking my womb. He told me how glorious I was, and I tried to imagine what he saw: a naked woman, shrouded in semidarkness, her limbs spread across his lap.

He put his hand against my mound and rubbed me while we mated. He'd been born to be my lover, to pleasure me, just as I'd been born to arouse him.

"We'll start tonight," he said.

I knew what he meant. After we climaxed, we would slip outside for his first dance lesson, to absorb everything we could from each other.

From now until the day he went away.

CHAPTER FOURTEEN

Jared was gone. He'd left town to attend a horse auction and wouldn't return until Monday. But for now it was Friday afternoon, and Mandy was at work with the phone cradled to her ear.

"Are you ready to shoot some Blow Jobs?" the female voice on the other end of the line asked.

Mandy bit back a grin, thinking how odd the invitation sounded coming from a woman. Then again, it wasn't just any woman. It was Amber Pontiero, the spoiled, sexy heiress who used to sleep with Jared.

"When?"

"Tonight. You can bring a friend, too. We can make it a ménage, metaphorically speaking."

Mandy immediately thought of Kiki. "I know just the girl."

"Perfect. Meet me at Clay's Corner at seven. It's a little place on the outskirts. Do you know it?"

"I've heard of it."

"Take a cab. Or hire a chauffeur. We're going to get obnoxiously drunk."

"That sounds good to me." Mandy needed a girl's night out, especially since Jared was gone.

"Do you want to do some Cocksucking Cowboys, too?"

Mandy blinked. "What?"

"Cocksucking Cowboys."

"Please tell me that's a drink."

Amber laughed. "It is."

"At the masquerade, you said that mixing cocktails isn't a good idea."

"It's a fine idea when you're planning to get drunk enough to dance on the tables. To flash your panties at other patrons."

Mandy crossed her legs, even though she was alone at her desk. She couldn't imagine dancing on tabletops. "I think I better wear pants."

The other woman laughed again. "Spoilsport." Her sexy accent drifted through the phone. "You're such a good girl, except for when you're with your man."

"He inspires me."

"Is that all he does to you?"

"I don't know what you mean."

"Are you falling in love with him? No offense, but you seem like the type."

Mandy's heart punched her chest, and she stalled, unable to answer the question, to consider the possibility. Instead, she fidgeted with a paperweight on her desk.

Amber went silent too, as if she were contemplating the delayed reaction. "Maybe you should fuck someone else. Maybe even have a real ménage."

Just in case she was falling in love? "That wouldn't work. Besides, I don't want anyone else."

"What about Pink and Red? I can arrange for you to be with them."

"I was only attracted to them because they looked like Jared."

"They can put their costumes back on."

"Honestly, I'm not interested."

"All right, darling. But you don't know what you're missing. I already fucked them, and they were fabulous. I'll give you the details when I see you." A smile sounded in Amber's voice. "Until tonight. Ciao."

Mandy didn't have time to say good-bye. The line went dead. She stared at the phone. A second later, she snapped out of her trance and dialed Kiki's extension, inviting her to join the drinking, tell-all sex fest.

Kiki accepted readily, and at precisely 7:00 p.m., they entered Clay's Corner, a woody establishment with a jukebox in front, a billiards table in back, and ceramic chili peppers decorating windowsills and doorways.

Mandy and Kiki snagged a booth. Clay's served appetizers, too. They ordered potato skins and chips and salsa. The food arrived before Amber did. Apparently she intended to be fashionably late.

Kiki lifted a potato skin from the platter and dunked it into the dipping sauce. "I'm anxious to meet this girl."

"I don't even know what she looks like. Not beyond her costume at the ball. Or those killer legs."

"You didn't Google her?"

"No." Mandy reached for her glass. They'd gotten ice water to drink. They didn't want to start boozing until Amber showed up.

"I did, and there are quite a few pictures of her on the Net. She's a gorgeous, short-haired brunette."

"Her hair was long and blonde at the party, but I suspected that it might be a wig."

Kiki leaned in close. "Can you believe she slept with your guys? Do you think she did it at the ball?"

"They aren't *my* guys."

"Not technically, but they *were* masquerading as Jared. Can you imagine having multiple partners? I can't."

"An orgy crossed my mind at the party. Which Jared is which? Maybe I'll take all of them. But in reality, I never would have done it. I'm too monogamous."

"So am I. But I think watching other people would be hot. Threesomes, foursomes, fivesomes." The redhead clamped a hand over her mouth, mumbling her shame. "I can't believe I just told you that." She freed her mouth. "Is fivesomes even a word?"

"I don't know. But don't worry about it. You can tell me anything. Besides, we all have fantasies."

"Lately I've had some doozies."

"Me, too." Mandy thought about the fantasy Jared had yet to fulfill. "Sometimes we even shock ourselves."

"No kidding." Kiki flashed a cockeyed grin, returning to her usual self. She glanced up. "Oh, wow. Our drinking buddy just arrived, and she's even more gorgeous than her pictures."

Mandy turned around. Sure enough, Amber Pontiero had

walked through the door, causing everyone in the bar to look her way. Sporting a white tank top, a denim skirt, and wedged sandals, she was a sight to behold. She wore her short, dark hair in an angular-cut bob, a style originated by Vidal Sassoon in the 1960s. Amber was still a mod girl, with or without the long blonde wig, fishnet stockings, and go-go boots.

As for her unmasked face, she had bluish green eyes smudged with nutmeg shadows and smoky liner, a slightly crooked nose, and a full mouth. All of it worked on her.

Amber smiled at a trio of male admirers at the bar and headed for Mandy and Kiki's table.

Mandy made the introductions, and Amber settled deeper into her seat. "Are you ladies ready to get drunk and cause a scene?"

Kiki drenched a tortilla chip with salsa. "You're already causing a scene. Just look at you."

"You, too. A genuine redhead. I know a dark and brooding artist who gets off on girls like you. Those cute little freckles across your nose would drive him mad. You wouldn't happen to be into bondage, would you?"

Kiki nearly choked on her chip. "Why? Is that his fetish of choice?"

"That's what he paints. BDSM depictions."

Mandy stifled a laugh. Kiki looked as if she'd been sucker punched. Apparently she hadn't taken her erotic fantasies quite that far. Or maybe she had, but she wasn't willing to admit it.

A round of Blow-Job Shooters was ordered, and upon their arrival, Amber instructed Mandy to go first.

"Make us proud, darling."

"I'll do my best." Mandy put her hands behind her back, leaned forward, and gripped the glass with her mouth. She struggled for balance and prayed that she didn't drop it all over herself. She could hear Kiki cheering her on.

"Come on! You can do it."

Mandy went for it. She tilted back her head and drank. By the time she was done, she had whipped cream all over her face. She wiped it off and grinned. The cocktail had tasted pretty damn good, but the process of drinking it was even better.

Kiki took her turn. She struggled and made a mess, too. But in the end she accomplished the task, receiving high fives from her companions.

Amber didn't spill a drop. She sucked and swallowed like a pro, treating her shot like the biggest, hottest, cream-filled cock she'd ever tasted.

"Good Lord." Kiki all but gaped. "If I were a guy, you would've given me a boner."

The three of them burst out laughing.

"The same drink with a cherry on top is called a Muff Diver," Amber said. "I've watched Jared down a few." She addressed Mandy. "As you recall, he got me into erotic-named drinks."

"And now I'm going to be hooked. Not to mention drunk and hungry for him. But he's out of town."

"So you can take him muff diving when he gets back." Amber flashed a knowing smile. "He's good at it."

"Really good," Mandy admitted. By now they were referring to the real deal.

Amber kept the party going. She flagged down the waitress and ordered Cocksucking Cowboys, shots made with two parts butterscotch schnapps and one part Irish cream. The Irish cream floated on top.

Amber lifted her glass in a toast. "To old friends and new acquaintances."

"Hear, hear." Kiki clanked her glass.

So did Mandy. Socializing with Jared's former lover wasn't the least bit awkward. Amber was so casual about the affair she'd had with Jared, Mandy didn't feel threatened by it.

"Tell us about Pink and Red," Mandy said.

"Oh, yes. My new playmates. They didn't have anything to do after you figured out who Jared was, so I hit on them." She winked teasingly at Kiki. "What man in his right mind would turn me down? Right, darling?"

"Right," the redhead confirmed. She seemed to be enjoying the other woman's vanity-driven charm.

Amber turned toward Mandy. "At that point, you and Jared were off somewhere."

"We were in the garden. That's where we spent the last half of the party."

"Ah. Then that explains your missing whereabouts. Well, anyway, I invited Pink and Red upstairs to my suite. It's not as if they were strangers to me. I knew their real identities. I'd helped Jared hire them."

"What do they look like when they're not in costume?" Mandy asked.

"They're both L.A. actors. Pink has light brown hair and a scrumptious tan. He surfs and snowboards and does all of those sexy California things. Red is part Native American and is originally from the South, so the accent wasn't much of a stretch for him. He also has a naturally exotic flair. Without the mask he looks more like Jared than Pink does. It took a bit more work to transform Pink."

"Your makeup people did an amazing job," Mandy said. "I was stumped when I saw all of them together."

"That was the idea. Do you want to know their names?"

Mandy nodded.

"Pink is Jay, and Red is Luke. But I did my darnedest to forget who was who. When I slept with them, I told them to keep their masks on. It seemed more fun that way. We kept the lights off, too."

"You did two masked men in the dark?" Kiki asked.

Amber nodded. "At first we just stood in the room and kissed. I was in the middle, and they were on either side of me. I kept turning to kiss one, then the other."

Kiki went after a handful of chips. Mandy followed suit, riveted by Amber's story.

"They undressed me, and one of them dropped to his knees. I can't tell you how aroused I was."

Mandy had to ask, "What did the other man do?"

"He stood behind me, kissing my neck, rubbing my nipples, playing with my belly button. There I was, getting oral sex from one lover and getting teased by the other."

Kiki asked the next question. "Did they switch places?"

"Oh, yes. They took turns, one right after the other. I gave both of them head, too. Speaking of which—" She stopped talking and ordered a third round of drinks, waited for them to arrive, and made sure that everyone did a Blow Job before she continued.

Mandy wiped the whipped cream from her chin and down the front of her blouse. Her shots were getting messier. Kiki's, too. Even Amber had to lick white froth from the corners of her lips.

"They didn't take their clothes off when I gave them head. They undid their pants and sat on the edge of my bed."

"Oh, my goodness." This from Kiki. "You went back and forth?"

"Yes, I did. Right there on my knees. I didn't do it long enough to make them come. I knew we'd be crawling all over each other later."

Mandy stuffed a potato skin into her mouth. "I'm calling Jared when I get home. I don't care if he's out of town. After all of this, I'm going to need to hear his voice."

Kiki scowled. "Who am I supposed to call? The Maytag repairman? Oh, I know—how about the Mac computer guy? He's young and hot. Of course, with my luck, the PC guy would answer instead."

Amber looked at Mandy, and they sputtered into laughter. Kiki rolled her eyes, but she laughed, too.

"There's always the artist I told you about, darling."

"Mr. BDSM?" Kiki looked downright panicked. "I think not getting laid is safer."

"He's not as dangerous as he sounds."

"Says the ménage mistress."

The storyteller laughed again. "You're so adorable. So feisty. I can just see him trying to restrain you."

"Don't even think about setting me up. That's all I need. A blind date with a guy who'll want to blindfold me."

"You think I'd set you up?" Amber batted her lashes. "*Moi?*"

"Yes, *moi*. Now finish your ménage. I want to hear the rest."

"But of course. Jay and Luke got undressed, and we climbed into bed. We started kissing again. They put their hands all over me, and I caressed them. Strong shoulders. Muscled abs. Big, silky cocks. And those masks. I think that was the sexist part of all."

"What about your mask?" Mandy asked.

"I ditched it. I'm not sure when, but by the end of the night, it was gone. The foreplay was incredible. Luke straddled my face while Jay went down on me." She made a confused expression. "Or maybe it was the other way around. All I know is that I was giving and getting at the same time."

She paused to reminisce. "I had condoms in my dresser, so I fitted both of them. They took turns, bending my body, spreading my legs, telling me how perfect I was. It was the most romantic threesome I've ever had. All that kissing, all that caressing. They even sent me flowers the next day. Pink and red roses." She tucked a strand of her choppy hair behind her ear. "Not that flowers matter that much to me. But it was sweet."

"Sometimes flowers matter," Mandy said, thinking about Jared. "Sometimes they're really important."

Amber shrugged, and Mandy considered the bouquet the other woman had received. Pink roses meant "grace and beauty" and red embodied "love and passion."

"We're all so quiet now," Kiki said.

Amber nodded, but she didn't comment. Mandy got the impression that the heiress wasn't as indifferent as she seemed, that in her own way, she'd gotten attached to Jay and Luke.

Finally Amber spoke. "Let's have one more round. I don't think we're drunk enough."

Mandy and Kiki agreed, but the tone of the evening didn't change. After they quit drinking, the tipsy trio hugged and said a girl's-night-out good-bye, then went home with an assortment of men on their minds.

Mandy entered her condo and peeled off her clothes. Naked, she brushed her teeth and wiped off her makeup, gazing at her hungry image.

Once she was in bed, she grabbed the phone and dialed Jared's cell.

He answered on the third ring. "Multiorgasmic Mandy," he said by way of a greeting.

She got warm inside. She even parted her thighs ever so slightly, making the sheet pool at her hips. "Is that how you have me programmed into your phone?"

"No, but I should put you in that way. How are you, baby?"

She tried to picture him in his hotel room. Was he naked, too? God, she hoped so. "Drunk and horny." Emotional, too. But she left that part off.

"Really?" He sounded amused. "How'd that happen?"

"Amber did it to me. With Blow-Job Shooters and Cocksucking Cowboys. Kiki was there, too. Amber told us a sexy story. Do you know what she did?"

"No, baby. What did she do?"

"She had a threesome with Pink and Red. At the ball. And they sent her flowers the next day."

He didn't respond, and she wondered if the call had gotten dropped.

"Did you hear me?"

No more humor. Irritation edged his tone. "Yeah, I heard you."

Mandy frowned at the phone. He was jealous of his ex being with two men who'd been masquerading as him? "Thanks a lot, Jared."

"I'm not pissed at what she did."

"Then what are you pissed at?"

"If I know Amber, she probably suggested that you fuck them, too. She probably offered to arrange it."

Mandy snapped at him. "So what if she did? I'd never do it."

"You wouldn't?"

"No." And she wasn't about to mention why Amber suggested that she mess around with Pink and Red. She might be drunk, but not inebriated enough to admit that the other woman thought she was falling in love with Jared.

Silence hung in the air, until he said, "I've done it."

"Done what?"

"Had ménages."

"With who?"

"I'm not bi, so being with two girls works better for me, but I've shared my lovers with other men. I'd never do it with you. I'd freak out if I had to share you with another guy. Or even another girl. I couldn't handle watching you with someone else."

"I couldn't handle you with anyone, either." Just thinking about him kissing another woman made her stomach churn. But even so, she didn't want to consider why their affair had gotten so intense, so committed, so emotional. "Are you going to go back to having threesomes when we stop dating?"

"I don't know. I doubt it. It's been a while since I've done it. Mostly I was experimenting, just being wild, I guess. Are you still horny? Or did I kill it for you?"

"It's dead."

"Sorry."

"It's okay."

"Want me to get you there? To talk you back into it?"

She smiled in spite of herself. "As long as it's just the two us. No talk of other people."

"That's more than fine with me. Are you on speaker?"

"No."

"You're going to need to have your hands free."

She egged him on. "To do what?"

"To bang yourself, baby. With that big, blasting dildo you made of me. This is our phone-sex ménage. You, me, and him."

She laughed. "So much for not involving anyone else." She hit the speaker button. "I'm ready."

"Get the dildo and the lube."

She stood up and went to her dresser, retrieving the necessary items. She even stroked the rubber phallus. "He's already hard for me."

"So am I. Now lie down and open those pretty legs."

She got back in bed. "Are you going to touch yourself, too?"

"Not this time. I'm going to save it for when I come on you. You still want me to jerk off on your tits, don't you?"

"Yes." Oh, God, yes. "But first you have to do it over my face so I can watch."

"I know. I remember. I'll do it exactly the way you want it. Now grease down the dildo."

She slathered the lubricant over the copy of his cock, her pulse already pounding at her clit. "When are you going to slip into my room, Jared? When is it going to happen?"

"Soon."

She fondled the pierced head. "How soon?"

"As soon I get back in town. Is the dildo ready?"

"Yes." She slid the phallus between her thighs, and he proceeded to give her orders, to make her wet and aroused, to tell her how deep and fast to use it.

Drunk and naughty, she fucked herself while he listened to every hot, hammering breath she took. She loved what he was making her do. But she refused to believe that she loved him more than the sex, more than the addiction.

Even if she didn't want to hang up the phone when it was over, even if she couldn't bear to let him go.

CHAPTER FIFTEEN

We lit a brass lamp and got dressed. I paired my nightgown with satin slippers, and Atacar climbed into the blue jeans I'd purchased for him in town. He wore his work boots, the only shoes he owned. He didn't bother with a shirt. We glanced at each other and smiled. Our dancing attire was most unusual.

We took the lamp outdoors to illuminate our way. As we walked arm in arm scouting our farmland ballroom, a gentle breeze enhanced the summer air, making scents from the night sweep and swirl.

We chose a spot near the barn. Atacar placed the lamp on a tree stump, and I admired him. As always, he looked stunning in the kerosene light.

I moved forward, running my hands along the masculine contours of his chest, encountering his nipples and the slightly raised ridges of old scars. My fingers trailed to his stomach.

"Is this what you do to all of your dance partners?" he asked.

I knew he was teasing me. "Only those I fancy."

"I like being fancied."

I was tempted to slip my hand lower, to invade the waistband of his pants, but I stepped back to regain my composure. "We'll start with the waltz."

He nodded, eager to learn. His attention was rapt, his gaze unwavering.

First, I taught him the proper way to bow. As he stepped to the side, closed in, and made the gentlemanly motion of bending forward, I smiled. He looked far more handsome than any man with whom I'd ever danced, even with his bared chest, blue jeans, and work boots.

I recalled the Indians who'd performed with Buffalo Bill and wondered how long it had been since Atacar had worn tribal adornments.

As we proceeded, I said, "The waltz is a turning dance in three-quarter time."

He gave me a quizzical look.

"The main pulse of the music is every three beats." I demonstrated, humming a song and counting off the beats, emphasizing the pulse.

He understood instantly.

I taught him the song so he could hum it, too. He was quite musical, and our voices blended in chilling harmony. I suspected that once he mastered the steps, we would partner in dance as splendidly as we partnered in bed.

With the Texas soil beneath our feet, I encouraged him to lead me into a basic waltz. We did quite well until he moved forward when he should have moved backward, and we bumped into each other.

We laughed and resumed the lesson. He was determined not to repeat his error, but he did it again.

"I'll get it right," he said.

I marveled at his focus. We practiced for hours, but he didn't want to stop. He continued to learn from his mistakes.

I instructed him in a polka-dot waltz, teaching him how to embellish the footwork. It was one of the sweetest, shortest versions of the dance, and I thought it suited us.

Afterward, we stood beneath the sky, our bodies pressed close. He ran his hands through my unbound hair, and I slipped my arms around his waist.

We separated, and my thoughts drifted to my youth, to the balls, soirees, and dinner parties I'd attended.

"I came out when I was seventeen," I said.

"Came out?"

"Formally presented to society. With the purpose of landing a husband," I added. "But I wasn't interested in marriage. Not at the time."

He didn't comment on my "Not at the time" remark. Instead, he said, "My people have a similar practice. We have a ceremony that announces when a young girl is ready to marry. At the end of the ceremony is the lover's dance, and that's when a man can propose. If she accepts, he consults her father and bargains for her."

"Did you propose to your wife at this ceremony?"

"No. Our marriage was arranged in a less romantic fashion."

I waited, hoping he would offer to teach me the lover's dance, but he didn't. He'd already made me ache when he'd declined to take me to Mexico, and now he'd made me hurt again. But what did I expect? For him to get an impulsive notion? To propose?

"Are you weary?" he asked. "Do you want to end the lesson?"

"I'm fine," I lied. I hadn't meant to make him aware of my distress. "I'd like to keep dancing."

"So would I." He began humming the song I'd taught him.

I curtsied to his bow, and he led me across patches of dirt and grass. Crickets chirped from their hiding places, making music with other nocturnal creatures. I looked for courting insects, but I didn't see any.

"In England, we call them glowworms," I said, thinking out loud.

Atacar blinked at me.

"Fireflies," I explained.

He didn't respond, but he stole a kiss while we waltzed, his mouth warm against mine.

"I want you to paint me," he said suddenly.

I faltered on my next step, gripping his shoulder to keep myself steady. He had gotten an impulsive notion, not to take me to Mexico, not to marry me, but to be the subject of the portrait I'd been longing to create. Although the woman in me wanted more, the artist in me nearly wept. He'd just eased a portion of my ache.

"You'll sit for me?" I asked.

"Yes."

"What if I need more time to paint you? Will you stay longer than you originally intended?"

Our dancing ceased, but we continued to hold each other. "I'll stay until you complete it."

The breeze turned stronger, blowing my hair and making my nightgown cling to my body. "What made you change your mind?"

"When I go away, I want you to keep part of me, to have it for all time."

I couldn't seem to find my voice, to engage in a response, not with my heart clamoring to my throat.

Atacar didn't fault for me for my silence. As I nestled against him, he rocked me in his arms, even after the lamplight went out, leaving us in the dark.

~

Groggy, Mandy awakened in the dark. She blinked at the shadows in her bedroom. Why did it seem as if she wasn't alone? As if someone was watching her?

Jared, she thought.

No, that made no sense. He was still out of town.

She squeezed her eyes shut. She was losing it, imagining Jared's presence when he wasn't even there.

"Mandy," a man whispered. Deep, low, sensual.

Oh, God. Her eyes flew open, and she shifted her gaze in the direction of his voice. He was standing in an inky black corner of her whitewashed room. He looked like a ghost, a hazy apparition. "You really are here."

"I came back early."

She inhaled a choppy breath and glanced at the digital clock on her nightstand: 2:58. "How long have you been standing there?"

"A while. I've been watching you sleep."

She followed his footsteps, trying to focus on his long, lean, shadow-shrouded body. This was her fantasy, the one she'd been waiting for. He was here to make it come true.

And now she was nervous. Anticipation curled low in her belly, and even lower, pulsing in reckless invitation. Jared had taught her to talk dirty, to think dirty, to be his bad, bad girl.

Then why did this feel so forbidden? She should be used to her nasty urges by now. But she wasn't. The conventional side of her rebelled, and she clenched her thighs. But that only managed to intensify the hunger.

Jared turned on the light, and the brightness illuminated the room in a blinding glow. She squinted, struggling to make her eyes adjust.

He walked toward the bed, stopping just short of it. Mandy sat up and leaned against the headboard, the sheet twined around her legs. She glanced at the clock again: three on the dot.

Her gaze drifted back to his, and boom! Her heart hit her chest. Beautiful Jared. His hair was combed straight back, plaited into its customary braid, exposing chiseled angles and sun-burnished skin. He sported a denim shirt and timeworn jeans. Like the cowboy he was, he'd looped a distressed leather belt with a traditional Western buckle through the frayed waistband. She zeroed in on his fly. He already had an evident bulge.

"What are you looking at?" he asked.

Desire pounded at every pulse point of her body. She didn't respond. They both knew exactly what she was looking at, what she wanted, what the naughty girl inside her craved.

He raked his lethal gaze over her, and she fidgeted with her oversize nightshirt, a faded garment with an image of Tinker Bell splashed across the front of it. Beneath it, she wore thin cotton panties.

"Interesting pajamas," he said.

Dare she admit that she had a Sleeping Beauty ensemble, too? "I wasn't expecting company. You tricked me by coming back early."

"And now I'm going to peel those sweet clothes right off you."

He climbed onto the bed, scuffing her sheets with his boots, adding another dimension to the game. The flecks of dirt aroused her. The roughness. The maleness.

"Lift your arms," he said.

She obeyed his command, and he tugged at her Tinker Bell top, lifting it over her head and messing up her already sleep-tousled hair.

He bared her breasts and stared at her nipples. He kept staring until they stood at attention.

If he touched them, she would cream the bed.

But he didn't. He merely took his visual fill, making her desperately aware of her fantasy. She could barely wait for him to take off his clothes, to kneel over her, to stroke himself.

But he wasn't ready. He was still teasing her. He hadn't even removed her panties, and according to the scenario she'd created, she was completely naked before he masturbated on her.

Damn. That sounded so dirty, so hot, so nasty.

"You're blushing, baby."

"No, I'm not."

"Yes, you are."

She quit protesting. Being at his mercy was driving her crazy. "You're making me wet."

"How wet?" When she just sat there, he tore away the sheet. "Show me."

She spread her legs, revealing the crotch seam of her underwear, letting him see what he was doing to her.

"Naughty miss. You've got a damp spot."

He latched on to her panties. Working them off, he skimmed them down her hips, her thighs, her knees, and then over her feet.

"Lie down," he told her. "And keep your legs open."

Blatantly bared, she scooted onto a pillow. She waited for him to get undressed. Instead, he slid his fully clothed body between her legs, his denim fly almost chafing her delicate skin.

Almost.

He kissed her, slanting his mouth over hers. That hadn't been part of the fantasy, but it was so warm, so tender, she nearly melted. Now she was romantically aroused, too.

"My Mandy," he whispered.

Yes, she thought. She was his. She belonged to him. He nuzzled her neck, and she could smell the woodsy scent of his cologne. She touched his cheek, skimming her fingers along his jaw.

"I've never done this before," he said.

Stunned, she met his gaze. "You've never touched yourself for any of your lovers?"

"Yes, but not like this. Not so"—he paused, his voice quiet—"intimately."

She understood what he meant. Even with all of his sexual experience, with all of his bad-boy wildness, he'd never stroked himself so close to someone's face. "Do it for me, Jared."

He kissed her again. "I will. All over you."

Mandy shivered. Already her skin felt warm and liquid soft. She could only imagine how it was going to feel after he ejaculated on her.

He sat up, and his demeanor changed. He was rough again. Hard. Demanding. The slight edge of shyness was gone. She shifted her legs a fraction, and he grabbed her ankles.

"Stay put."

She wasn't about to move. She was more than willing to lie there with her heart pounding and her fingers itching to calm her clit.

Eager for more, she watched him get undressed. He did it roughly, tugging off his boots, pulling at the snaps of his shirt, thrusting open his belt, jerking down his pants, and freeing his cock.

Mandy's breath lodged in her lungs. His big, erect cock. Barely able to contain her excitement, she waited for him to put it in her face.

"Are you ready?" he asked.

"Yes." Please, yes. Her clit throbbed like a bitch.

He crawled over her, and she fisted the sheet strewn at her side. He got into position, planting his knees.

More throbbing. More hunger.

His penis, surrounded by a dark patch of hair, jutted forward, the pierced head aimed right at her. Like a missile, she thought, primed to launch.

Not only could she see his heavily veined cock, she could see the weight of his balls. He looked so powerful, so strong and masculine she couldn't take her eyes off him.

He licked his hand and lubricated his palm, and when he gripped the thickness of his shaft, Mandy caught her breath.

This was a first for him, but it was an even bigger first for her. Aside from a few scattered X-rated movies, she'd never witnessed male masturbation, and even in the movies she'd watched, the men hadn't done it from start to finish. A few strokes were all she'd seen.

But now . . .

She loved how aggressive Jared was. He treated himself as if he were his own prey. Although he moved his hand slowly at first, he was rough.

Kneading his thumb over the head, he pressed the piercing. His crown prince, she thought. She couldn't wait until it jeweled with come.

He stroked harder and faster, and Mandy moaned her pleasure. He glanced down at her, and their gazes locked.

"You're going to lick me," he said. "I'm going to move closer, and you're going to use your tongue."

Yes, she thought. *Yes.* When she'd relayed her fantasy to him, she'd told him that she'd wanted to lick whatever parts of him were closest to her mouth.

He widened his knee stance and moved lower, positioning his balls within her reach. She separated the tender sacs and laved each one, inhaling his musky scent. It was far more primitive than his cologne, but just as appealing. She buried her face against him, and he bucked like a stallion.

"Oh, fuck, baby. That feels good."

A wicked thrill spiraled through her. He was still stroking himself, moving his hand in a rapid motion. Empowered, she ran her tongue along his perineum, the sensual seam between his genitals and his ass, and he rocked against her touch. She knew it was a highly sensitive area. Sometimes when he gave her oral sex, he licked her there. Women had perineum regions, too.

Mandy didn't stop. She put her mouth all over his hot, male flesh. While she tortured him with her tongue, he kept milking himself, fulfilling her fantasy.

On the brink of ecstasy, he pulled back to show her his cock. Pearly drops of pre-come moistened the tip and leaked onto the barbell.

He rubbed the moisture against her lips, and she tasted the salty flavor. Together, they made ragged sounds. Desperate for relief, she reached down and stroked her clit, creating feminine friction.

"Naughty girl," he said.

"Naughty boy," she parroted.

They masturbated in unison. Mandy slid her fingers from her clit to her opening, smearing her juices, and he leaked more and more come.

"I can't hold on . . . I'm going to . . ."

She braced for the ultimate orgasm, for getting splashed with his semen. He moved down and ejaculated on her breasts, soaking her with his essence.

She went mad, coming when he did. In the silky minutes that followed, she massaged his seed over her nipples, across her stomach, and between her legs. She used it like lotion, just as she'd been dying to do.

He watched her, a dirty-boy smile on his handsome face. "You're incredible, baby."

She purred her pleasure. "I'm not done yet."

"You're not?"

"No." She wanted to have another orgasm, so she rubbed the milky wetness in tiny circles around her clit, renewing her arousal.

"Lord have mercy, woman." Jared sat beside her, taking in the show.

She noticed that he was still half-hard, that his erection wouldn't go away. Focused on his cock, on the memory of his warm, wet ejaculation, she frigged her clit until she ached, until she shuddered and thrust her hips in the air.

Slowly, slowly, the peak subsided, and she smiled at her lover. "Promise we can do this again."

"I promise." He looked as if he could barely breathe. "Any-time."

Feeling playful, she grabbed him and pulled him on top of her, gumming their naked bodies together.

"Shit!" He cursed in her ear, but he laughed, too.

They rolled over the bed, bunching the sheets and knocking pillows onto the floor.

Finally he pinned her down, cuffing her wrists with his hands. "I'm going to get you for that."

She feigned a struggle. "You and whose army?"

"Okay, now you did it. Now you're going to get it even harder."

But even as he professed his machismo, he released her from his bonds and kissed her, holding her close, so close she couldn't distinguish her heartbeat from his.

In that life-harrowing moment, she feared the worst. That she was a stone's throw from falling in love with him.

CHAPTER SIXTEEN

As I prepared my studio for Atacar's first portrait sitting, my confidence wavered. I'd been desperate to paint him since I'd first laid eyes on him, but now that the time was here, my nerves threatened to shatter.

This portrait was all I would have left of my lover after he was gone, and I wanted everything to be perfect. What if I didn't do him justice? What if I couldn't capture his true spirit? What if my talent wasn't worthy of him? I'd been convinced in the past that he would be my greatest work, but what if I'd been wrong?

Frowning at a chair I'd strategically placed in front of a blank wall, I moved it ever so slightly, reangling its position.

I thought about my previous works, portraits I'd been commissioned for in Paris. Female artists weren't sought after, but I'd managed a small measure of success, even with the restrictions of my gender. Yet here I was, losing faith in my ability.

"Catherine?"

Atacar's voice sounded behind me. I turned to look at him. Up until now, he'd remained quiet, clutching his rifle, waiting for me to make my final adjustments.

"Yes?" I responded.

He leaned his gun in a corner of the room. "I can't do this."

My heart dropped to my stomach. Had he lost confidence in me, too? Or had his original concern resurfaced? Was he uncomfortable about leaving a piece of himself behind? "You won't sit for me? You won't allow me to begin your portrait? Last night you said that you would."

"I'm not going back on my word. I was talking about leaving you behind after the painting is complete."

A gust of breath left my body. I reached out to grip the edge of the easel where I'd placed the canvas for his picture. Had I heard him correctly? Was he considering an alternative?

"I kept telling myself that creating a life with you would be wrong," he said. "But leaving you behind feels wrong, too. I want us to have more than memories. More than my soul locked inside of a painting."

I whispered a prayer to the heavens. Another gust of air expelled from my lungs. "Are you asking me to go to Mexico with you?"

He nodded. "If I had columbine and pennyroyal, I would give them to you."

Tears flooded my eyes. The sentiment attached to columbine was "I cannot give thee up," and pennyroyal meant "Flee away."

"What would you give me?" he asked.

I moved closer to him. By now I was trembling, but somehow

I was floating, too. As if I were in the midst of a dream. "Dandelions."

"To say that your wish has come true?"

"Yes." I took another heart-winging step in his direction. "I would give you red chrysanthemums, too."

Atacar's boots vibrated the floor. He was moving toward me, as well. Red chrysanthemums meant "I love you."

He reached for me, and I practically fell into his arms. His chest rose and fell; his breathing quickened.

"I love you, too," he whispered against my hair.

I lifted my face to his, and we kissed, the taste of our commitment rising like a wave. My fear of losing him was over. He was mine. He belonged to me.

"Nanny will come with us," he said.

"Yes, of course. She'll be pleased to be part of our future." I clutched him as closely as I could. I inhaled his scent, too. He smelled like the elements: the wind, the earth, the fire in his blood.

He kissed me again, deeper this time. We separated, our hearts full. We agreed to begin his portrait as we'd originally intended. Only now, when the painting was complete, we would be leaving for Mexico together.

He retrieved his rifle, and I instructed him to sit forward on the chair. He followed my direction, gripping the barrel of his gun and resting the butt on the floor.

He lowered his chin and looked up at me. The effect was stunning. For a moment, I could do little more than stare.

Daylight scattered across his shoulders, and shadows hollowed his cheekbones. His gaze caught mine, his eyes dark and serious.

Faint lines bracketed his mouth, fading into the sun-cloaked texture of his skin.

I approached the canvas, the passion I felt for him bubbling inside me.

He didn't move. He didn't flinch. His expression remained constant. He was the most brilliant model who'd ever sat for me. I opened my paint box, ready to work.

To capture every detail, every nuance of the warrior I loved.

Mandy wasn't going to let it happen. She wasn't going to fall in love with Jared. Yet here she was, drenched in his semen and emotional from the tender way in which he held her. Surviving a mundane marriage had been easier.

He lifted his sticky body from hers. "We need a shower. Or a bath. Or both. Do you want to rinse off in the shower, then take a long, hot bath with me?"

"That sounds good." Too good, she thought. But refusing wasn't an option. They couldn't sleep the way they were. "We'll have to change the sheets, too."

"You think?" He shook his head, laughed a little. "I can't believe you did this to me."

It wasn't as bad as what he'd done to her. At least he wasn't worried about falling in love. She stalled and gazed into his eyes. Or was he? She didn't have a clue what went on in Jared's mind.

"Do you want to light some candles in the bathroom?" he asked. "We could use the ones from Black Magic." He turned toward her dresser, motioning to the trio of candles they'd bought at the sex shop. "We could have a drink, too. Brandy, wine, whatever you've got."

She fought a frown. "Are you trying to be romantic?"

"I guess, yeah. Is that a problem? I thought you liked it when I did nice things."

"I do." Trapped in turmoil, she put her arms around his neck. "I do."

"Then why are you so tense? What's wrong, baby?"

"Nothing. Honestly, I'm fine." To prove her point, she pressed her lips to his, warning herself to accept their affair for what it was, to quit stressing about the tightness in the vicinity of her heart.

The kiss seemed to satisfy him, to solidify her sincerity. He reached for her hand, and they entered the kitchen and uncorked a bottle of sparkling rosé. Upon gathering the wine and two glasses, they returned to her room and collected the candles.

After rinsing off in the shower, they filled the tub, poured the wine, and enhanced the air with scented wax.

Jared sat down first and bent his knees, making room for Mandy. She slid into the open space he'd provided and leaned against him, the back of her head nestled in the crook of his shoulder. Even in the tight quarters, they were comfortable. Cozy, she thought.

As she sipped her wine, she weighed the past with the present. She'd wanted these sorts of moments with Ken, but he wasn't the bath-and-candle type.

"Do you believe that people have a compatibility quotient?" she asked.

"I don't know. I suppose they do." Jared skimmed her nipples, then lowered his hand and drew imaginary rings around her navel. "We're sexually compatible."

She sighed from his touch. "Do you think we have anything else in common?"

"We love Santa Fe. Neither of us will ever leave this place. We've made it our home."

She wanted him to keep going. She wanted to hear more. Needing to concentrate, she abandoned her wine, placing the glass on the side of the tub. "Anything else?"

He circled her navel again. "We appreciate art, music, and flowers. We have a similar sense of humor, and we make pigs of ourselves when we eat dessert." He stilled his hand. "We don't like to talk about our feelings, but we end up doing it for each other anyway. But most of all, we crave excitement. If we didn't, we wouldn't be having this affair."

She sat up and turned around to look at him. "I never thought of myself as a thrill seeker." Nor had she expected him to say such poignant things.

"Are you kidding? The good-bad girl?" He smiled and flicked some water at her.

She smiled and splashed him back. He always managed to make her feel young and vibrant. "If Ken had been more like you, he would have been a heck of a lot more fun."

Jared ended the swashing game. "You do that a lot."

"What?"

"Compare me to your ex."

Damn. "I'm sorry. It's a bad habit. I'll try not to do it again."

"Its okay, I guess. I'm learning to deal with it."

"Me and my crummy marriage?"

He shrugged. But a second later, he zapped her with a personal question, an issue they'd never discussed. "Why didn't you have kids? Isn't that what most couples do? Start a family, even if their marriage sucks?"

Mandy couldn't deny his logic. There was truth in his words, in his assumption. "We decided in the beginning that we would wait until we established our careers. And then we just let it pass. We didn't talk about it anymore."

"What about now? Would you take another stab at marriage and babies if the right guy came along?"

Oh, God. She went flip. If she didn't, she feared her feelings for him would betray her. "Is there such a thing as the right guy?"

He considered the question. "Probably not. But I've heard women talk about it. Even Amber says that kind of stuff. Of course, she's probably looking for two Mr. Rights."

Mandy couldn't help but laugh. Jared laughed, too. But their mirth died as quickly as it had erupted. In the interim, she reached for her wine.

He cut into the quiet. "I almost donated my sperm."

"What?" She gaped at him. "To who?"

"A sperm bank."

She drained her glass. He was full of surprises. "When?"

"I'd just turned eighteen, and I was saving money to move here. I heard that sperm donation paid about seventy-five to a hundred dollars per specimen, and that it required weekly specimens for up to six months. When you do the math, it sounds pretty good. But it's not that simple. They reject ninety to ninety-five percent of the applicants."

"Were you rejected?"

"No. I passed all of the screenings. I was young and genetically healthy. I hadn't gotten tattooed or pierced yet. Not completely. I had my ears done, but they were old. So that wasn't a concern."

"Why? Is there a time frame involved?"

He nodded. "You can't be tattooed or pierced within a year of the donation. I think the same rule applies to giving blood. Or it used to. It might be less time now." He shifted his legs, bending his knees a bit more, making Mandy aware of his height, even in his seated position. "But passing the screenings didn't matter. I backed out on my own. I couldn't go through with it."

She assumed he was talking on a deeper level, more than ejaculating in a cup. "What made you change your mind?"

"I didn't want to procreate that way. I didn't want to look back years later and wonder if I had a kid out there."

She battled her next question, hoping his response, regardless of what it was, wouldn't affect her. That she wouldn't get emotional about it. "Do you think you'll ever settle down? Maybe have a family of your own?"

"I don't know." He made a perplexed face, as if no one had ever asked him that before. "But I'll tell you this much. I'd be the best dad I could be. I'd never do what my old man did to me."

So much for not getting emotional. She wanted to put her arms around him and never let go. "Of course not. You're a good man."

"I'm not that good."

Needing a diversion, Mandy tried to focus on something else. To her, he was starting to seem perfect. Searching for a change of topic, she glanced at his matching armbands. She took a quick perusal of his jeweled penis, too. She could see it below the surface of the water.

"So, when did you get your Prince Albert and your tattoos?"

He glanced down. "I got the royal treatment a few months after I decided not to donate my sperm." He looked up and met her gaze. "I was going through a rough time, trying to identify myself, to get rid of the old me, to bury the kid my dad used to kick around."

"And getting an intimate body piercing helped?"

"Yes, it did."

"What about the tattoos?"

"I got inked after I'd been in Santa Fe for a while. I couldn't afford any major artwork until then." He turned one of his arms toward her, explaining the design. "This represents White Painted Woman. She's a deity who bore a child from the rain." He indicated a symbol that represented rain. "She called him Child of the Water. My mom used to read me folklore about him. The slaying of monsters was my favorite."

"It's nice that you remember her reading to you."

"Yes, but it's scattered. Not the stories. My memories. I kept up on the folklore myself. I kept that part of my culture alive. My dad certainly wasn't going to do it." Jared lifted his wine and brought the rim of the glass to his lips. "Dad didn't follow the old ways, and neither did his family. They're not spiritual people. They're hard and violent."

And he'd disassociated himself from them a long time ago. "Your tattoos are beautiful. Thank you for telling me about them."

"You're turning out to be a pretty good friend. You know that, Mandy?"

She warned her heart to be still. "You, too."

They went silent until he asked, "Do you think the water is getting cold?"

"Maybe a little."

"Should we refresh it, or do you want to get out?"

"We can refresh it." She didn't want to break this bond with him. "If that's okay with you."

"It's fine. The bath was my idea."

She drained most of the water and added more, and he refilled their wine. Once the tub regained its warmth, she returned to her original position of leaning back against him. The candles continued to burn, making shadows dance on the shower curtain.

Jared circled her waist. "That looks ghostly."

"It does," she agreed before she closed her eyes and sank into the haunting comfort of being wrapped in his arms.

I asked Atacar to bathe with me, so we hauled the tub into my room and filled it with hot water. We lit some candles, too. At one time, candles had been a primary source of household lighting. Now they seemed old-fashioned and romantic.

The tub hadn't been constructed for two people, but we made do. We leaned back and sat across from each other with our legs bent. Some families had piped-in water and built-in tubs, but not in this area. This was as close to luxury as we got.

"Are you going to sell the farm?" Atacar asked.

I shook my head. "I don't own it outright. I'm making payments to the bank. They can reclaim the property after I'm gone."

"I can repair your old wagon to take to Mexico."

Ah, yes, I thought. The broken-down vehicle the previous owners had left behind.

"I can paint it so it looks good," he said. "And I can make a top for it."

"That's a brilliant idea." I could afford to buy a covered wagon, but Nanny kept warning me that the income Papa had provided for me wouldn't last forever, and I should be more frugal. Besides, if I purchased a shiny new wagon, the townsfolk would wonder why I needed it, and Nanny and I were keeping our move a secret.

Atacar planned our trip. "I'll have to stay in the back of the wagon when we're on main roads. But we'll still need to be cautious."

"We will. We'll be careful."

"When the time comes, you should darken your hair. You'll be less noticeable in Mexico. We'll want to attract the least amount of attention possible."

I patted my blonde mane. I'd piled it on top of my head for the bath. "Do you know of a plant that will make it brown?"

He nodded and leaned forward to give me a gentle kiss, reassuring me that everything would be all right.

"Turn around," he said. "I'll wash your back."

I changed my position, and he ran the soap along my spine. He nibbled the side of my neck, too.

"Will you marry me when we're in Mexico? Will you become my wife?"

His words, his proposal, made me shiver. I latched on to his arms and wrapped them around my body.

"Yes," I said. "Oh, God, yes."

He continued to nuzzle, to nibble, to graze my damp skin. "We'll have beautiful children, Catherine. Babies for Nanny to spoil."

I tightened his hold on me; I made certain that he didn't let go. "We'll have a perfect life. We'll be together until we're old and gray."

"We can farm in Mexico. We can do what we're doing here. And we can pick variegated dahlias and put them in glass jars all over our house. To think of each other constantly."

"We can pick yellow dahlias, too." They meant "I am happy that you love me," and Atacar and I would always be happily in love.

Wouldn't we?

"Promise that the army will never find us," I said. "That they won't take you away from me."

"They won't," he whispered. "This is meant to be. We are meant to be."

As water lapped at my body, Atacar shifted me to my knees. I pitched forward and gripped the tub. I could feel his cock pressed against me. He was on his knees, too.

The arms that had been circling my waist dropped lower, a strong hand slipping between my legs. He stroked the bud of my womanhood while he entered me.

He thrust deeply, and I watched the candles burn, mesmerized by the erotic drip of wax. I arched my hips, wanting to feel more of him. He pushed all the way inside, riding me full hilt.

The candles flickered. The water sloshed. My mind spun.

"Who will marry us?" I asked.

"A mission priest," he responded.

I wasn't Catholic, and neither was he, but that was the faith in Mexico. I suspected it would become our religion, too. Our baptism. "I'll have to improve my Spanish."

"I'll give you lessons." He tugged on my hair, loosening pins, making strands fall. "Turn your head. I want to kiss you."

I angled toward him, and his mouth crushed mine. Our tongues twisted and danced, the sensation warm and wet. He pumped into me, swaying back and forth. I reached back to cup his balls.

I knew how he liked to be fondled. I knew almost everything about him, sexually and otherwise. He was more than my lover. He was my dearest friend, too. There was nothing I wouldn't do for him.

He thrust in and out until I climaxed, until flames burst in front of my eyes. But he didn't stop. He kept moving at a feverish pace, pushing toward his own release, filling me with his heat, his passion, his seed.

Afterward, we slid into the tub and steadied our breaths. I turned around to face him, and we completed our bath, drying off with the same towel and kissing each other again. From now on, we would share everything.

Our future, I thought, as I hugged him desperately close. The rest of our lives.

CHAPTER SEVENTEEN

The following week, George and his family came to visit, and we enjoyed a lighthearted afternoon. Nanny prepared a picnic-style meal, and the men moved the dining table outside. The weather was lovely, perfect for a social gathering.

We weren't far from the house, just a short distance from the porch. A butterfly winged its way past the table, and little Peter tried to catch it. He was Alice's youngest son. At two years old, he was an active child with rosy cheeks and wispy brown hair. Jack, the four-year-old, had a similar look. He was more interested in the pie Nanny had baked than helping his brother snare the butterfly. I could hardly blame him. The aroma of sugared apples wafted through the air.

Atacar glanced at me and smiled. The children were a pleasant reminder of the family we hoped to create someday.

We confided in George and Alice about our plans to move to Mexico, and they supported our decision. George promised to help us acquire extra horses. He offered to help Atacar repair the old wagon, too.

After everyone finished eating, I discussed my upcoming nuptials with Alice. As a second-time bride, she was an accomplished wedding organizer.

She accompanied me inside, and we sorted through my gowns to choose one in which I could be married. I wanted to be prepared for my special day. As soon as Atacar, Nanny, and I arrived in Mexico, we intended to arrange the ceremony. Atacar already knew the town in which we would settle.

I opened a wooden trunk that housed my best gowns, and Alice sucked in her breath.

"Oh, my," she said.

"Most of them are from Paris. Some were featured in fashion magazines."

"They're exquisite." She placed a pink dress on my bed, followed by a yellow, then an emerald green. "But you should wear white."

"Even if I'm not a virgin anymore?" I teased.

She gave me a conspiratorial smile. "Neither was I the first time I married. I was already carrying Jack in my womb. But I wasn't far enough along to show."

It felt wonderful to have a new friend, a young woman willing to share her secrets with me. "I've been drinking a preventative tea."

Alice tilted her head. "I've never tried anything like that. When Rowan, my late husband, and I were courting, we practiced coitus interruptus. Withdrawal," she clarified. "But it wasn't effective every time. That's how I conceived Jack."

I analyzed the science of intercourse. "Some of Rowan's seed must have leaked out before he withdrew."

She nodded. "There are physicians who say that coitus interruptus can be detrimental to men's health, and others who believe it isn't so. Rowan didn't behave any differently when he spilled inside of me or when he withdrew. He derived the same pleasure."

"Atacar and I want to conceive after we're married." I considered the alternative. "But it would be all right if it happened sooner. The way it did with you and Rowan."

Alice glanced at the flatness of my stomach. "You'll know if you miss your menses."

"I haven't yet."

"Then the tea must be working." She paused, smiled. "But no matter, you'll have charming children."

"You have charming children. Your sons are adorable."

"I love them dearly. I want to have another with George. Hopefully a little girl. But after that, I'd like to stop." She furrowed her brow. "Maybe I should try your tea. They don't sell preventatives in town, and it's illegal to obtain them through the mail. Such nonsense. Such prudery."

In her own quiet way, Alice was as independent as my bohemian friends. I would miss her once Atacar, Nanny, and I were gone.

"I'm glad we're getting to know each other," I said.

"Me, too."

"I'd offer to write to you, but I don't know how reliable the postal service is in Mexico. Besides, I—"

"Worry that soldiers could intercept the letters?" she provided.

I nodded. "Atacar says we'll be safe in Mexico, that the U.S.

Army has no power there. But how can we be sure?" I sighed, hating to lose touch with her and George. "Maybe you can visit us. That way we could see each other again."

She brightened. "That would be lovely. Maybe we can plan a trip for next year and bring the boys."

I shared her enthusiasm. "I'll look forward to it."

We proceeded to sort through my gowns. I had three white dresses. The design that seemed the most appropriate for a wedding had a trained underskirt and yards of lace. Alice thought it was breathtaking. It was a favorite of mine, as well. With a bouquet of flowers and a delicate veil, I would make a stunning bride.

As for Atacar's attire, I would ask Nanny to make him a white shirt and a black jacket. We could buy the materials in town and say they were for a tailored suit for me. Some modern girls were wearing mannish skirt ensembles. They even sported bow ties at the collars.

Alice helped me put away my gowns, and we sat quietly for a moment.

"How did Rowan leave you widowed?" I asked.

"He was thrown from a skittish horse and broke his neck. I miss him something fierce. But I'm grateful I have George now."

I, too, was glad that she had George. But if I ever lost Atacar, I could never replace him. I'd just as soon die.

We returned to the outdoors and found the men playing games with the children, behaving like boys themselves. As I watched Atacar with Peter, my heart went pitter-patter. The two-year-old toddled on his chubby legs, and Atacar scooped him up and made him squeal.

Nanny sat in the shade, monitoring the activity with a smile.

George turned and noticed Alice and me. He'd been spinning Jack like a windmill. "Our womenfolk are back."

Atacar turned, as well, making my heartbeat stronger. "So they are. Your wife and my betrothed."

His betrothed. I walked toward him, a lump forming in my throat, a prayer for our future.

"Play some music," Alice said to her husband, lightening my mood.

George complied, entertaining us with his fiddle. His wife danced with Jack, and Nanny gave the youngest a twirl, bouncing him in her arms.

Atacar bowed to me, and we joined in the fun, doing a whimsical polka we'd been practicing.

As the day quieted down and the children grew sleepy and napped on the grass, Atacar requested one last song.

A romantic waltz. Just for me.

"Are they doing a country western waltz?" Mandy asked.

Jared glanced at the dance floor. While a cover band played honky-tonk ballads, jean-clad couples moved counterclockwise in a promenade position. "Yep. That's what they're doing."

"It looks fun."

He returned his attention to Mandy. She sat across from him at a rustic little table. He'd invited her out for a night on the town, so here they were at one his favorite cowboy haunts. "I can teach you, if you want to learn. It's similar to a ballroom waltz, but it doesn't use as many diagonal patterns, and it's more relaxed."

"Sure. You can teach me. After I finish this." She lifted her Silk Stockings, an iced cocktail that paired tequila with cream and cinnamon.

Not that Jared minded watching her sip a lingerie-inspired concoction. He'd started the sexy-drinks cycle with her, just as he'd done with Amber.

"So where did you learn to ballroom waltz?" she asked.

"I took lessons."

"For the masquerade?"

He nodded. "But I've been country dancing most of my life, and as I said, it's not that different."

"Your ballroom technique was amazing. I was impressed."

"Thanks." Uncomfortable with her praise, he glanced away. Atacar had been a natural-born dancer, too. "Maybe it's in my blood."

"Did the other men take waltz lessons for the masque, too?"

The other men. She meant Pink and Red, or Jay and Luke, as they were known in the real world. "Yes, but Pink wasn't picking it up fast enough, so that's why he never got his turn to dance with you."

She laughed. "God forbid that one of your impersonators would be stepping all over my feet."

He laughed, too. Even if he felt serious inside. "That would have blown the polished Victorian image was I was trying to create."

"So what's your image tonight, Jared?"

"Nothing. I'm just being me." Before he frowned, he swigged his beer, quenching an uneasy thirst. Was there even such a thing as being himself anymore? He'd gotten so caught up in the journal, in mimicking Atacar, in comparing himself to his ancestor, he was starting to wonder who Jared Cabrillo was.

And then there was Mandy.

He studied his lover, with her mink brown hair and pretty blue eyes, wondering when he'd gotten so attached to her, when she'd started to matter so damn much, when she'd become more than just a hot lay.

She returned his intense gaze, and he kept his hands wrapped around his beer, clutching the base of the sweating bottle.

"Are you all right?" she asked.

"I'm fine."

"Are you sure?"

"I was just thinking about how powerful women are." Especially her. If she wasn't making his dick hard, she was making him emotional. "Have I ever told you about Coyote?"

"No. Is that a woman?"

"He's a trickster in my culture."

"What does he have to do with women being powerful?"

Jared tried to ignore the music. The band was playing a twangy version of "Could I Have This Dance," a song about falling in love on the dance floor. "Coyote discovered the power of a woman." He scooted his chair closer to the table, bumping the edge of it. "Of her pussy."

Mandy's glass rattled. She grabbed it and gave him a suspicious look. "Are you making this up?"

"It's folklore." But it was starting to seem frustratingly real. "Coyote found a pretty woman and wanted to have sex with her, but he got scared because he saw teeth inside of her vagina."

She raised her eyebrows, but she didn't comment.

"When the woman wasn't looking, Coyote got a long stick and a rock. Instead of inserting his penis, he put the stick inside of her." Jared paused, frowned. "Her pussy ground up the stick, so Coyote was glad he hadn't used his cock."

She winced. "I'll bet."

He made a face, too. The fall-in-love song was still being sung. "Coyote used the rock next. He used it until he knocked off all the teeth, until her vagina became what a woman's is today." Soft and warm, he thought. Alluring.

"So did Coyote ever have sex with her?"

"Yes. And do you know what she told him when he was done?"

She leaned closer. "No. What?"

"She said something like, 'Hereafter I shall be worth a lot. Many horses and many things.' "

"Smart girl." Mandy angled her head. "Is that the folklore behind Apache men offering gifts for their brides?"

Jared nodded, grateful when the romantic song ended. "But I think it's just another way of paying for pussy."

She toyed with the cherry garnish in her Silk Stockings, teasing him, going coy. "Maybe I should start making you pay. You've got lots of horses."

Was she kidding? He was already paying, sitting here with his heart twisted around his cock.

The band slid into another love song, and Mandy showed him that she'd finished her drink and was ready for her county western waltz lesson.

He stood up and offered her his hand, wishing she had teeth in her vagina. If she did, he would know better than to get bitten.

But it was too late for that. Because when he took her in his arms, all he wanted to do was keep her.

Hours later Jared drove Mandy to a secluded spot with a hilltop view. He parked his truck, and they gazed out the front windshield. He wasn't sure why he'd brought her here. Maybe it was to look at the stars.

"This makes me feel like a teenager," she said. "Like we're high school sweethearts."

He turned toward her, thinking how pretty she looked in the moonlight. He considered lifting the hem of her dress and sliding his hand along her thigh, the way a teenage boy would do, but he tempered the urge.

Instead he asked, "What was your favorite subject?"

"In high school?" She provided a ready answer. "I took an art appreciation class that blew me away."

"That makes sense. Considering your career path."

"What about you?"

He didn't glance back at the stars, but they were there, scattered across the night sky. "Astronomy. But I liked anatomy, too."

"Human anatomy, I'll bet." Her smile went crooked.

"Are you accusing me of stealing kisses between the lockers?" The urge to lift her dress returned, but he held off. "I partied and played around, but I managed to stay on track. I got good grades in all of my classes. I didn't mind studying. It gave me something to focus on."

Her voice went soft. "Other than your dad and the way he was mistreating you?"

Jared nodded. "No one expected a kid like me to be an honor roll student, least of all him. He wanted to see me fail. It pissed him off when I didn't."

"Nothing you did made him proud."

"No, nothing." He shifted the dialogue to her family, needing to rid his mind of his. "So, do your parents ever come to visit? Or any of your brothers or sisters?"

"Not too often. Mostly I go back to Iowa since everyone still lives there."

"I wonder what they'd think of me." He got closer to sneaking his hand up her dress. "The cowboy you're boning."

"Since you put it that way . . ."

"What?"

"Truthfully? My parents would think you're too young and too wild for me, my brothers wouldn't trust you, and my sisters would whisper to each other about how gorgeous you are. Then they'd warn me to be careful."

He tried to shrug it off. He was often judged in that manner. But deep inside where it counted, her honesty stung.

"I'm sorry," she said. "That sounded harsh. But I come from a conservative family. Their opinions are predictable."

"It's okay," he lied. "It doesn't matter."

"Yes, it does. If you ever did meet them, I'd insist that they give you a chance. That they look deeper. That they see you for the man you really are."

"I'm just a guy who's fucking you, Mandy."

She shook her head. "You're more than that. You're strong and kind and wonderfully impulsive. You're thoughtful and romantic, too. You've done things for me no man has ever done." She cleared her throat, battling a sudden hoarseness. "Amber even accused me of being in love with you."

Holy shit. He tried to breathe, but he couldn't exhale. His lungs expanded like a balloon.

"But I'm trying not to love you," she added quickly. "I'm trying not to complicate our lives that way."

"Good. Good." He released a chop of air, then another. Finally he steadied his breathing. "Sex is best. Lots of sex." But even as he said it, he knew they were spiraling toward more.

The balloon came back.

He should end it now. He should take her home and never see her again. But he was still itching to touch her, to slide his hand under her dress, to claim her under the stars.

He scooted across the bench seat of his vintage truck, moving closer. Then he did it. He hiked up her hem and exposed her panties.

She parted her legs, letting him have his way. But that was the dynamic of their relationship, the heat that drove them.

"Are your panties blue or purple?" he asked, creeping his fingers along her thigh. It was too dark to distinguish the color.

"Blue."

"You'll have to get a purple pair, too."

"Why?" She widened her thighs a little more.

"There's a drink called Purple Panties." He eased toward the waistband. "Vodka, triple sec, pineapple juice, grapefruit juice." He slid inside the fabric. "You shake the ingredients with crushed ice, then add seltzer and lime."

"That sounds refreshing." She tightened her rear, pushing her pelvis toward his hand.

He stalled, teasing her, making her wait. She was trying to get him to make contact with her clit.

He told her, "Pink Panties and Edible Panties are drinks, too."

"I wear lots of pink underwear. But I've never worn the edible kind." Another pelvic lift, another attempt to make him comply.

He didn't give in. He let her crave his touch even more. "What about Slippery Panties?"

Her head seemed to be swimming. She gave him a dizzy look. "What?"

"Slippery Panties. That's another drink."

"If you touch me, my panties will get slippery. Creamy. Wet. Please, Jared. Move your hand. Do something."

He let it happen. He stroked her, and the energy between them splintered. His cock went hard, straining against his zipper. But he wasn't looking to get himself off. It was her he wanted to please.

He dipped into Mandy's center, spreading her juices while he thumbed her ever-swelling clit.

She still had her ass flexed. Tight and sexy. He leaned in to French her, to capture her mouth. As their tongues tangled, the pressure built.

They stopping kissing, and their aroused breaths steamed up the windows. By now her thighs were wide-open. They could have been teenage sweethearts, he thought. Getting nasty on a school night.

She climaxed in a feminine flurry, biting down on her bottom lip and making girl-sweet sounds. He didn't remove his hand until the shuddering stopped and he'd absorbed every gentle quake.

In the afterglow, she leaned her head against the back of the seat and smiled at him. Miss Blue Panties. He gave her a chaste kiss and righted the hem of her dress.

"What's your full name?" he asked, realizing that he didn't know one of the most basic things about her. "Is it Amanda?"

"Yes, and my middle name is Lynn."

"Amanda Lynn Cooper." He turned the key in the ignition and set the defroster. "Is Cooper your maiden name? Or is it left over from Ken?"

"It's my maiden name. I went back to it after the divorce. What about you? What's your middle name?"

"Michael." He watched the windows clear. "Jared means either to rise or to descend, and Michael was an archangel. It's a strange combination."

"No, it's beautiful. Jared Michael. Will the angel rise or will he fall?"

He didn't comment on being called an angel. "Remember when you asked me if the Apache believe in Heaven and Hell? Christian Apache do. And those who follow the old way believe in the underworld. It's a place where spirits go, with mountains, rivers, and trees. Whatever you did on earth, you do there. If you were a warrior, then you stay a warrior. You're the same, only you're dead." He paused, fought a self-induced chill. "A ghost."

"Do you think that's where Atacar went after he died?"

"I don't know." He hadn't instigated this conversation to pull Atacar into it.

"If he did, I hope Catherine was able to meet him there."

"What makes you think she died, too?"

"She had to have died eventually. It's been over a hundred

years." Mandy sighed. "But I still wish I knew what happened to her. That her journal would surface."

Jared turned toward the stars, feeling guilty for keeping secrets, feeling sad for knowing the truth. "Like you said, eventually she died, too. Eventually it was over for both of them."

CHAPTER EIGHTEEN

I set down my brush and stepped back. The portrait was finished. I'd reached my artistic vision. Everything I'd ever learned, my entire craft, seemed centered on this moment, on this painting.

I told Atacar, and he responded, "Truly? It's done?"

I nodded and smiled.

He rose from his chair and leaned his rifle against the wall, coming around the other side to view his image. I hadn't allowed him to see it before now. I'd been keeping it covered in between sittings.

But this was the final unveiling.

He didn't speak, not at first. He gazed at the canvas for what seemed like a very long time. Suddenly I got nervous. While I waited for his reaction, my pulse bumped like a rough carriage ride.

"It's me," he said. "Only better." He turned toward me. "Because it came from you. From your heart, from your hand."

"It's the man I love."

"It's the man who loves you, too." Atacar turned back to the painting. "You captured him."

He was right. I did. I captured him in every way possible. "The seriousness in his eyes, that comes from the pain in which he has lived. But it comes from the power of who he is, too. The warrior who escaped. The Chiricahua Apache who found his freedom."

"He found more than freedom. He found a woman. The perfect woman."

"Perfect for him," I said.

"Yes, for him."

He leaned in to kiss me, and I looped my arms around his neck. His clothes smelled of the herbs he sometimes burned when he prayed.

I wondered if there was another couple in the world who loved each other as much as we did. I didn't think it was possible, but I was biased.

We separated and faced his portrait again. I could still taste him on my lips, lingering, always lingering. I got eager for nightfall, for the things he did to me in the privacy of our room.

"We should show the portrait to Nanny," he said. "She'll be impressed."

"Yes, we should." Nightfall was hours away.

We went into the parlor, where Nanny was using her sewing machine, a hand-operated model we'd purchased from a catalog. She glanced up, with spectacles clipped to the bridge of her nose. They were a common style of eyeglasses, and she wore them to read and to sew. She couldn't see well close up.

"The portrait is complete," Atacar said.

"Is it?" Nanny pushed away from her chair and got to her feet, anxious to view what I kept telling her would be my greatest work.

She removed her spectacles, which were attached to a ribbon around her neck, and abandoned her sewing.

The three of us entered my studio, and upon seeing the painting, my dear old nanny pressed a hand to her heart. She got teary-eyed, too. She'd never expressed that kind of emotion in front of me before, and certainly not over one of my paintings or sketches.

"It's grand," she said, her voice awed. "Oh, it's so grand."

I thanked her, humbled by her praise. Atacar smiled at me, and I reached for his hand.

We returned to the parlor, where Nanny resumed her sewing. I offered to prepare supper, and she and Atacar exchanged a humored glance.

I rolled my eyes. I was a pitiful cook, but I could manage cold meats and cheeses. I could slice fresh fruit and arrange it festively on a platter, too.

I donned an apron, intending to look official, as wifely as I could. Beneath the practical cover-up, my work clothes were mottled with paint. I was a silly sight.

But somehow I was enchanting, too.

I knew this because when I glanced back over my shoulder, my future husband was admiring me.

~

Later that night, Atacar guided me to the mirror on my wardrobe cabinet and stood behind me. We were fully clothed, but I could tell that he had other intentions.

I gazed at our reflections. I'd never considered making love in front of a mirror. But it was titillating, so very right for me. I liked to envision how we looked while we mated, and now I would be able to watch, to see everything.

He slipped his arms around my waist and turned his head to kiss the side of my neck, to graze me with his teeth.

In the glass, my expression went soft and womanly. He undid the tiny buttons that marched down the front of my dress. His technique was slow and painfully sexy. The more buttons he worked, the more my dress gaped, exposing my corset cover.

He paused to nibble my neck again. He was torturing me purposely, making the process last. Finally, he removed my dress, peeling it down my body and allowing it to pool at my feet. I stepped out of the circle of fabric and waited for his next move.

He pillaged my hair, one pin at a time. I was wearing a la concierge, a style in which my long hair was pulled to the top of my head and fastened into a knot.

Silky strands tumbled in disarray, making me look like a siren. I was more beautiful than I'd ever been, but my beauty was coming from him, from what he was doing to me, from the way he was making me feel.

He divested me of my corset cover and petticoat, leaving me in my ribbon-trimmed corset and lace-hemmed drawers. On the day I'd met him, this was how far I'd gotten in my state of undress before we'd been forced to hide in the trees.

I searched his gaze in the glass. My Atacar. My love. Someday I wanted to take him to Paris, to show him the city that influenced me. Eventually I wanted to take him to London, too. Home, I thought. To introduce him to Mama and Papa and my brother, Paul. I didn't know if they would accept him any better than they accepted me, but it would be nice to form a bond with my family, especially for the sake of the children I hoped to have.

Atacar removed a buttercup from his pocket and tucked it behind my ear. I'd been wearing a buttercup in my hair every night, but today I'd gotten sidetracked by our guests and had forgotten to pick one from the nearby field where they grew. My lover had remembered for me.

His seduction continued. He opened the front closures on my corset and caused my breasts to spill out. He caressed me, rubbing my nipples, then moved forward and bent his head, taking a pointed tip into his mouth.

My reflection went breathy, and I put my arms around him, holding him close. As I watched, I listened to the sounds of his suckling. He shifted from one nipple to the other, enjoying his treat.

I waited for him to move lower, to give me cunnilingus. He teased me instead, kneeling to toy with my navel, to dart his tongue in and out of the indention.

"Does this feel good?" he asked.

My voice vibrated. "Yes."

"Are you getting wet?"

"Yes."

He undid my drawers, pulling them down my hips. Once they were all the way off, he faced me forward. By now, I was completely naked, desperate for him to lick me.

But he didn't. He stood up, approached my vanity table, and retrieved my hand mirror, an ornate object with silver backing.

He returned to his knees and positioned the small mirror between my legs. I tried to remain poised, to not seem shocked. But I was. Shocked and curious.

"I want you to see what I see when I look at you there," he said.

I glanced down and saw my nether lips, surrounded by a tuft of blonde hair. I took a swift breath and looked up at my head-to-toe nakedness. Then down again at my private place. I was wickedly aroused.

Atacar kept the hand mirror in place, angling it just so. "Use your fingers. Open yourself up."

I obeyed his erotic command. I exposed my dewy folds. The flesh inside was soft and pink. I imagined Atacar's tongue delving into it.

"Keep looking," he said. "Keep touching."

I rubbed my clitoris, making it swell.

Finally, too aroused to continue, I begged him to lick me. Atacar discarded the smaller mirror and gave in to my plea, grasping my hips and pulling me toward his mouth. I shivered, wildly excited.

I watched from the bigger mirror as he made his luscious foray. I pressed closer to him, rocking in a forward motion. I sank my hands into his hair, fisting his scalp.

He painted me with saliva. He sucked and nibbled. He did everything imaginable with his hot, hungry mouth.

I climaxed like a tornado. Before I pitched over, he steadied me, sliding his hands along the sides of my body as he rose to his feet.

"We're not done yet," he said, passion alight in his eyes. "We're just getting started."

I curled up to him, purring my pleasure, a wind-ravaged kitten anxious for more. "Are we going to use the mirror again?"

He nodded, opening his shirt and pushing down his pants. "And the floor and all of the furniture in the room. I'm going to press you against the wall, too." He spun me around and made my heart hit my chest. "I'm going to take you as many ways as I can."

"Forever," I gasped.

"Yes," he responded. "Forever."

Jared closed the leather-bound book and returned it to the floor safe in his closet, spinning the combination lock until the numbers blurred before his eyes. He'd been reading Catherine's journal, as he often did when he was alone. But this time, he panicked.

Forever.

The word reverberated in his mind. He couldn't do forever. He couldn't make that kind of commitment, and if he kept mimicking Atacar, that's what would happen. He would get so far into Mandy that he wouldn't be able to live without her.

The other night beneath the stars, he'd considered ending their affair. But he hadn't done it, even after she'd admitted that she was trying to keep herself from falling in love with him.

So what the hell was he waiting for? For her to stumble and fall? To love him?

He needed to let her go, for both of their sakes. No more dancing. No more candlelit baths. No more language of flowers.

He reached for the landline phone on his nightstand, prepared to ring Mandy, to tell her that they should call it quits. But he stalled. Already his body was craving hers.

One last time.

All night, in every position imaginable, the way Atacar had taken Catherine: in front of a mirror, straddled on a chair, up against a wall, on the floor . . .

Shit.

He glanced around his room. He couldn't do it here. He needed to make a clean break, which meant her condo was off-limits, too.

A hotel, he thought.

The first time they'd fucked had been at a hotel, so why not let it be their last?

He got out the phone book and dialed the place where they'd started their affair. Focusing on the tightness beneath his zipper, he requested the same accommodations. He didn't stop to consider why he remembered their old room number, other than that his first night with her had been pretty damn memorable.

There, he thought, as he hung up, the wheels were in motion. He ignored the other tightness, the clenching near his heart, and called Mandy, catching her on her cell phone.

She answered in a customary greeting. "Hello?"

"Meet me at the Hôtel de Terrasse. The same room as before."

"Jared?"

"Who else would it be?"

"What's going on?"

"I just said what's going on. Meet met at the hotel. Room four ten."

"What for?"

"To have sex." He glanced at his watch: 2:04. Check-in was at three. "In an hour."

"You sound strange. Are you all right?"

"I just need to get laid. We're going to do it all night, over and over, as many times as we can."

"Oh, my goodness. Are you at least going to buy me dinner first?"

He could tell that she was teasing him, joking about his impatience. But she was right. He needed to slow down, to catch his breath. Besides, food was fuel, energy to keep going. He'd meant what he'd said about making it a marathon. "We can order room service."

"I was kidding, Jared."

"I know, but I think we should eat. I think dinner is a good idea."

She didn't disagree. "I need to get ready. And to pack a bag."

"So do I. I'll see you at three."

He ended the call and threw his belongings in a leather satchel. He wasn't going to tell Mandy that this was their last date, the end of their relationship. He would do that in the morning, when the sex was over, when he could think clearly.

Atacar would hate him for this, and so would Catherine. But they'd been dead and gone a long time. They weren't in any position to save him.

An hour later, Jared got to the hotel and checked in. Mandy was late, so he waited. The familiar room, with its hand-painted furniture, beamed ceiling, and kiva fireplace, did nothing to ground his emotions.

He walked onto the balcony. He could see a view of the Plaza, where historical Santa Fe sprawled out before him.

Finally Mandy arrived, and he greeted her with a powerful hug. "Thank you for doing this," he said. "For being here."

She gave him a passionate kiss. "I promised that I'd never say no to you, remember? Besides, why wouldn't I want to be here?"

"No reason." He hugged her again, holding her as if he would never let her go. But letting her go was exactly what he was doing. After tonight, he thought. After he thrust his desperate cock inside her.

He stepped back. "Let's order dinner."

They scanned the room service menu and chose the same meal: mango gazpacho and beef fajitas. For dessert, they ordered chocolate mousse.

Jared admired his companion. She looked amazing in a backless dress, a halter or whatever it was called. He'd never seen her in anything that required her to go braless.

"That's sexy," he said.

"Thank you." She turned in a pretty pirouette. "It's new. A gift to myself."

"It suits you. The good-bad girl." What the hell was he going to do without her?

Get on with his life, he told himself a second later. Become a bachelor again.

"You look sexy, too," she said. "All rough and ready."

Jared ran his hand along his jaw, where he'd neglected to shave. He would probably give her a beard-stubble burn. Everywhere, he thought, all over her naked body. But he doubted that she would complain. He suspected that she would like it.

He frowned, wondering who would share her bed after he was gone. Envisioning another man in his place packed a punch, in more ways than one. It made him want to rip the nameless, faceless guy apart.

Christ, he thought. He needed to get a grip.

A short while later, a knock sounded on the door. Jared dashed off to allow their food server into the room.

Once they were alone, Jared and Mandy settled in to eat. She spooned into her gazpacho, a cold soup designed for warm weather. He tasted his, too.

"This is good," she said.

Good?

No, he thought, his chest going tight. This was bad. The shittiest thing he'd ever done. He was going bang her in nearly every sexual position known to man, and in the morning when she was wrapped securely in a hotel-monogrammed robe, he was going to break up with her. He deserved the bastard-of-the-year award for that, and he would probably get it, too. She would probably hate him forever.

Forever.

There was that word again. The word that panicked him. The word that Catherine and Atacar had tried—and failed—to claim as their own.

They kept eating, and when they were nearly done with their meal, Mandy said, "It's been almost two months."

Jared glanced up from his dessert. "What?"

"Since we first got together." She looked toward the bed. "Since our affair started. Being in this hotel feels like an anniversary, especially in the same room. It's nice that you remembered."

He didn't want to talk nice. Because he didn't feel nice. Because he wasn't. "I just want to touch you, Mandy."

She swallowed the last spoonful of her mousse and stood up.

He pushed back his chair and tugged her onto his lap. With the flavor of chocolate on their lips, they kissed.

He skimmed a hand down her back, where the dress left her skin exposed. She straddled him, rubbing against his jeans.

"Guess what color my panties are," she said.

His thoughts drifted to the other night. "Purple."

She shook her head.

"Pink."

Another headshake.

He didn't guess again. "Why don't you show me?"

She climbed off his lap and lifted the hem of her dress, inch by inch. He waited for a color to appear. But what he saw was her Brazilian-waxed pussy, sans underwear. She'd gone commando for him. His mouth all but watered.

He shoved their dishes aside, making room for his lover. "Take off your dress and sit here."

She blinked. "On the table?"

He nodded. "With your legs open. I want to eat you."

She did it. Only she placed her dress below her, using it like a napkin between her ass and the tabletop. He smiled, thinking how mannered she was.

He sat in front of her, lowered his head, and feasted like the sexually starved man he'd become. She was better than the chocolate, better than anything he'd ever tasted. He glanced up and noticed how willing she looked, spread out like a sacrifice.

He returned his attention to the dampness between her thighs. He licked and swirled. He kissed and nibbled. He ate her as erotically as Atacar had eaten Catherine in front of the mirror.

"Have you ever looked at yourself?" he asked.

"Looked?"

"In a mirror."

She nodded, seeming shy yet seductive, Mandy at her most alluring. "Sometimes when I . . ."

"Touch yourself?"

She scooted closer to his mouth. "Yes."

Damn. He pushed his tongue all the way inside, and she thrust her hips in a bang-me motion. He made her come, but he didn't give her time to rest. Right after she shuddered and shook, he lifted her off the table started the sex marathon.

Jared peeled off his clothes, and they christened the floor, where he penetrated her, doggy style, with him kneeling behind her. He wanted to start this way because they could watch themselves in the closet-door mirror.

As he pumped into her, their gazes locked in the glass. She was on all fours with her little tits hanging down and her hands and knees ground into the carpet.

But she liked it. He could see how turned on she was. He clutched her hips and thrust harder. She moaned and lowered her head and torso, making the position even more exciting.

Hotter. Naughtier.

He didn't care if he came a hundred times tonight, if he used up every ounce of semen his body could produce. All he wanted was her—Amanda Lynn Cooper—in every dirty, sexy way he could take her.

They stood up, and he fucked her against the wall, backward, where he was behind her. But soon he spun her around so they faced each other and one of her legs was wrapped around his waist.

"You feel so good," he said. "So good."

"So do you." She kissed him, making his head spin.

They tumbled into bed and went missionary for a while, then she straddled his lap and rode him home.

He came in an explosion of lust, and she collapsed on top of him. He held her, their bodies slicked with sweat.

They stayed that way, nuzzled close, then cooled off with ice cubes, rubbing each other down, letting the frozen water melt and drip.

She leaned over to suck him, getting him ready for a second round. He stroked her hair and watched her blow him.

Within no time, they were at it again, going for an edge-of-the-bed position with a pillow propped under her hips and him standing over her. All she had to do was put her legs in the air and let him hammer away.

Which he did, as deeply as he could.

He tried not to think about anything but his primal need, his hunger. Tomorrow he would deal with the ache of letting her go, of freeing himself from emotional bonds. Tonight, all that mattered was being tangled up in her sinuous body.

She arched and flexed, and they found their way into a kneeling lotus, a soft and gentle position that made Mandy sigh. They kissed and caressed, but it was still sex, Jared told himself.

Just sex.

His partner climaxed, rocking back and forth. She moved like a mermaid, fluid and luxurious. He could feel every sway, every rhythm of her wavelike peak.

He gave her a minute to snap out of her trance, and she graced him with a smile. Before he lost what was left of his needing-to-escape heart, he pulled her back into down-and-dirty fucking.

They used every stick of furniture at their disposal. They even boffed on the balcony, where evening had crept in, shrouding their nakedness.

Hours later Jared struggled to sleep. He lay awake for most of the night. But his lover didn't. She nodded off in his arms, unaware of what morning would bring.

CHAPTER NINETEEN

Mandy awakened next to Jared, the smell of sex clinging to her body. She looked longingly at her partner in crime. He was still crashed out, his hair covering half of his face. A portion of his braid had come loose.

Although she tingled to touch him, she let him sleep. She eased away from the bed and headed for the bathroom. She took a long, hot shower and toweled off. She brushed her teeth and combed out her shampooed hair, too.

Getting cozy, she slipped on a thick, white robe provided by the hotel. Then she made a pot of coffee and poured herself a cup.

She returned to bed and sat on the edge, steam rising from her cream-doctored brew. What a night. She was sore, but it was a good kind of ache.

Jared squinted and opened his eyes. Mandy smiled, thinking how rough and rumpled he looked, a sexy male in his prime.

"Hi," she said.

"Hey," he rasped back.

As he sat up and leaned against the headboard, the sheet circled his waist. His penis was hard, tenting the fabric. But she knew it wasn't for her. Fully functioning men got erections during the dream stage of sleep, even if their dreams were nonsexual. Jared had awakened with what was commonly referred to as "morning wood."

He jabbed at the loose strands of his hair, struggling to smooth it in place. "You're wearing one of the hotel robes. Just like I figured you would be."

She angled her head. He sounded odd, dark and pensive. "Isn't that why they give them to us? To wear?"

"Yes, of course." He glanced at the clock. "I hadn't meant to sleep this long."

She checked the time, too. "It's still early. How about some breakfast? We can order in."

"I'm not hungry. But you can get something if you want."

"I made coffee." To her, he seemed like he needed a caffeine boost. "Do you want a cup?"

He shook his head. "I just need a shower."

She understood that he was groggy and tired from their marathon, but his moodiness was killing her morning-after glow.

He stood up and paused for a moment, as if he meant to touch her, to twine a finger around her damp hair, to fold down the collar of her robe, to kiss the pulse at her neck, to show her affection.

But he didn't. He grabbed his overnight bag and disappeared into the bathroom.

Okay, so fine. Maybe he would feel better after he showered. In spite of his refusal of food, Mandy ordered a continental breakfast big enough for two, in case he gained an appetite. An assortment of rolls, bagels, and pastries might do him some good. The fresh-squeezed orange juice would be an extra pick-me-up, too.

She didn't get dressed. She stayed belted in her robe, intent on remaining cozy. She'd always enjoyed the hotel experience. Refusing to sit in a dimly lit room, she opened the drapes, allowing the sun to shine through the sliding-glass balcony door.

Jared emerged from the bathroom, fully dressed with his hair rebraided and his jaw free of day-old whiskers. She caught a whiff of his cologne, a spicy, sea-breeze scent. As crisp as he looked, as fresh as he smelled, he still seemed sullen.

"What's wrong with you?" Mandy asked.

"I can't do this anymore," he responded.

"This?"

"Us." Nerve-frazzling seconds ticked by. "I think we should stop seeing each other."

She gripped the back of a dining chair. "You're ending our affair? After a night like last night? After . . ." The guilt in his eyes hit her square in the stomach. The wariness. The betrayal. She released the chair and clenched her middle. "You did this on purpose, didn't you? You planned it. That's why last night happened the way it did."

"I'm sorry. I just needed—"

"To fuck me over? Literally and figuratively?" Her breath rammed out her lungs, scratching past the lump in her throat. She shouldn't care. She'd always known an end was in sight, but not like this, never like this. "Is it because of what I said about trying not to fall in love with you? Is that why?"

He thrust his hands in his front pockets, hunching his

shoulders, going James Dean. "That's part of it. We weren't supposed to get close enough for either of us to worry about falling in love."

She fought to steel her reaction, the way she'd been fighting her feelings for him. She wasn't going to let him see her come unglued, even if she was headed toward destruction. "And the other part?"

"I feel as if I'm losing my identity. Like I don't even know who I am anymore. I need to go back to being Jared. The old me."

She studied him: deep-set eyes, slightly winged brows, hard-cut cheekbones, a sensual mouth. He looked the same, but she knew he was referring to the party boy, the man who didn't cuddle at night.

A knock rattled the door, and they both flinched. She'd forgotten about breakfast until a disembodied voice announced, "Room service," from the other side.

"I have to get that," she said.

Jared stepped back, and she answered the summons. Instead of allowing the server to come inside, Mandy took the tray and placed it on the unmade bed.

After signing the bill, which would be charged to Jared's credit card, she closed the door and left the food untouched. She wasn't the least bit hungry. Not anymore.

She gazed at her now former lover, and he frowned.

"I'm sorry," he said. "But I think it's better this way."

Better for whom? The ache between her legs throbbed, but the pain that knifed her heart was a thousand times worse.

"If it's over, it's over." She made a sweeping gesture. All she wanted was for him to go away, to vanish before she cried.

He stalled, almost as if he couldn't bear to leave on such a hard, cold note. That gave her a gleam of satisfaction. The jilted woman.

With a snap of feminine bravado, she carried her continental breakfast to the table as if she meant to eat it. When she turned her back on him, he released a jagged breath.

But he didn't apologize again. Nor did he change his mind. She heard him gather his last night's clothes, which were still strewn on the floor, and shove them into his overnight bag. She heard him place something on the nightstand, too. She suspected it was the key to her condo.

She waited, the sound of his booted footsteps moving farther away from her, and with the click of the door, he was gone.

~

The time had come. We were leaving for Mexico. Instead of traveling at first light, we'd chosen to depart in the afternoon, so our friends could see us off. Alice was already at the farm, and George was scheduled to arrive later, after his workday ended.

Up until today, Nanny and I had been sorting through what seemed like an endless amount of personal effects and supplies. We were leaving many things behind, but it didn't matter, as long as Atacar and I were going to be together.

"I'll miss you so much," Alice said, as she glanced around the partially barren house.

"I'll miss you, too," I responded.

"We'll visit when we can. But for now, it's going to be difficult to say good-bye."

I hugged her, and Peter toddled between us, eating a treat Nanny had given the boys. His face and hands were sticky. He grinned at us with his tiny teeth. Alice and I laughed, and she cleaned him up.

I went outside and approached Atacar, where he was fastening a wire chicken coop on the back of the wagon. We were taking our chickens, as well as our cow. Nanny intended to cook some of the chickens along the way, and the cow would provide milk on our journey and in Mexico.

Atacar smiled at me, and I returned his affection. The sun shimmered, highlighting the blue blackness in his hair. He was so handsome, so big and strong, and he was mine. All mine.

The sound of hoofbeats snared our attention. We spun around and saw George racing toward the farmhouse.

Panic rose in my bones. "Something is wrong." The other man had left work early.

We dashed toward him, and he reined his horse to a frantic stop and dismounted. Nanny and Alice appeared on the front porch. They'd heard the thunderous hoofbeats, too. The children followed, but Alice shooed them back inside, protecting them from the drama that was about to unfold.

"An Indian was spotted near the watering hole this morning," George said.

"Oh, God." I clutched Atacar's hand. He'd gone to the stream earlier to gather the spiritual herbs he used when he prayed.

"There was no one around," my lover said. "How could I have been seen?"

George explained. "A couple of boys was hiding in the trees. They'd sneaked off to chew tobacco and have a spitting contest. They didn't tell nobody at first. If they admitted that they'd seen you, then they would've had to tattle on themselves, to say they wasn't home doing their chores."

"But they did tell." This from Alice.

George nodded to his wife. "After their pappy discovered their chores wasn't done, they spilled the beans, and their pappy took them into town to talk to the marshal." He addressed Atacar once again. "The boys wasn't sure if the man they seen was you. But they was sure he was Indian. And when they described him to the marshal . . ."

I clutched Atacar's hand more tightly.

George continued. "The town is all abuzz. I came here as soon as I heard."

"Did the marshal telegraph the army?" Atacar asked.

"Yes. And now soldiers are going to be searching this area again, from here to the border."

Which meant that Atacar needed to travel alone, to mount a horse and ride as fast as he could, to take the back roads, to make headway. The wagon would be too slow, too cumbersome for him to outrun the army.

I turned to my lover. "You leave now, and Nanny and I will head out on our own. We'll meet you in Mexico."

He touched my cheek, making me ache. "Promise me you and Nanny will be safe."

"We came to America by ourselves. We won't falter on this trip." Tears flooded my eyes. "Promise me the same thing."

"I'll do whatever I can to make our destination." His hand lingered on my cheek. "For you. For us."

George helped Atacar pack his saddlebags, and Nanny provided him with dried meat and hardtack. Within minutes, he was ready for his lone journey.

He kissed me, more deeply than he'd ever kissed me before. "I love you, Catherine."

I put my arms around his neck, my voice quavering. "I love you, too."

As I watched him ride away and disappear in a cloud of dust, my knees threatened to buckle.

Silence fractured the air. Nanny put her hand on my shoulder, and Alice and her husband stood like scarecrows.

George finally spoke. "You have to unpack his portrait," he said to me. "You can't take it with you. If you encounter soldiers along the way, they might stop you and search the wagon. They might search every wagon they see."

As a precaution, I thought. To be sure no one was harboring a runaway Indian. Or that he wasn't a stowaway without the traveler's knowledge.

"I understand," I said. If the army uncovered Atacar's portrait in my possession, they would know I was willingly connected to him. "What about my journal? I keep a memorandum book. It's filled with his name, with my thoughts, my feelings."

"Is it small enough to hide on your person?" Alice asked.

I nodded, deciding that I would tuck it into the waistband of my drawers. Soldiers would never look beneath a woman's skirt, not unless they intended to rape her, and I would fight to the death if they attempted to violate me.

"What shall we do with the portrait?" Nanny asked.

"We can hide it here," George responded.

We went inside, and he removed a row of boards in the parlor wall. I placed the carefully wrapped painting inside and watched him hammer up the opening.

That was it. The final act before Nanny and I bade our friends farewell and began our journey.

Without the man I loved.

Mandy stood in front of Atacar's painting, gazing at his image. A wall of glass protected him from the modern world, from vandals, from thieves. But a safety shield hadn't surrounded him when he'd been alive.

She looked into his eyes and battled an ever-present ache, an emptiness that grew deeper with each day. She missed Jared. She missed him so much. Two weeks had passed since he'd ended their affair, and she couldn't stop thinking about him.

Footsteps echoed off the museum floor, and she turned to the quick-paced sound. Kiki headed toward her in a gypsy-inspired dress with her hair rioting around her face.

"I figured I'd find you here," the other woman said.

Mandy nodded. She visited Atacar for a few minutes every day. But she'd always done that.

Kiki sighed. "You look sad."

"I'm hanging in there." Mourning a man who was still alive. How lovesick was she? How lost without him? God, she hated herself for that. She glanced at the painting. Was being near Jared's ancestor making it worse? Or better? At this stage, she didn't know how to feel.

"Sometimes life sucks," Kiki said.

Mandy nodded, still gazing at the portrait, still locked within its oil-on-canvas embrace. "Do you think the old army report about Atacar is accurate?"

"That he aimed his rifle at the soldiers who attempted to apprehend him, and they returned fire in self-defense?" The historian went silent for a moment. "I don't know. But I could see him doing that. Fighting to maintain his freedom."

"So could I." According to the report, he'd taken several bullets to the chest, one of which had been fatal.

Before Mandy's mind wandered further in that direction, Kiki exhaled an audible breath and said, "I hate to do this to you right now, but we need to talk. There are some things I need to tell you."

"About what?"

"The journal. First of all, I located one of Nanny's ancestors. A cousin, a working-class Londoner. He says his family doesn't know anything about it nor do they have it in their possession. If they did, they would've sold it to the highest bidder long before now."

"Do you believe him?"

"Yes. But it doesn't matter, because I think your former lover has it."

"Jared?" His name all but bruised her lips. "Oh, my goodness. Why?"

"Because Nanny's ancestor told me that he heard a rumor that Jared stayed at Minerva Burke's estate when he was in England."

"Catherine's grandniece? The reclusive old lady who won't speak to anyone about Catherine?"

Kiki nodded. "I checked into the rumor, and it's true. From what I uncovered, Jared has been to England twice."

"Yes, he told me that."

"Did he also tell you that on his first trip, Minerva contacted a historian, and she and Jared had something authenticated?"

Mandy's pulse jiggered. "Something?"

"I wasn't able to find out what it was. But I'd bet my ass in a sling that it's the journal. What else could they possibly have in common?"

Mandy's stomach clenched. "If it is the journal, then Jared lied to me the entire time we were together."

"I hope you're going to confront him."

"Damn right I am. Oh, God. I feel so betrayed. On every level. What was he trying to prove? What kind of game was he playing?"

"I have no idea. But he sure played it well."

A tour guide entered the room, and when she led her group toward Atacar's exhibit, Mandy and Kiki moved out of the way.

"I'm so sorry," her friend said, as they stood off to the side. "I wish I'd delivered better news."

"Me, too." As strangers gathered around Atacar, Mandy noticed their heightened interest in the tour guide's commentary about the warrior's rumored romance with the artist who'd painted his portrait. "Me, too."

While en route to Mexico, I darkened my hair with the plant dye Atacar had suggested. I did everything I would have done if my lover had been with me. Everything except lie in his arms, except touch him, except listen to him breathing while he slept.

I missed him painfully, and I prayed for every mile of our trip that he would be there when we arrived.

No one stopped us, and no one searched our wagon. We passed other travelers, but we didn't see any soldiers. Nanny kept saying that was a good sign, but I wasn't sure.

We crossed the border on a gruelingly hot day. Amid the countryside, I saw dahlias growing wild, rich with color. I insisted that Nanny stop so I could pick some. I gathered them in my arms, as many as would fit.

"They're for Atacar," I said.

"You'll see him soon," she responded, reminding me that we were on our way to the region where he would be waiting, the town in which we'd agreed to make our home.

I clutched the flowers, holding fast to their sentiment: "I think of you constantly."

We drove to our final destination, the wagon bumping along dusty roads, where farmland and orchards shimmered in the distance.

My lover was nowhere to be seen, and within days, the dahlias wilted. I spoke to everyone in town, describing his appearance in my limited Spanish. The mission priests were especially kind. I told them of his true identity, and they offered to help me discover what had happened to him.

Nanny tried to reassure me. "If he was captured and taken to Fort Sill," she said, "he'll find a way to escape again."

But he never did. Because the priests learned that he'd been shot and killed. That he'd died right before he'd reached the border. He'd fallen from his horse and bled into the earth with his rifle by his side.

CHAPTER TWENTY

"I'm going to tell her," Jared said. He was on his cell phone, talking to Minerva Burke, doing what he'd been doing for the past two weeks: missing Mandy.

"Her?" the elderly woman asked. "The museum director?"

"Yes."

"Why?"

"Because I . . ."

"Love her?" came the inquisitive reply.

He stalked the office in his barn, where ribbons and trophies boasted his horse-industry status. He was supposed to be working, catching up on paperwork.

"I don't know," he said.

"Yes, you do. Or you wouldn't have called me. And certainly not at this hour."

He winced. He'd forgotten about the time difference between New Mexico and England. He'd probably gotten Minerva out of bed. "Sorry."

"Do you love her?" she asked again.

He wanted to curse, but what good would it do? He'd been having this conversation with himself, over and over, until his mind threatened to burst.

"Yes," he said, finally admitting it out loud.

"Does she love you, too?"

"She told me that she was fighting it."

"Then do what you have to do to make things right, even if means making Catherine's memorandum book public."

He stopped pacing. Aside from the British historian who'd authenticated the journal and whose job it was to keep quiet, Minerva and Jared were the only people who'd read the book in its entirety. "You'd be okay with that?"

Her voice didn't slip. She maintained the same polished tone. "Truthfully? I'd prefer that it remain private, but not at your expense. When I asked you to keep it a secret, I never expected it would cause you so much pain."

"It didn't. Not until I fell for Mandy."

"Yes, and now I feel responsible for your troubles. You wouldn't have lied to your young lady if it weren't for me."

He thought about his deception at the hotel. "This isn't your fault. I did things to her that have nothing to do with you." And he could only hope that Mandy would forgive him.

After work, Mandy went home to change her clothes, to freshen up, to take a deep breath before she climbed back in the car and drove to Jared's house.

She considered calling to tell him that she was coming over, but she decided the element of surprise would work in her favor. If she caught him off guard, it would be easier to catch him in his lie. Or so she hoped. He'd done a damn good job of fooling her into believing that he didn't have the journal. That he didn't even believe it existed.

He was in possession of the one thing she wanted most, not only for the museum, but for herself. He knew how much Atacar and Catherine meant to her, how deeply she'd become rooted to uncovering their past, but he'd breezed in and out of her bed without saying a word. The way he'd used her and cast her aside, especially their last night together, hurt beyond words.

Mandy opened the door to leave and—

Boom!

There he was: a tall, dark mirage standing on her stoop. Talk about getting caught off guard. Suddenly she couldn't think straight.

Silence slammed between them, and they made rocky eye contact. She forced herself to take the lead, to speak first. "I was just on my way to see you."

"Then my timing is okay?"

He sounded humble. Too humble? Was he here to embark on another game, another lie? To seduce her back into his handsome clutches? "Your timing has never been right. You always seem to get the upper hand."

"I'm so sorry I hurt you, Mandy. What I did to you—"

She cut him off, stopping him from taking advantage again. "Do you know what I found out today? What Kiki figured out?"

He made a face. "That I have the journal?"

Lucky guess, she thought, giving him a sarcastic look. "Kiki said that you and Minerva Burke had it authenticated."

"We did. But only because Minerva wanted proof that it was real. I already knew it was authentic. I'm the one who found it, who brought it to her."

"And now you're on my doorstep on the same day I discovered the truth. How convenient for you."

"Maybe it's coincidence. Or fate. I don't know. But I came here to tell you everything. The whole story."

Mandy didn't soften her expression.

"You don't believe me? Why else would I be here?" He made an open gesture. "With my heart in your hands?"

She wanted to trust him, but she was afraid of letting go. How many nights had she hugged her pillow and wished it were him, had she cried herself to sleep?

What if he hurt her again?

Once bitten, twice shy. She'd never quite gotten the impact of that idiom until now.

"Give me a chance, Mandy. Please."

Oh, God, she thought. He was making this difficult, so damn hard. She allowed him into her condo. He sat on the sofa, and she took the chair farthest from him, struggling to keep her distance.

He cleared his throat, and his Adam's apple bobbed, making him seem boyish, nervous. He blew out a rough breath. "Remember the trinket box I told you about that belonged to my mom? That I broke earlier this year?"

She nodded, and he continued. "The journal was inside of it. When I knocked the box onto the floor and the wood splintered, I discovered that there was a sealed compartment."

She scooted to the edge of her seat, envisioning what he was describing.

"I can't even begin to express how I felt. I'd been searching for Catherine's journal for most of my adult life, and there it was right under my nose. I sat down and read it, every word. I've read it hundreds of times since. It's beautiful, Mandy. Sexy, romantic, sad. Catherine and Atacar loved each other so much."

"Why didn't you trust me with the truth?"

"It wasn't a matter of trust, not in the way it seems. I'd agreed to keep the journal a secret before I met you. I promised Minerva that I wouldn't make it public. She's been avoiding rumors about Atacar and Catherine for nearly forty years, since his painting was found at the farmhouse, and she was worried the journal would stir up everything again."

"The proper, prestigious Burkes." Mandy heaved a sigh. "Even after all this time, they still want to sweep Catherine under the rug."

"That's what I thought at first, too. But once I got to know Minerva, I realized it went deeper. She resembled Catherine when she was young. In her family, that was a cross to bear."

"I know," Mandy said. Kiki had mentioned that a while back, when they'd first discussed Catherine's grandniece.

Jared explained further. "Minerva won't admit it, but somewhere deep inside, she identifies with Catherine. I think Minerva would have run free if she thought she could have gotten away with it, but she followed the rules of society instead. I think she's afraid of the journal going public because it represents everything she isn't supposed to feel. Or wasn't supposed to feel when she was young."

"Why did you show her the journal to begin with?"

"Because I discovered that I was related to Minerva, to the Burkes." He held Mandy's gaze. "Catherine is my great-great-grandmother." He paused, still making eye contact. "And Atacar is my great-great-grandfather, not my great-great-uncle."

"Oh, my goodness." Her heart bumped her chest. "They had a baby? And you're a descendant of that child?"

"Yes." Jared's breath went rough again. "But Atacar didn't know about the baby. Catherine didn't find out that she was pregnant until after he died."

Without Atacar, I wanted to die. Life was a seamless blur of pain. I cried endlessly for the man I loved. I mourned him every day, alone in the dark, clutching our wedding clothes against my body.

Nanny tried her best to console me, but she missed Atacar, too. She'd treasured him like a son, and now he was gone.

Instead of getting our own farm, we stayed at the mission. I donated money to the church, and Nanny cooked and cleaned for the priests. I tried to paint, to put brush to canvas, but I couldn't. I was empty inside.

Then everything changed. My menses that month never arrived. I told Nanny, and we waited for signs of life to appear in my womb. When I struggled through bouts of dizziness and nausea, we rejoiced. In my final days with Atacar, the preventative tea I'd been drinking had failed, and I've conceived his child.

I wrote to Alice. I was no longer worried about the army intercepting my correspondence. My whereabouts wouldn't interest them, not without Atacar by my side.

Three months later, I received a reply from Alice. She was thrilled about my baby. She gave me news from Texas, too.

She wrote, "George and I heard about Atacar soon after he'd been shot. The army notified the marshal that the 'Runaway Apache' was dead. George and I mourned him silently. We were heartbroken for your loss."

She added, "The bank already sold the farmhouse, and as far as we know, Atacar's portrait is still there, hidden in the walls. Now, in retrospect, it seems like a grave. But George says it's all right because Atacar had been happy at the farmhouse, so it's a good resting place for his picture."

I folded the letter and pressed it against my heart. Alice promised to visit this summer with George and the boys. She was anxious to see Nanny and me. By then, I would have the baby, and all of us could be together.

Atacar wouldn't be at our reunion, but he was never far from my thoughts. When I went to sleep each night, I rubbed my protruding tummy and whispered to the little one about its father. I had a reason to keep living, to be happy once again.

"Was she happy?" Mandy asked, after listening to Jared recount Catherine's story. He'd given her a condensed version of what had been written in the journal, retelling it in his own words.

"She was happy while she was pregnant, but she never got to raise her son. She died in childbirth."

Mandy turned emotional, deeply pained inside. Hurting for Catherine, she walked onto the patio to get some air. Jared followed her, but neither took a seat at the colorful mosaic table. They stood on a small slab of concrete, near a potted plant, and gazed at each other.

"Did Nanny stay in Mexico?" she asked.

"Yes, but soon after the baby was born, she became ill. Her life was ending, too."

"So there was that little boy with no one."

"The priests took him to an orphanage."

"What was his name?"

"Adán. It's the Spanish form of Adam."

"How you know all of this? Did Nanny document it before she died?"

"It was Alice," he said. "She wrote the last entry in the journal, summing up what happened and how she felt about it. When she and George arrived in Mexico to visit Catherine and Nanny, they were met with tragedy. Catherine was gone, Nanny was gravely ill, and the baby was at an overcrowded orphanage."

A breeze stirred the air, blowing a strand of Mandy's hair across her cheek. She tucked it behind her ears, concentrating on Jared's tale. "What did Alice and George do?"

"They stayed with Nanny until she passed. But before she died, they promised her that they would find a loving home for Adán. They wanted to keep him, but they couldn't."

"Because of his heritage?"

"How could they bring a dark-skinned baby home and raise

him? They knew that he would be scorned. That he wouldn't be accepted. So they devised a plan to take him to Fort Sill to be with Atacar's sister and her husband."

Mandy frowned. "Wouldn't that make Adán a prisoner of war?"

"Yes, and Alice struggled over that, but she decided that Adán should be with Atacar's family, even if it meant being under military custody."

Mandy pictured the fort as it had been. From what she knew, the prisoners lived in picket houses, raised cattle, and farmed. Later, after their captivity ended, they were supposed to acquire Fort Sill as their permanent home, but they never did.

"Alice and George pretended to be missionaries," Jared said. "That gave them opportunity to roam freely and sneak Adán inside. They located Atacar's sister and gave her the baby. After that, they all sat down and composed a lie, working out details of how to pass Adán off as Tiana's child."

"Tiana? That's Atacar's sister?"

Jared nodded. "This is the story they came up with: Tiana would approach the fort officials and reveal that she had a two-month-old baby, but that she'd kept her pregnancy and Adán's birth a secret because she was trying to avoid registering him. All of the prisoners were supposed to have enrollment numbers. Births and deaths were supposed to be reported."

Mandy contemplated the lie. "I can see how she fooled the fort officials, but what about the people Tiana was close to? Friends? Family? How did she fool them? Wouldn't they have known that she wasn't pregnant? Or nursing?"

"Apache women wore full skirts and long, loose blouses. Her figure wouldn't have been an issue. As for nursing, she was able to feed Adán from her breast. She had another child who was still taking milk from her. A daughter who was about fifteen months old. Women nursed their kids for a long time in those days."

"Do you think Tiana or her husband ever told Adán the truth? About who his real parents were?"

"I doubt it. The whole point was to protect him from being labeled a half-breed. In that environment, Adán would have been treated badly for his mixed genetics, not just by the military, but by other Apache."

When Jared stopped talking, another question occurred to her. The final one. The end of the saga.

"What about the journal?" she asked. "Who put it in the box? Who sealed it?"

"Alice asked George to make a box to preserve it. Then she gave the box to Atacar's sister for Adán when he grew up, to treat it as a family keepsake. That was Alice's way of honoring Catherine without anyone knowing that her journal was being passed from generation to generation."

Now that the story was over, Mandy went silent. She couldn't think of anything to say. But apparently Jared could.

"I'm sorry I lied to you," he told her. "And I'm so sorry for what I did at the hotel."

She longed to touch him, to hold him, but she didn't. She questioned him instead. "Is your heart really in my hands?"

"Yes. Totally. Completely. I love you, Mandy."

He ventured closer, and the heat, the scent, the familiarity of him made her ache. But she didn't reach for him, so he stopped moving toward her.

She needed to know more, to be sure that what he claimed

was real. "On the night you broke up with me, you said something about losing your identity. What did you mean?"

"I seduced you because your interest in Catherine and Atacar intrigued me. But later, I got confused." He squinted into the waning sun. "I started living through the journal. I created parallels, similarities between their affair and ours. I mimicked Atacar. I behaved the way he did."

"Then maybe you're still confused. Maybe you're mimicking Atacar now."

"I'm not. This is coming from me, not from the journal." He thumped against his chest, his heart. "Me," he reiterated with another light pounding. "I broke up with you out of fear. I was fighting my feelings, but you said that you were doing that, too."

Her breath hitched. "I was."

"Are you still?" He searched her gaze. "Or did I blow it? Is it too late for you to love me?"

"No, it's not too late." She couldn't stop herself from latching on and closing the gap between them. "It's not too late at all."

"Will you say it?"

She was grateful that he needed to hear the words, because she needed to say them, to let herself feel them, to stop fighting what was in her heart.

"I love you," she said. "I do."

He wrapped his arms around her. "I'm never letting you go again."

"I'm never letting you go, either." She put her head on his shoulder. "I want us to have what Catherine and Atacar lost."

"The chance to stay together? We'll have that and more." He

paused. "But we'll have to decide what to do about the journal, whether to keep it private or make it public. I spoke to Minerva earlier, and she's willing to go public, but she'd only be doing it for me."

"You care about her, don't you? That's why you kept the journal a secret for her, why you protected her feelings."

"The first time I went to England was to show her the journal and see how she would react to me. The second time, she invited me back so we could try to get to know each other a little better. So, yes, I care. She's cautious and reclusive, but she seems to care about me, too."

"Then it's your choice what to do about the journal, Jared. I won't intervene. I'll respect your wishes, no matter what they are." She reached for his hand and led him to her bedroom, hungry to have him, to make every being-in-love moment count. "All I want right now is you."

Jared was desperate for Mandy, too. To breathe her into his pores, to press his body against hers.

"I feel like a kid who's going to come too fast," he said.

She teetered toward him, reaching for the buttons on his shirt. "We don't even have our clothes off yet."

"That's what I mean." He nudged her hand down, encouraging her to cop an intimate feel. "See? Instant hard-on."

"Like that's anything new." She smiled and cupped him through his jeans. "You're the most hard-on guy I know."

"Because you're the most orgasmic girl I know. We've got this chemistry thing going." Love, he thought. How amazing was that? He stepped back, stopping her from undressing him. He wanted her naked first. "Strip for me. Let me look at you."

"Are you going to make me get in bed and spread my legs? Are you going make me touch myself?"

Damn. He more than loved this girl. She was the epitome of lust, of sin-swept temptation. There she was, his Mandy, with her eyes bright and blue and her hair caressing her shoulders.

"Yes," he said. "I'm going to make you do that."

She took her sweet time removing her blouse. He waited and watched. Her expression turned soft and sultry, like twilight, like the hour between waking and sleep.

He imagined spending the rest of his life with her. Commitment, he thought, in the midst of erotic dreams.

"This is going to work out just fine," he said.

"What is?" She dropped her blouse on the floor.

He admired her, standing before him in her bra, a modest piece of lingerie with soft cups and a bit of lace. "Us."

Ziiip. She went after the front closure of her pants, tugging the linen garment down her hips. Her panties exhibited the same innocent appeal as her bra.

His hard-on got harder.

Off came her undergarments.

She was beautiful, so damn beautiful with her small, flushed breasts, slim waist, and curvaceous hips.

"I kept my favorite toy," she said. "But I didn't use it when we were broken up. I was afraid it would make me miss you even more."

He knew she was talking about the dildo they'd made of him. "Use it now, baby. Get naughty for me. Be my bad girl."

That was all it took. She got the device, climbed in bed, and lubed it. Once it was slick and wet, she rubbed the pierced head over her nipples, down her stomach, and around her clit.

She spread wide, exposing her labia, letting him take a greedy look. She made the insertion, and desire fevered through his blood, making him hotly, romantically aroused.

She bit down on her bottom lip, and her breathing elevated to shallow pants. But before long, she was inhaling and exhaling in a deeply sensual way, in and out, like the motion of the dildo.

Jared removed his clothes and got into bed. He stretched out next to Mandy and gripped the toy, taking over for her. She moaned low and sexy, and her eyelashes fluttered. She was close to coming, but not quite there.

He ditched the rubber phallus and fitted himself between her thighs, giving her the real deal. She wrapped her legs around him, and they kissed . . .

And kissed . . .

And kissed some more.

He rocked his hips, claiming her in ways he'd never claimed her before. The carnality was the same as it had always been, but the feeling was new.

Heart sex, he thought.

She climaxed with his cock thrust full hilt, and while it was happening, they looked into each other's eyes. This was it. Love in its deepest, purest, most primal form.

Jared resisted the urge to come. He took it slow, setting a sinuous rhythm, wanting to give Mandy another orgasm before he let himself fall.

The onset of dusk seeped through the blinds, shadowing the

room. He wasn't looking for a marathon, just more of her, of what she made him feel.

She was warm and silky soft, and they moved fluidly together. He linked both of his hands with hers, holding on to a word that was no longer forbidden.

Forever, he thought, as he kissed her again.

Forever.

EPILOGUE

ONE MONTH LATER

"Are you nervous?" Kiki asked.

"A little," Mandy responded. She and Kiki were at the museum, standing in front of Atacar's portrait and waiting for Jared and Minerva. He was picking up Minerva from the airport, and this would be Mandy's first time meeting her. "I want to make a good impression."

"You will."

"I'm going to try." Jared had left the fate of the journal in Minerva's hands. And after much thought, the older woman had decided that it should be made public and that Jared should proclaim his birthright. But before Catherine's memorandum book was turned over to the museum, Minerva wanted to meet Mandy and discuss the details of how it should be exhibited. Minerva wanted to see Atacar's portrait, too.

"I appreciate you hanging out with me," Mandy said. "For helping me wait out my nerves."

"No problem. I'll just say a quick howdy-do to Minerva and scoot off afterward."

"Thanks." Mandy started another conversation, killing time. "So, what's going on with you? Anything new?"

"Except for Amber calling me all the time and bugging me to meet that guy?"

"What guy?"

"You know, Mr. BDSM. The bondage artist."

"Oh, that's right. The one who has a thing for redheads. Are you going to take a chance and meet him?"

"Are you kidding? I'm not setting myself up for something like that." Kiki lifted her wrists above her head, as if she were being restrained. "Could you see me like this? Strung up in some wacko's playroom? Begging him to do Lord only knows what to me?"

Mandy laughed. "Actually, I could."

"Oh, shut up." The historian laughed, too. Then she made a guilty face. "I checked out his art."

Aha, Mandy thought. Curiosity in bloom. "In person or online?"

"Online. I have to admit, his work is amazing. I saw his picture, too. Jet-black hair. Sizzling blue eyes. And get this—according to Amber, he's a history buff. He just bought a house that used to be a turn-of-the-century hotel. Of course, he can buy whatever he wants. He inherited billions from his family."

"Wow. He sounds like quite a catch."

"Oh, right. He's a dream, except for the whips and chains and muzzles and gags part." Kiki glanced toward the door. "Speaking of rich families . . ."

Mandy turned and saw Jared and Minerva enter the museum.

Kiki leaned over and whispered, "Look at her. It's like we're holding court for a royal."

"Shhh." Mandy nudged her friend, even if the same thought had just crossed her mind. At eighty-three, Minerva carried herself like a noblewoman. Sheathed in an elegant dress and a triple strand of pearls, she clutched Jared's arm. Her snow-white hair was classically coiffed.

Jared escorted his elderly cousin closer, and Mandy took a deep breath. After the initial introductions and small talk were exchanged, Kiki excused herself and slipped away. As for Jared, he turned quiet, letting Mandy and Minerva get acquainted.

"You're lovely," the older woman said to her.

Mandy relaxed. "Thank you. So are you." She wondered if Catherine would have aged in a similar manner if she'd gotten the chance to grow old, if her hair would have turned a brilliant tone of white, if her eyes would have faded to a paler shade.

"I packed a family photo album in my luggage," Minerva said, as if she sensed that Mandy had been comparing her to Catherine. "With pictures of my ancestors. And me when I was young."

When she'd resembled Catherine, Mandy thought. "I'd love to see the album."

"And you shall." Minerva turned toward Atacar's portrait. "Oh, my. He's stunning, isn't he?"

"He made my heart pound the first time I saw him," Mandy responded. "I can only imagine what he was like in person."

"I suspect that he was as captivating as Catherine described. Can you fathom what she felt for him? What he felt for her?" She turned back to Mandy. "Well, of course you can. Jared and you . . ."

Yes, Jared and me, she thought. He'd made her heart pound the first time she'd seen him, too. She glanced at him, and he smiled. They were living together now. She'd rented out her condo and moved in with him, becoming his partner in every way.

As Minerva studied the portrait again, Jared said, "The journal itself should be exhibited here, but I don't think we should make all of it available for the public to read. We should protect Catherine and Atacar's most intimate moments."

The Burke matriarch agreed. "All we need to do is release excerpts that will prove what they felt for each other was real."

"Very real," Mandy said, as the three of them gazed into the warrior's painted eyes.

"Do you think this will reunite them?" Jared asked.

Mandy reached for his hand. "I hope so." They were giving Atacar the journal, every word Catherine had written about their life together.

To stay beside him for all time.